Best Wishes,
Shirley Mays

Also by this Author:

Outer Banks Piracy
Where is My Son Jeffrey?

Outer Banks Piracy II

Drugs and Political Corruption

Shirley Mays

authorHOUSE®

AuthorHouse™
1663 Liberty Drive
Bloomington, IN 47403
www.authorhouse.com
Phone: 1-800-839-8640

First published by AuthorHouse   5/11/2009

ISBN: 978-1-4389-8135-2 (sc)

Printed in the United States of America
Bloomington, Indiana

This book is printed on acid-free paper.

Contents

Dedicated To My Wonderful Daughters

Tatiana And Melinda

Introduction

Edgar Styron, Jr.

A deliberate attempt was made by Edgar Styron, Jr. of Hatteras, North Carolina to deceive the United States Coast Guard into believing that Jeffrey Mays and Ted Wall were at sea in trouble when in fact he knew it was a lie. He was piloting *The Easy Ryder* on November 13, 1980 and was one of the last persons to talk to the boys. At the time, Edgar was a drug dealer working directly under Harry Williams.

Harry Williams

Harry Williams is the brother of H. P. Williams, the District Attorney for the first prosecutorial district of North Carolina. He was caught drug dealing while driving the DA's Buick in June of 1991. He was sentenced to one year in jail, four years suspended and five years probation, out of a possible 15 year prison term.

Jock MacKenzie

Jock MacKenzie owned *The Easy Ryder* and was aboard on November 13, 1980. He and Edgar Styron, Jr. were the last two people to see Jeffrey Mays and Ted Walls offshore. He was the brother-in-law of Lt. Robert Eck.

Lt. Robert Eck

Lieutenant Robert Eck was with the Dare County Sheriff's Department. He worked with the Organized Crime Drug Enforcement Task Force for the Eastern District of Virginia. This task force was created in 1982 by President Reagan and the Attorney General to disrupt narcotics trafficking by organized criminal groups.

Jeffrey and Ted

Jeffrey and Ted Wall were last seen about 1:30 p.m. on Thursday, November 13, 1980 about 16 miles southeast of Hatteras Inlet. Edgar Styron, Jr. told the Coast Guard that he helped the two repair the engine of Jeffrey's 23 foot boat, the Sea Ox. He reported that they went south.

The search for the missing men and boat began about 9 that evening and continued for two weeks. Coast Guard boats, Navy, Marine, Air Force and Coast Guard helicopters were used to cover more than 211,000 miles of ocean. Jeffrey's boat, the Sea Ox, was considered unsinkable. The Sea Ox boats are filled with foam flotation that can keep them just under the surface even when swamped. The lost boat had a 280-horsepower engine. Authorities didn't find anything from the boat, which was unusual.

Many fiends and family of Mays don't believe Jeffrey is dead.

In 1995 during a meeting at Jock MacKenzie's house, Jock told Dick Ruffino of Missing Persons and Shirley Mays, mother of Jeffrey Mays, that Edgar told him, *during the search* that the boys were OK.

In 2004, Harry Williams personally told Shirley Mays that the boys were at Edgar's place in Avon, North Carolina earlier that fatal morning of November 13, 1980. He told her that Edgar was *under* him.

She has committed her life to finding Jeffrey or finding out what happened to him. She wrote her first book "Outer Banks Piracy, Where Is My Son Jeffrey?" hoping the book would open up some doors in her search for her son. She is willing to tell the public some more facts in hopes of opening up the final door with information that will bring closure to her family. She lives with the hope that Jeffrey is alive and safe somewhere in the world but in any case, she is ready for the truth.

She wants justice.

One way or another.

This is her story.

Main Cast of Characters

OUTER BANKS, NORTH CAROLINA

Tom White, Attorney
Ray White, Banker
H. P. Williams, District Attorney
Harry Williams, brother of District Attorney
Edgar Styron, Jr., Fisherman
Jock MacKenzie, Boat Owner
Lt. Robert Eck, Drug Task Force Team

ELIZABETH CITY, NORTH CAROLINA

John Morrison, Attorney

RALEIGH, NORTH CAROLINA

Rudy Renfer, Civil Chief, NC US Attorney's Office, qui tam case
Tom Manning, Attorney, Local counsel, qui tam case

WILMINGTON, NORTH CAROLINA

Gary Shipman, Attorney, qui tam case

WASHINGTON, DC

Frank Hunger, Attorney. Department of Justice, Head of qui tam case
Justin Castillo, Trial Attorney, Department of Justice, qui tam case

The true story you are about to read involves drugs and political corruption and the effect they have on the banking system and families everywhere.

"The truth will set you free!"

"Not if the government or law enforcement gets involved"
said Shirley Mays in the year 2009.

The following story is one of a missing son whose fate got involved with the political corruption, the drug dealing, and the money laundering on the Outer Banks of North Carolina, the area in which he lived. Jeffrey Mays was just 21 years old; a little fish in a very big pond that day 16 miles off Cape Hatteras in international waters when he disappeared.

Shirley Mays, in her search for her son gets entangled with many of the modern Outer Banks pirates; the lawyers, bankers, accountants and developers who were involved with drug dealing and who used drug money to buy valuable coastal properties during that time and later.

Searching for Jeffrey lead her into discovery of the drug dealing being conducted right out of the local Great Atlantic Savings Bank, FSB in Manteo, North Carolina. She became a whistleblower who filed the biggest qui tam case ever filed in the State of North Carolina. It was all about bank fraud.

The Resolution Trust Corporation was an agency formed by the Federal Deposit Insurance Corporation to manage the sale of the assets from the defunct Savings and Loans Banks. The RTC was a total failure and the FDIC falsified the officially owned databases to block the trail of value of assets from 747 institutions in order to cover up the actual damages. The FDIC used these falsified databases to compile reports to Congress.

Her case was covered up at the highest levels of government because of the involvement of so many high elected officials.

The taxpayers of America deserve to hear her story.

Chapter One

In the Beginning

In the wee hours of the morning on November 13, 1980, just as the dawn was breaking, Shirley's son Jeffrey and another young man, both 21 years of age, left the Cape Hatteras Marina in Hatteras, North Carolina. They were following the Atlantic Fishing Fleet heading southeast towards the Gulfstream fringe around the end of Diamond Shoals towards good fishing grounds. The two boys were in Jeffrey's 23 foot cream colored Sea Ox. They never returned to shore that afternoon. She has spent 29 years of her life chasing the mystery of Jeffrey's disappearance. The unknown changed her life and that of her family forever. She was determined to fight the environment of drugs and organized crime that surrounded Jeffrey in Dare County at that time and continues today in the year 2009.

In 1985, she became involved in a real estate white collar crime lawsuit in Dare County that lasted until 1991. In the legal circles of North Carolina, the case was well known as *The Neimay Lawsuit.* It was a lawsuit against the estate of George Neighbors, the general partner who died in 1983. George was a real estate scammer who migrated to the Outer Banks from the Eastern Shore in the mid seventies. He was a real estate scam teacher to many locals. His estate file remains open. The lawsuit was one of the longest running cases in Dare County, North Carolina. She was after the local pirates.

In 1996, she filed the first <u>qui tam</u> case, also known as a False Claim Act or a whistleblowing case in the state of North Carolina, or so she was informed when she went to the federal courthouse in Raleigh to walk her case through the complicated process. She is a real estate broker and an environmental consultant and is certified to bid on contracting work with the government. Her <u>qui</u> <u>tam</u> lawsuit involved the contracting process within the FDIC and the RTC. It involved the Savings and Loan debacle of the 80s and 90s which was the biggest real estate scam this country had ever seen. She sued sixty-five corporations and a dozen FDIC employees. She is considered an "insider" because she was certified by the FDIC as a minority contractor. She was also after the national pirates.

Actually, these two involvements coincided because the same lawyers, bankers, accountants and developers were involved with both the Neimay Case and the defunct Great Atlantic Savings Bank, FSB in Manteo, North Carolina which was taken over by the FDIC and the RTC. It was all happening at the same time.

The Department of Justice (DOJ) and the FDIC continues to obstruct justice by covering up her discovery.

That is how she got to where she is. It is a very complicated story. Her life story is what it is because of her insistence on being true to herself.

Jeffrey Mays

Chapter Two

Jeffrey was born in Bloomington, Indiana when his Dad was a senior at Indiana University. Shirley was getting homesick for her Tar Heel State of North Carolina. After graduation, he agreed to accept a job with a company based in Greensboro, North Carolina that sold business machines. Bud was a marketing major and was hired in sales. After training in Greensboro, he was offered a choice of territories, one being in Wilmington, North Carolina.

Wilmington was a fast growing little town on the east coast in southeastern North Carolina and only about four hours from her hometown of Elizabeth City. There was a University of North Carolina extension located in the area and a community college located downtown on the waterfront. The movie studios were beginning to blossom and become a big part of the future for the area. Wilmington was indeed an artsy place to live.

Two of the best years of her life were spent on Harbour Island, the little piece of land between the mainland of Wilmington and Wrightsville Beach, North Carolina. She had spent her summers growing up on the Outer Banks of North Carolina in Nags Head and dearly loved the coast. When they moved to Wilmington, they lived as close to the ocean as they could get.

She didn't work so she and Jeffrey spent all of their days together. Soon after moving to Wilmington, she became pregnant with their second child. They took daily walks to the beach during her entire pregnancy. They always ended up at the charter boats so Jeffrey could watch the big fishing vessels coming in after a long day at sea. He loved fish and he loved to watch the fishing boats bring in their daily catch. Those memories are precious for her.

One day a dear friend of Bud's from college who was traveling north after being in Florida dropped by to visit and talked him into leaving his present company and going to work for Wolverine Shoe Company. That is how the Mays ended up in Ligonier, Pennsylvania.

Jeffrey started kindergarten and finished high school in Ligonier, a beautiful little village in Western Pennsylvania with less than two thousand residents.

While living in Ligonier, Bud left Wolverine Shoe Company and started a business of his own with a friend who worked for the Xerox Corporation. It was a manufacturing toner supply business based in Latrobe, Pennsylvania. At the time of this bold new business struggle, Jeffrey was a little boy. He was only about seven years old and was already a truly dedicated fisherman. The Mays lived in a lovely neighborhood on the top of a hill in Valley Heights. They had a fresh water stream stocked with trout rushing briskly at the foot of their property. It was quite safe in Ligonier during those years for him to go fishing alone with his young buddies. He would haul his fresh catch home daily and proudly present them to his mother. She was the only one in their family who loved to eat fresh fish.

Bud was from the Midwest and was raised on meat and potatoes. Money was scarce for the Mays when they first went into business for themselves so sometimes they would cut back on the high cost food items. Shirley ate like a queen because of Jeffrey's daily catch of fresh fish. He was proud of his contribution to the family's welfare and Shirley was very proud of her little fisherman.

Bud named his new business Imaging Systems. He started it about the same time Jeffrey started school. It was a very successful business when he sold it to his partner in 1974.

Back in 1970, the Mays bought the Kitty Hawk Coast Guard Station in Kitty Hawk, North Carolina. Shirley had no idea at the time they purchased the Station that a few of the Kitty Hawk officials had their eyes on it for a Welcome Center. They bought it from a friend of her family, without the knowledge of the public.

It was their summer home and their favorite vacation spot. She can still visualize Jeffrey and his buddies fishing hard in the mornings, playing football in the surf in the afternoons and chasing the girls at night while growing up. They were indeed very healthy and happy youngsters. As they ventured into their teens, the boys would sit on the top porch, directly under the crows nest, with binoculars and weed out the bathing beauties until one would catch their attention. Then they would send his sister and her friends down the beach to meet those beach beauties and arrange a date for them. The boys had no intentions of being turned down while making the first big contact.

After the sale of Imaging Systems in January of 1974, it was natural for Bud and Shirley to head to their Coast Guard Station in North Carolina for a little R&R and for an opportunity to see what was up in the real estate world of the Outer Banks. They had some investment money from the sale of their business and were itching to find some good real estate. Real estate had proven to be one of their best investments.

It was quite natural that she would spot a real estate sign being pushed into the sand just a short distance from their Station. The sign read, "Tract of Land (45 acres) Ocean to Sound, Estate Property, Contact Bank." They stopped in the closest real estate office to inquire about the land. The broker said, "I was told that the bank was going to notify me first about that tract. I developed the tract next to it. Are you interested in forming a Limited Partnership with me?"

They were interested so the developer came up with a partnership whereas he, George Neighbors, the broker became the general partner and Bud became the limited partner. They named the partnership Neimay after both of them.

The Mays had no plans at that time to leave Pennsylvania. The partnership was to last for ten years from 1975 to 1985.

Jeffrey graduated from Ligonier High School in 1977 and decided to attend college at East Carolina University in Greenville, North Carolina which was only about two hours from her hometown of Elizabeth City. The Pennsylvania winters became very bitter so Shirley suggested to the family that they move south to be closer to Jeffrey. In the summer of 1977, they made the big move.

Bud owned an office supply business in Los Angeles, California which was a spin-off company of Imaging Systems. He decided to move that business to the East Coast just to have something to do.

They bought some prime commercial properties on the waterfront in downtown Elizabeth City. In the past, the buildings had housed a John Deere dealership and an old Cotton Mill. They were quite historic and interesting properties. They were in a wonderful downtown location. Both buildings had been owned for a very long time by a prominent local retired businessman. Shirley's mother knew the owner and had made the suggestion that they consider talking to him about purchasing the properties.

They had been fortunate in Ligonier to be able to purchase the General St. Clair Farm, a very prominent 60 acre farm one mile from the Diamond which was the center attraction of the downtown. They were exceedingly lucky to purchase the Coast Guard Station in Kitty Hawk. It was a most historic property and was next door to the original Station where the Wright Brothers had sent their telegraphed message about the first flight. Now they had the good fortune to purchase another one of a kind property in Elizabeth City, the building for the oldest John Deere Dealership in North Carolina and the Cotton Mill building next door. Both buildings were mostly over the waters of the Pasquotank River directly on the path of the Intra-Coastal Waterway.

Shirley had no idea when they purchased the John Deere building and Cotton Mill that the town officials had their eyes on the location for a public park. The properties were on pilings and mostly over water but no one had said that was a problem. There were no restrictions on the deeds.

John Morrison, a local attorney they engaged to close the deal was also the seller's attorney. He didn't inform the Mays of any problems when he performed a title search. He certainly didn't inform them about a state Submerged Land Program that targeted over 10,000 waterfront properties in the coastal towns of North Carolina. The State of North Carolina had worded the newspaper article to make it appear that the properties were grandfathered in if you registered before a certain date. The Mays found out later that the previous owner made sure he didn't miss the deadline.

They were not aware of any of these problems at the time of purchase. They had no problem getting title insurance. They were convinced that they had bought prime downtown property with the best view in town.

They bought the waterfront properties in 1977 before the regulatory bodies like Coastal Area Management Act (CAMA) became an issue. Soon after they bought this desirable waterfront property, the regulatory bodies, local, state and federal, appeared to become "born again." The agencies seem to just keep growing and growing, eliminating rules and changing rules and nothing appeared to be carved in stone. Dealing with the environmental folks in the 70s and 80s was like playing a game of darts and it was a very, very expensive game. Every throw was different.

They found out that it was very costly to own a waterfront property, especially one that had been targeted for public use. The financial regulatory pressures never let up from the beginning of the sale. Her hometown didn't want change so any regulatory agency, local, state or federal, that entered the picture and helped the local government stop progress was fully supported by many of the local elected officials.

The Mays received a very costly education. They are aware that governments have all the resources necessary to wait you out. It is only a matter of time before government gets whatever properties government wants.

Drug dealing was beginning to become a big problem for small towns like Elizabeth City. In the late seventies, the Universities also became targets. Marijuana was the drug of choice. By 1980, students and professionals alike were beginning to use and sell cocaine. Many of the young professionals in her hometown were involved. She was never exposed to drugs but she certainly heard the rumors. She could hardly believe the prominent local names involved. If Jeffrey was involved with any drugs at college, she never suspected it. She was very naïve about drugs and drug dealing during his college years.

She was too busy working and trying to make a difference to see what was happening right in front of her eyes. Many other people were so busy that they too did not see the country changing. Drastic changes were taking place involving the drug trade all over the United States. The corruption that followed was devastating.

A few police in her hometown were rumored to be involved with selling drugs and antagonizing the young people who were competing with them. What a mess! The national press said it was happening in many small towns all over the nation. Elizabeth City was no exception.

In the summer of 1980, Bud was looking for a business that Jeffrey could inherit and enjoy. Bud knew very little about the fishing business but he knew a lot about sales and felt sales were the key to any successful business. He was visiting George Neighbors one day at the Outer Banks, when George told him about this "one of a kind" fish business in a great location that was owned by a longtime prominent fisherman.

Shirley didn't trust George Neighbors and warned Bud that a seasonal business at the Outer Banks would really tie him down.

George never thought the Mays would be moving to North Carolina. She later found out that he was known for picking partners who were little old ladies with lots of money in other states. He didn't like anyone looking over his shoulder.

Bud was a marketing major from the Midwest. The third and fourth generation fish owners looked at him like a foreigner. He bought the retail business from Charles Nunemaker, a well known fish dealer whose wife was stealing him blind, unbeknownst to the Mays. It was a cash business. She was best friends with George Neighbors.

In fact, George had lunch with Harriet Nunemaker most days. Charles and Harriet sold the retail part of Nunemakers to the Mays through George Neighbors, their broker and retained their Nunemaker wholesale business. Part of the deal was that Bud would buy fish from Charles' wholesale business. Charles Nunemaker had been a friend of Shirley's parents. He was known to be a good man. It was the farthest thought from her mind that he would cheat them.

Kitty Hawk Coast Guard Station

Chapter Three

The Year 1980

Jeffrey left East Carolina University in his senior year to move to the Outer Banks to help with the new fish business. His parents made him a partner. He was willing to work seven days a week helping his father at the fish market. He had always been a very hard worker since he was a little boy. The fish house gave him a new sense of purpose. After all, he had been a successful fisherman since he was about six or seven years old. He was very excited about the purchase of the fish market. His parents bought him a cream colored 23 foot Sea Ox after Jeffrey convinced his Dad he could set nets with it and in a small way become another supplier for the business.

Most watermen will tell you a Sea Ox is a fine boat, particularly the one that Jeffrey had. His was designed especially for commercial fishing. It was tough, rugged, powered with a Volvo inboard-outboard of 280 horsepower. Most importantly, watermen will tell you a Sea Ox is unsinkable because of built-in foam flotation.

Shirley was in Elizabeth City running the office supply business and wasn't even aware of the day to day business at the fish house, fifty miles away. She wasn't aware that Bud had hired Ted Wall, the young son of her Elizabeth City High School classmates. Ted's father, Franklin had been a football star and his mother Verna was their class valedictorian. They were fine people and she hadn't seen them since high school.

You can imagine the shock she had on November 13, 1980 about 8:30 at night when the phone rang. "Shirley, this is Franklin Wall and I think our boys are in trouble." She was bedridden. She was the sickest she can ever remember. She thought it was the flu. "Wait a minute Franklin. Bud has come up from the beach and he is here." She did not realize that Jeffrey and Ted were staying in Hatteras at Franklin and Verna's trailer while they were fishing for the business. How could she know that when she didn't even know Ted Wall had been hired? What trouble could they be in and why was Franklin calling so late? Jeffrey had never been in any trouble before so how bad could it be?

Bud hung up the phone and left the house abruptly. Shirley was in a world of hurt. The next ten days or so were like a bad dream. In fact, in the year of 2009 she is still waiting to wake up. "Bad dreams can't last this long, can they?" she has asked the Lord every day for 29 years. Bud headed straight for the Coast Guard Station Hatteras Inlet. Franklin had told him the boys went out fishing early that morning and did not return at the normal time, about 6:00 or 6:30 p.m. in the afternoon. This was the time all the charter boats came in flying their flags, flaunting their catch of the day.

Franklin and Verna had gone to Hatteras on Nov. 12th, because Franklin was feeling sorry for the boys and wanted to go down and cook them a good meal. He had been real tough on them the previous week when Jeffrey and Ted were spotted at the local shopping center in Elizabeth City. They should have been fishing out of Hatteras.

Shirley and Bud were in Los Angeles visiting their oldest daughter. Franklin spotted them at the shopping center in Elizabeth City, told them to get to his house immediately. He gave them a good dressing down and reprimanded them because they were on Bud's payroll and should have been in Hatteras fishing. He had been tough on the boys and worried about it for a couple of weeks. He wanted to make it up to them so he and Verna headed to Hatteras on November 12 to surprise the boys and cook dinner for them.

Early morning on November 13 Frank went over to his trailer where the boys were staying, to help them rig the Sea Ox and get the equipment on board ready for a big day of fishing. He and Verna were staying at a friend's house. Usually the boys would ask Franklin to go out fishing with them but that day, for some reason, they didn't invite him to go along.

Later that afternoon, Franklin was standing on the shore, waiting for the boys to come back in with the fleet. He knew most of the Sea Captains so he asked each and everyone, "Where are my boys?" Each gave a different report; last seen heading north, heading south, heading east. Still another said he had seen them circling a big freighter. Several of them reported that the boys appeared to have some boat trouble but just as Edgar Styron, Sr. was heading for them, his son Edgar, Jr. called on the radio and said "We've got them." That was at 1:30 pm, 16 miles offshore, in the Gulf Stream. November 13, 1980.

That was the last time they were reported to have been seen.

There were many, many conflicting stories about what happened that fateful day. They all seemed to have their own theory.

For twenty nine years now, Shirley has checked out as many of the stories as possible.

After questioning the fishermen, Franklin and Verna rushed over to Edgar Jr.'s house. They knew him and the area well because Verna was an Austin from Hatteras. The local sheriff was an Austin. There were many Austins in the Hatteras area. The area was full of Midgetts and Austins. In fact, the Midgetts and Austins were the local backbone of the Coast Guard and the Coast Guard was the area's claim to fame.

Everybody in Hatteras knows everyone else and you can rest assured they also know the strangers who don't live there. They can spot them in a hurry. Franklin went to Edgar Jr.'s house and excitedly said to him, "We have to get the Coast Guard to start looking for the boys." Verna told Shirley that she was waiting in their car at the time and she saw a man hurry by with a briefcase. The man walked up on Edgar's porch, cupped his hand and whispered to Edgar, Jr. Edgar Jr. turned hurriedly to Franklin and said, "I'll be back in an hour. I have to go to Avon with Harry." Franklin was extremely frustrated about getting a search started for the boys but what could he do? Edgar, Jr. was the key to pin pointing where the boys were last seen. He reportedly had been the very last person to talk to them at 1:30 that day.

The search was delayed for several hours because of Edgar Jr.'s unexpected trip to Avon with Harry and his briefcase. It was after this visit to Edgar, Jr.'s house when Franklin called Bud in Elizabeth City. "I think our boys are in trouble." He had plenty of reason to be worried about that after meeting with Edgar, Jr. and witnessing the briefcase encounter. It didn't make any sense at all to Franklin that a trip to Avon could be more urgent to a seaman than reporting a troubled boat offshore. In fact, why did that seaman even leave the troubled boat?

Bud arrived in Hatteras in record time. Shirley was in bed beginning to have the worst nightmare imaginable. Their oldest daughter was living in California and their youngest one was at home with her. She could put that much together. Everything was happening at once and she desperate wanted it to go away. She told everyone not to call her daughter in LA because she was so far away and she would worry over nothing. Everything was going to be all right in the morning. It was all just a mistake.

In the morning, their daughter was there.

Was she dreaming? Shirley doesn't even know who called her or how she got there. She only knew that she was still having a nightmare and couldn't get out of bed.

The nightmare got worse.

The phone wouldn't stop ringing. It seemed like hundreds of people were downstairs. Why were they there and what did they want? All of Jeffrey's friends from college were calling, especially one from Carolina

Beach, North Carolina and one from Dunn, North Carolina. Jeffrey had mentioned them but neither she nor Bud had met either one of them. Many friends called from Pennsylvania. Shirley's friends from growing up and Bud's friends and family from Indiana all either called or were on their way there.

All she knew was that her entire family was there in full force. Her Mother Fannie was a Seymour and when the Seymour family gets in full force, you have an army, a very good and efficient army. Shirley was in very safe hands but why was everyone so concerned about Jeffrey?

She actually doesn't remember how long this part of her nightmare lasted but she remembers her sister Pauline coming upstairs. Shirley said to her "let's go." She and Pauline were very close sisters and Pauline got her to the Rescue Center in Hatteras as fast as she could. Many of the family members were gathering in the big assembly room. The search was in full force. The Hatteras Coastguardsmen took in at least twenty relatives of the Mays and Wall family. They cared for them tenderly, always gruffly hearty and optimistic.

She thinks it was only the next day but how could that be? It had to be a week or month or year later. It seemed a lifetime since that dreaded phone call. That twenty-four hours or less immediately after Franklin's call to them is lost forever in her mind. After all, no one can remember all the bits and pieces of a dream, especially when it turns into a nightmare.

When Shirley and Pauline arrived at the rescue center, she remembers seeing her oldest daughter standing in the middle of a circle with the Coast Guard rescue pilots, praying for their successful efforts to find her beloved brother. She and her brother were extremely close. What a nightmare this had to be for her. She was only 19 years old. Those rescue pilots, the ones looking for her brother, the ones who huddled in a circle with her in the middle praying, would later avoid her like the plague at the end of each and every search day. They just knew every minute they would spot him and bring him back to her and her family because Edgar had reported the exact location of the troubled boat.

The United States Coast Guard has the best rescue pilots in the world and if Jeffrey was out there, they would find him.

How could they not find him? After all, Jeffrey and one of his buddies from Ligonier were leaving in a few days to go see his sister on the West Coast. They were all going skiing at Tahoe. He needed to be home soon.

She also remembers, in her dream, no, in her nightmare, that the loudspeakers kept blaring out about the search saying that they found a shoe or something else but never anything from the Sea Ox that Jeffrey owned and was running that day.

The Sea Ox Company was so upset that they sent a representative to Hatteras during the search. They felt certain that the Sea Ox didn't go down at sea. They met with the owner of a Marina in Hatteras where Jeffrey had recently had some repairs performed on his boat. They both decided after studying the entire situation that the boat did not go down at sea. Even the sea-wise executive officer of Group Cape Hatteras who was in charge of the search, was deeply puzzled. "That boat is still afloat. I think those boys are okay. I just can't understand why we haven't found them." He came from an Outer Banks island and he owned a Sea Ox. "That boat is still afloat" he kept repeating during the search.

If the boat did not go down at sea and nothing aboard was found in the search and the weather was beautiful that day, then what happened? How do people just disappear from the earth without leaving any trail of evidence? Shirley knew, without a doubt, that was not the situation with her son Jeffrey. Jeffrey was a survivor. They would hopefully find him soon, but when and where?

On the seventh day of the search, a reporter friend from the Outer Banks, who knew the Mays family well, wrote a three page story which headlined "WHERE? A LONG SAD SEA HUNT." Half of the front page showed a satellite picture of the entire East Coast. The second page had a picture of Jeffrey's cream colored 23 foot Sea Ox. Shirley read the article and wondered how she was going to be able to handle this biggest challenge of her life. The possible loss of her only son. She left the room and got sick to her stomach.

The search was one of the largest ever at that time on the East Coast. It lasted almost two weeks. After they stopped searching from the Hatteras Station, the search was moved to the Coast Guard Station in Elizabeth City. The officials there brought in a Chaplain to inform the mothers that they had to end the search. Shirley panicked and refused to talk to the Chaplain. She and Verna met with a retired Captain, a friend of the Seymours, who was there with the search party and she convinced him that they were not searching in the right direction. They needed to look south, towards Wilmington, North Carolina. The retired Captain came forward and said he had not draw up a flight plan in years but would be personally willing to draw one up now. Using his plan, the Coast Guard searched longer and in a different direction.

Elected officials from both political parties got involved. Everything was done that could be by the Coast Guard. Everyone involved went way beyond the call of duty. Everyone and that included family, friends, elected officials and that retired Coast Guard Captain.

During the last search days, while the operation was being directed out of Elizabeth City instead of Buxton, Shirley could hear the C-130s flying directly over her riverfront home heading for the Hatteras area. She prayed and prayed and prayed and still couldn't wake up from that horrible nightmare. She remembers seeing herself in that dream with her chin on the winder sill, in the middle of the night, waiting for Jeffrey's car to drive up. One night she held his picture against her heart and felt his heartbeat. That was no dream to her, it really happened. It woke her up in a hurry.

She knew Jeffrey was alive. She just didn't know where.

One incident in particular stands out in her mind about the search while it was being conducted out of Hatteras. About two days before the families left the area, Dale Winslow, one of Ted's best buddies arrived and just sat around with Ted's family. He was like a son to them. He wasn't there at the beginning of the search. He just showed up a few days later. He didn't jump up every time the families did when an important announcement came over the speaker. It was almost as if he knew it wouldn't be true. One of the first rumors that Shirley heard after the search was called off was that Dale Winslow was involved with whatever was going on that day and that Dale knew where the boys were. It is a fact that shortly after the search, Dale left the area, went south to Florida, west to New Orleans, Texas and California, headed north and ended up in Alaska. He appeared to be on a mission.

The Mays family joined the local Methodist church when they first arrived in Elizabeth City in 1977. The church had a beauty little red velvet chapel where you could be by yourself and never feel alone. Shirley managed to drive there after the Coast Guard had to stop the search. She remembers almost crawling in on her hands and knees into the chapel while praying to the Lord, "Please dear God, if you will just take care of my son Jeffrey, I will do anything you want, I promise."

After that moment, her life was never going to be the same. She had given it to God and she would never betray him. After all, she had always been true to her commitments in life. Commitments were sacred to her and were never taken lightly even if they took longer than she had planned. This commitment was going to be very, very different from all of the rest.

Church would never be the same again for her. Every time she attended, she could feel the entire choir staring at her. Even if they were not, she felt that they were so her attendance became less and less. Besides, who wants to see someone crying in church all the time? To see her crying would be depressing when they should be rejoicing. Surely, people should get over tragedies but it is really hard when there are no answers and everything is unknown.

She felt like an outcast who didn't fit in or belong anywhere anymore. Someone she loved very much was in that church choir. It was her high school band director, and he was always looking straight at her, feeling her hurt. He had a similar situation and had walked in her shoes. His youngest son had disappeared for quite awhile. His son also attended East Carolina University. His son's disappearance was involved with drugs. Was Jeffrey's? If so, Shirley was not aware of it. At that time anyway. Her band director's son got in trouble while at East Carolina and had to go to court. He made a trip to Greenville to attend court with him. During court, his son pointed out a lawyer who was deeply involved with drug dealing at the university. After that court action, his son got in trouble again and the local law went to his house to arrest him. He jumped out the window and swam across a body of water. They had helicopters and dogs after him. His son got away. It is an amazing story that was told to Shirley by the bank director who was a dear friend.

First they received a postcard from him saying that he was OK but the band director didn't think it was his son's hand writing. Out of the blue one day, his son called from Canada to say he was OK. He said that he had a job with a contractor and he would be leaving the area and going to a city about 1000 miles away. He gave them a last name for the contractor. His father only had little bits and pieces of the puzzle. He took a pencil and string and drew a circle about 1000 miles from where the call came. There was only one city that appeared to fit the bill. It was Toronto.

He and his wife went to Toronto. They got a phone book and looked up the name of the contractor. They went to his home and an older woman was sitting on her front porch in a rocking chair. The bank director asked her about her husband. She said her husband had worked for the railroad. He was dead but she had a son named after him. She said that her son always talked about a good friend from North Carolina whose father was a band director. She said he was at work but if they wanted to wait, her son would be home in a short while.

They waited until the son came home and he told them that their son was down the road just a short distance at a motel. They went to the motel and sat in the car waiting for him to appear. When he saw them, he immediately went into shock and turned to run. They had found him. He was extremely paranoid. They went to a restaurant so they could relax and be with their beloved son who had been missing forever it seemed to them. The son insisted that they pick a table in the corner of the restaurant so he could see everyone coming in. His dad learned that he had been able to obtain a new identify before going over the border into Canada. He feared coming back to this country. His parents felt helpless in their efforts to convince him to return home.

The drug situation was beginning to infiltrate the college system all over the country. The temptations of big money was just too much for many of the young people.

That tragedy happened to the band director's son a couple of years before Jeffrey disappeared. Did Jeffrey get involved in drugs, with someone like this lawyer, when he was at East Carolina? How could these outstanding young men from nice, successful families get caught up in such a mess? Shirley had no hard evidence of any kind at that time. It was just one big puzzle, one big mess, one big disaster for their family.

Bud had bought the fish business at the beach in June of 1980. Jeffrey became missing in November of the same year. Shirley was struggling with the management of the business in Elizabeth City while Bud was struggling with life without Jeffrey at the beach. They were in different worlds at that point. This was a time of survival for their family and they knew it. They were both extremely strong, confident people but shattered like an atom bomb had hit them. Looking back on that time, she wondered how the girls survived with their parents in such a state. Life can deal some lousy blows and their young daughters were the biggest victims of all. Their beloved older brother had fallen out of the nest and their parents appeared to be lost at the same time.

Their Mother definitely was.

Shirley knew, without a doubt, if one of her girls had disappeared, she would be in an insane asylum, probably somewhere like Dorothy

Dix in Raleigh, North Carolina. At least Jeffrey was 21, strong and smart. Maybe he could have defended himself if he encountered foul play 16 miles offshore in international waters. She prayed that he had a chance to pull out of whatever had happened to him. She tried to return to normal for the girls. She struggled hard but when you are forced to live with the unknown, it is very difficult to return to anything even resembling normal.

Somebody mentioned to the Mays, "If anyone would know what happened to the boys, it would be Ted's close friend Rodney Matthews. Rodney is in Tortola in the British Virgin Islands surfing." They checked around and found out that a lot of the Dare County boys go to Tortola during the winter to surf.

Shirley called the State Department, told them her problem and asked for help. They said they would find out where Rodney Matthews was staying and would meet them at the airport and take them there.

She called her brother Ken in the Keys. "Meet us at the Miami airport. We're going to Tortola to look for Jeffrey." All three of them flew out of Miami to Tortola and were met by officials of the State Department. They were taken directly to the west side of the island to the house where Rodney was staying. He seemed quite startled upon seeing them. "I don't know where the boys are but if I did, I wouldn't tell unless they wanted me too."

Ken was furious. "If I ever find out that you do know, this universe won't be big enough for you." Shirley strongly suggested that Rodney come over to their motel room that night for further conversation.

That night in Tortola, a different country and many miles from home, they grilled Ted's friend until he confessed that Ted had dealt some with drugs in the past, wanted to go higher on the chain and always said he would like to disappear and get a new name. Rodney Matthews said he sincerely didn't know what happened to them that day offshore.

Sadly, they flew back home without any suggestion of what to do next.

They took part of their Cotton Mill on the downtown waterfront and built a three story brick home. They started planning for it right after Jeffrey was missing. It became therapeutic for Shirley. She needed a focus so she wouldn't lose her mind. They took half of the Cotton Mill building, dismantled it down to the river pilings and had a wonderful architect design them a colonial home which fit in perfectly with the historic district that her hometown was attempting to develop. It faded in with the other waterfront buildings and was truly a show place. The house and properties were in the middle of two very nice public parks.

During those years, Elizabeth City was having a lot of drug problems with users and dealers just like many other small southern towns. It was becoming blatant. She had a ringside seat from their properties, especially from their big front waterfront porches, and could easily view all of the activity in both public parks. In fact, it was hard for her to miss it. She kept the phone busy calling the police. The druggies pulled needles out and actually shot up right in the parks next door to her home, not even appearing to be concerned about getting caught by the local police.

On many occasions, she witnessed a seaplane landing in the water in front of their house and the parks, make a hand signal and then off in a southerly direction. She would then witness people leaving the park to go meet the plane.

She also saw foreign boats come in at dusk, without a mast, pull up near the local shipyard, walk over, get a mast and install it. She was later told by the FBI in Charlotte that some shipyards on the East Coast had been seized because of that same action. She kept good records and documented it all. She tried to work with law enforcement, local, state and federal, but was never aware of any actions taken on their part because of the information she gave them. It was very discouraging and hard for her to keep the faith.

Contrary to the facts, all of this information she was furnishing the proper officials seemed to be backfiring on her. With the exception of a couple of officers, one being a woman, the local police seem to resent her for calling them so much about drug problems downtown in the parks on the waterfront.

Chapter Four

The Year 1981

The insurance man was cruel. He was hesitating about paying the insurance for Jeffrey's boat because he thought they knew the whereabouts of Jeffrey. She will never forget that insensitive person. How could anyone be so cruel as to think that parents could be a part of the nightmare of losing their son? How low can people get? That insurance man's actions went completely under the radar. Shirley thought he was truly an indecent human being.

The first of the year 1981, a young man with a beard came into their Elizabeth City business. Bud was working instead of Shirley that day. He told Bud he didn't know Jeffrey but he knew Ted and he could put his hands on the boys. He said they were in trouble with the Mafia, owed them $100,000 and he could get them out of it if he had $100,000 to negotiate. He said not everyone could deal with the Mafia but he could.

He came back a second time when Bud was at the fish house in Nags Head and Shirley met with him. She had already checked him out, learned his name and that he was an informer with the local police. He lived in Currituck County, a couple of counties away and halfway to the Outer Banks. She also found out that he had attended a nearby local school with her brother Ken. He repeated the story to Shirley that he knew where the boys were and he could put his hands on them. "Good. Put your hands on them and take them to my brother Ken in Florida. Then you can get your $100,000." "Suppose they get away?"

27

"You know my brother Ken. You went to school with him and you know that won't happen."

That double dealing informer never surfaced again – until several years later. She should have called the FBI at that time but it was too soon for her to realize that what just happened might be an extortion attempt.

Chapter Five

The Year 1982

In 1982, the Mays sold the office supply business to their bookkeeper who moved it to another location. They had an empty John Deere building.

In October of '82, a major storm hit the Outer Banks. Their Kitty Hawk Coast Guard Station suffered some damage to the porches but their oceanfront neighbors were not so fortunate. Ten cottages on both sides were gone by the next morning, leaving scattered debris and exposed septic tanks. The tenacious old Coast Guard station remained sturdy.

Chapter Six

The Year 1983

In June of 1983, George Neighbors died unexpectedly of cancer. The partnership wasn't to end until 1985 so they were in a bind by his unexpected death. The partnership consisted of 45 acres of prime beach land from ocean to sound in Kitty Hawk, North Carolina. It was called Kitty Dunes West, Kitty Dune Village and Kitty Dunes Commercial on both sides of the by pass road.

In the state of North Carolina, a partnership automatically dissolves at the death of either partner. In the case of a general partner, the limited partner can take over and manage the business. Their initial partnership papers made sure that was the case. To do this, the limited partner must have the total knowledge of the books. Shortly after George's death, Shirley started trying to get information from their accountants; Jack Adams and Johnson and Burgess, the Neimay lawyers, Norm Shearin and Tom White, the Planters National Bank bankers Ray White and Chris Payne and John Neighbors, the son and the executor of the estate.

From the beginning, she was stonewalled by all. What she did not know at that time was that George owed Planters National Banks millions of dollars that had nothing to do with Neimay Partnership. And that he was in business with most of them in other development deals.

In early 1981, George had been involved with a fisherman who was indicted as a drug dealer. Shirley didn't have knowledge of this until many years later during the lawsuit against him. The local sea captain, Lunsford Crew, piloted a receiver-ship through local channels. The mother ship was located offshore Cape Hatteras.

In 1988 during the lawsuit, she read a local paper which said: "Lunsford Crew, 40, an Outer Banks resident when the offenses occurred between December 1978 and spring of 1981 pleaded guilty to one count of conspiracy to traffic in marijuana in return for having five counts of felony possession of over 10,000 pounds of marijuana dropped. As part of the plea bargain, he had agreed to pay a fine of $25,000 and any prison time should run consecutively with his federal term if the bargain is accepted. Crew was the local captain who piloted the receiver-ship through local channels, according to the prosecutor." The article further stated, "The group would load a mother ship with the drugs and this ship would cross the ocean to a point just off the coast where it would make contact with a smaller fishing boat which would pick up the marijuana and deliver it to port. There were nine boatloads in all. The boats brought as much as 25,000 to 46,000 pounds of marijuana per load to this area during the time the drug ring was in operation."

Shirley discovered, during the Neimary Lawsuit which she filed in 1985, that on May 19, 1981, George Neighbors had Lunsford Crew's properties put into his name by Tom White, Neimay partnership attorney. The indicted fisherman's father, who drew up all of the necessary paperwork for the transfer was a prominent attorney in a small nearby town.

It took her six years to get the cancelled checks from Ray White, President of Planters National Bank in spite of the court's order to release them. Ray White at the time was in business with some of the Neimay players in another company called Sea Ventures.

On 5-19-81 George Neighbors wrote the following checks on an account opened for him and his son John at Planters National Bank by Ray White:

- Check 2931 made out to PNB (Planter National Bank) for $9548.08 for a cashier check for Kellogg, White, Evans for *Crew*. The check was stamped **DO NOT RETURN** and the backside of the check read **Cashier's Check issued in lieu of**.
- Check #2932 made out to Tom White for $1169.50. No memo note.
- Check #2933 made out to Starkey Sharp for $241.48. The memo recorded it was for May pay –Bal.

The checks made out to Tom White and Starkey Sharpe were endorsed by them and deposited into the trust account of Kellogg, White, Evans & Sharp on May 20, 1981.

Shirley was aware, after finding checks like the ones above, that the banks were using cashier checks to hide transactions. She found quite a few of them in her discovery.

During the same discovery, she found a Planters National Bank deposit slip dated 2-11-81, three months earlier than the Crew transaction, in the same George and John Neighbors account with the following deposits:

- Check #13277 made out to George Neighbors for $1,747 from Nunemaker Fish Company, Wholesale Fish Dealers signed by Harriet Nunemaker, wife of Charles Nunemaker.
- Check #1362 made out to Nunemaker Fish Co. for $11,753 from Aylesworth's Trucking and Seafood Inc., St. Petersburg, Fla. . (This check was deposited directly into George Neighbor's account without being endoresed).

Those two checks add up to $13,500. These transactions by George Neighbors and Planters National Bank ran in and out of the Neimay accounts. They were really hard for Shirley to follow.

It looked like fish business running through real estate accounts to Shirley and it further appeared that George Neighbors had put the Mays smack in the middle of the action.

The discovery of these checks was at the same time she discovered that Tom White and Ray White were partners in business with George Neighbors on other real estate development deals at the Outer Banks.

It looked blatantly like Planters National Bank money laundering to her and Ray White, in his deposition, said he had been with Planters Bank for 24 years.

And it really bothered her that Jeffrey's boat had been docked at the Nunemaker wholesale fish house in Hatteras that fateful day of November 13, 1980 when he left to go fishing and never came home.

While finding this discovery in the late eighties, she found out that George had not only mixed their partnership money in with fish dealing and incorrect real estate deals but also with Planters National Bank accounts that had checks written for many gun purchases.

She had only been aware of two Neimay partnership accounts, one regular and one money market when in fact; she learned that George Neighbors had been commingling in more than eighteen Planters National Bank accounts. It took Ray White of Planters National Bank six years to give her these checks, in spite of a court order.

She started developing plans to build little shops inside the vacant John Deere building. They had a young man working for them fulltime almost since the day they arrived in town. His name was Billy Winslow and he was a whiz at carpentry. He could build just like the old master carpenters. Just sketch a picture and he could do it. His specialty was custom trim work. He did all of their work on the waterfront in Elizabeth City, the Coast Guard Station at Kitty Hawk and Nunemaker fish business in Nags Head, when it was turned into a restaurant and seafood bar. He was just like a son to her.

Billy was savvy about drugs. He knew the drug crowd and he was absolutely fearless. He got into a little trouble growing marijuana on his back porch during the time that he was working with them and had to spend a short time in prison. She didn't want Billy and his wife to lose their house so she brought his wife to live with her so they could rent their house. She arranged for him to get out of prison daily on work release. She drove to the prison every day. It was a good distance from Elizabeth City. She kept Billy busy working days either in Elizabeth City or at the Outer Banks and then would take him back to prison in the evening. She did this every day until he was released.

One day, while the John Deere building was still empty, she got a phone call from the local industrial developer who was a personal friend of hers. "Shirley, I got a strange call from a man in New Jersey. He said he was coming to Elizabeth City to start an investigative service and he is interested in buying a certain brick building on the waterfront. He described your exact building. I told him it was not for sale and he said everything has a price. What do you want me to do? I don't trust him." "Bring him here when he arrives." She didn't want the New Jersey guy to know that she didn't have a price.

Shirley was 24/7 looking for Jeffrey and she never knew when a piece of the puzzle might pop up.

The call from the industrial developer was in the middle of the week. On Sunday night, February 19, 1983 at 12:40 a.m, Bud was in Elizabeth City. They had just retired for the evening when the phone rang. She answered. "I know what you are doing, but you don't know what I'm doing." "You've got the wrong number." He said, "No, I don't. You don't know what I'm doing." He laughed like a hyena and hung up abruptly. She was shocked and couldn't speak. Again the phone rang and the same person said, "You have a son lost at sea. I sell drugs. Just call me Blow John." Bud jumped out of bed and said, "What was that?" Before she could answer, the phone rang again. Bud grabbed it. "Who is this?" The hyena just laughed and laughed and hung up without saying a word.

The next day she called the Elizabeth City Chief of Police who was one of her Mother and Dad's best friends. Everyone knew about Jeffrey's disappearance so no explanation was necessary. "Chief, would you please put a tap on our phone? We are getting some intimidating calls from a very strange man who is referring to Jeffrey." The Chief called back and said, for some reason that she never will understand, that he couldn't place a tap on their phone. She picked up the phone, called a relative who had owned the phone company and a tap was placed on her phone immediately.

Unfortunately, the hyena didn't call back the next day but she did get another call from her friend, the industrial developer who said, "I've called the Chief and told him I'm worried about you. This nut is in town and he has checked in the local hospital. He insists he's here to buy your property." About that time, she received a call from a real estate friend of hers. "Shirley, I've got this guy who wants to see your property. He's in the hospital interviewing girls to work with him. My daughter is one of them. He is promising big salaries and I don't know what is going on. What should I do? He told them that he was buying the big brick building on the waterfront, describing yours, and starting his investigative business as soon as possible."

She said to the real estate agent who was a friend of hers, "Bring him here." She wanted to see if his *voice* fit the Sunday night phone voice of the hyena.

Later that day, *the voice* arrived. Billy was out of prison and back on her jobs fulltime. She called him to stop what he was doing at her house next door and come to the John Deere building. She told Billy just to look busy but be there with her when this mysterious New Jersey oil rig business man arrived. When the real estate agent and *the voice* arrived, she rushed out to the car, extended her hand and quickly said, "We're so happy to have you in town. I have a son missing and I will probably be your first client."

The voice had icy blue eyes, was wearing a polyester suit and was a role model profile of a druggie. She was beginning to spot druggies in a flash. She had totally disarmed him and he sputtered, "Who is he missing with?" Strange question right off the bat. She gave him Ted's name. He wanted Ted's social security number. She told him she certainly didn't have that. Shirley and Billy together gave *the voice* a tour of the building and knew that he wasn't listening to anything that was being said. He was too busy trying to retrieve his mind. He left and she all but kissed him goodbye. He was definitely the hyena who had called them laughing about their son and disrupting their lives once again.

She thought, "You dirty dog, I am going to run a background check on you."

Strange things started happening. She called the local police immediately and told them about this man who was in town and telling many people that he was buying their building. She informed them that at that very moment, he was leaving town on the bus. The real estate agent had whispered that in her ear as they got in her car to leave. She was taking *the voice* directly to the bus station. Shirley was almost begging the Chief, "Can the police please check on this stranger because something is really wrong?"

Chief called back in a couple of hours and reported to her, "Sorry but we missed him." Somehow she wasn't surprised. It appeared she had been made a smoke screen for something big, maybe a big drug deal going down in Elizabeth City. After all, the town was having a big festival at the time and it would be easy for the drug folks to get lost in the crowds downtown and at hospitals and other places. What a rotten thing for *the voice* to do to the Mays. Using Jeffrey's family as a smoke screen like that was beyond cruel.

Two days later, Bud called from the beach and told her to be careful. His best friend, Eddie Miller, who had several restaurants at the beach, had just interviewed a man who said he was from New Jersey and that he was a chef. Eddie was very suspicious of him and asked for references. Eddie had been interviewing two young ladies from Elizabeth City at the time this man arrived and he excused himself to interview the "chef." After the guy left, the two young girls got very excited and said to Eddie, "That was the man who was at the hospital in Elizabeth City interviewing people and telling everyone he had bought the Mays' property on the waterfront."

Those girls should have known because they were the same ones interviewed by *the voice* at the hospital for those nice high paying jobs he was going to be providing for the area. Bud had told Eddie about the Sunday night phone calls from the hyena as soon as he returned to the beach. Eddie immediately called Bud as soon as the "chef" left and said, "That man is dangerous. Call and tell Shirley."

She called her doctor friend at the hospital who had attended *the voice* and told him she needed a name to give the police chief. The doctor knew all about Jeffrey's disappearance so he was more than willing to help her anyway he could. The guy had checked into the local hospital under an alias, Sean Demarr. The Chief ran a check and *the voice* had several aliases and had been in trouble all over the country, starting in Seattle, Washington. His real name was Sean La Moure. Appears he always had a guardian angel to bail him out. He never got punished by the law until getting arrested in North Carolina. He had just been released from prison somewhere in North Carolina for stealing a car in Hatteras. Eddie checked his references and tracked him back to a small restaurant in Cape May and an oil rig offshore in New Jersey.

Shirley had a few more pieces of the puzzle but the trail of *the voice* with the icy blue eyes and polyester suit grew cold mainly because she was unable to get any help from law enforcement. She felt sure neither she nor *the voice* would soon forget each other.

She and Billy started developing the little shops in the John Deere Building. All she had to do with him was throw a sketch on a small piece of paper and it became a reality. She had a little problem when she requested a door or window to be "crooked" because he was such a perfectionist. He soon learned to do the little crooked doors and windows exactly the way she wanted them. The little historic shopping center was a showplace and all because of Billy. He was truly a genius in his own field.

She was creating a space for a deli and space for about fourteen neat little specialty shops. At the same time she continued informing everyone, including the State Bureau of Investigation (SBI), Federal Bureau of Investigation (FBI) and the local police about the drug dealing activities surrounding her downtown properties. She even made a trip to Charlotte to tell the main FBI men, one in charge of drugs and the other in charge of political corruption about the out of control drug dealing in her hometown. When she left them, her developer friend from Canada who had accompanied her said to them, "What can you do to protect her?" They looked straight at Shirley. "Just keep on doing what you are doing. You are very high exposure."

Sure, she was high exposure because of the location of their properties and she felt strongly that she was doing their work and nobody cared what happened to her.

That trip to the FBI in Charlotte backfired on her also.

Within a very short time of the Charlotte FBI trip, she got a break-in at their shopping center. It appeared to be a setup rather than a normal break in. It was strange because the people or person breaking in got food from the deli, ate it in the area of a lot of cell phones and other technology and didn't steal a thing. When the local police came to investigate, one of the officers that she knew said, "Shirley, don't take everything so personal." She felt like saying to him, "and you tell your druggies to stay the hell out of my life."

One of the strangest incidents of all happened, about this time when she was sitting on her riverfront porch witnessing police cars on both sides of her house. One police car was in Mariner's Park, north of her, facing away from the river. One police car was in Waterfront Park, south of her, facing away from the river and still another police car was about a block away at the local Peoples Bank.

"What in the world is going on?" she thought.

She looked straight up the river in front of her house and saw a boat coming in at an extremely fast pace. Boats were not supposed to create much wake at that location but evidently somebody forgot to inform them. Curiosity got the best of her so she walked over to the big park south of her house, adjoining her property. She peeped down and looked into the police car parked there facing out and it was the local cop who came recently to investigate her break-in who thought she was taking things too personal. She nodded and continued her stroll over to the boat ramp. She watched the boat being pulled up and the windshield was shot all to hell. She shouted to the guy running the boat, "what in the world happened to you?" He looked quickly in both directions and sputtered, "Vandalism." It was a Marine Fishery boat.

"These environmental people must not always be safe out there doing research like they do," she thought.

The Marine Fishery guy and his boat were escorted out of town by those police cars so fast it would make your head spin. Shirley then turned to walk the short distance home and thought to herself, "And if you cops think I bought that story, I will sell you the Brooklyn Bridge."

Her puzzle was filling in and it appeared to her that the international drug center was moving out of the Outer Banks Oregon Inlet Fishing Center and inland into her hometown and the Mays' prime waterfront property had been targeted for their headquarters. It was such a prominent spot that many of the visiting boaters who moored for a night or more would ask if the Mayor lived there.

It sure appeared to her that a lot of people were trying to run her out of town. She saw cars from Louisiana, Florida, Texas and other southern states stopping in her driveway and taking pictures of the surroundings, including the shipyard, the public parks and her property. She stayed busy calling the Coast Guard to report strange boat activity and the local police about local drug activity. She knew she wasn't going crazy because the local papers were busy reporting the drug activity and even the Director of the S. B. I. said, "If things continue the way they are, we'll be living in one of the top ten most dangerous states at the end of the decade."

After visiting the FBI in Charlotte, several unusual things happened on the waterfront directly in front of their house. She wondered if they might somehow be on the scene without her knowledge. She doubted very much that they were. She felt all alone in her fight against the crime and corruption in her hometown and the Outer Banks. Many times she felt like no one cared but her. Shirley had huge porches facing the water and spent a lot of time there just thinking about her girls and how they had been tragically wounded by Jeffrey's disappearance. She felt like a lost mother with no control at all over her life.

Several days in a row, she spotted a car in the park south of her with a canoe tied to the top. She had not seen many canoes launched from that particular dock. It was the same dock that the Marine Fishery boat came in and out of so fast recently. The canoe caught her attention. One day, while the boating activity was busier than normal, she spotted the same canoe in the water in front of the shipyard which was very close to her. At the same time, she spotted a man standing next to a boat that was almost on her porch. He had something in his ear and he appeared to be talking to himself. She could hear him say, "They are pulling in, now backing up, lots of electronics, etc." She was concentrating so hard on him that she didn't see the canoe man pull up. He was looking straight up at her on her porch and shouted, "You can see a lot from down here." She shouted back, "And you can see a hell of a lot from up here!"

Disgust was dripping from her lips.

She believed the Mafia was in town on some of those big yachts with all their electronics and she was thoroughly disgusted that the volunteer welcoming committee from the city was feeding them free wine and cheese and crackers while thinking that they were just nice boaters passing through. She knew differently because she was beginning to be able to spot the bad guys in a flash. She saw two of them walking from the cheese party up to her property so she hurriedly pulled out her binoculars. She could not tell what they were saying but they were pointing to her house. She was hiding behind the curtains but she wanted to step out on her porch and shout, "She's a damn nice person, has a missing son and shouldn't have to put up with this drug activity on both sides of her property."

She had a notebook documenting many occasions similar to that one.

Chapter Seven

The Year 1984

Shirley continued trying to get partnership information. She was dealing with the same lawyers and bankers that handled George Neighbor's land transactions with Lunsford Crew, the local drug dealer. They were all frantically stonewalling.

During the year 1984, she kept herself real busy in Elizabeth City doing community work to keep from losing her mind. She was a charter member of the Committee of 100. That was a committee where you paid a hundred dollars a year to do volunteer work for the community. She volunteered to head up the Waterfront Committee. She helped develop the city park next door to her into free boat slips, where visiting boats could moor for a day and two and get to know her hometown. A few city officials were reluctant about letting her put in the boat slips on city property. They almost made her put in writing that she could prove it would be successful. After the slips became successful. Shirley was given the honor of 'Business Woman of the Year' from the Downtown Business Association.

In 1984, she co-chaired an event for the 400th Anniversary of the State of North Carolina. She and a friend from another small town in North Carolina volunteered their services to the State for two years to organize a flotilla during the event that would her depart from her hometown of Elizabeth City and sail to Roanoke Island, the Land of the Beginning. Jim Hunt was the Governor at the time. He invited Walter Cronkite to attend the event as Sir Walter Raleigh. Walter Cronkite was Shirley's houseguest for a couple of days in her waterfront home. The event was extremely successful and brought a lot of publicity to her town. She received the award of "Business Woman of the Year" from the Chamber of Commerce for that event.

It took a lot to keep her busy because Jeffrey was on her mind all the time. Where was he? What had happened? Why couldn't she get some information from law enforcement? Why was she always hitting steel doors while searching for answers? She and Bud were growing apart at this time, emotionally, physically and financially. They decided to split some properties because she had been approached by a businessman from Virginia, a General, who wanted to build some condos with her at the Outer Banks. She was a real estate broker and had some developing experience.

She and Bud divided most of their assets in late 1984 or early 1985. They really started growing apart at that time although they didn't divorce until 1987.

She tried to get Neimay discovery from Tom White, Ray White and Jack Adams from 1983 until 1985 at which time in March of 1985, they had no choice but to sue. When she and Bud split assets in 1985, she inherited the Neimay Lawsuit. At that time, she was on her own with the local Outer Bank boys and their very own judicial system.

In March of 1984, there was a huge drug bust at the Outer Banks. Twelve people were indicted in a $40 million dollar drug operation. The indictment followed a two-year investigation by the Organized Crime Drug Enforcement Task Force, which the Reagan administration created in 1982. One of the ships destined for the North Carolina coast, the Don Frank, was boarded and seized by the Coast Guard in December of 1980. The captain of that ship, not a local, was convicted of drug charges in 1981 and sentenced to five years in prison. In 1980 and 1981, the ring brought in three loads, one of 40,000 pounds, and used at least five vessels, including the Miss Michelle. The vessels were drug trafficking from South America to a series of landing spots in the United States. A few of the main landing sites, according to the grand jury, were a fish house in Stumpy Point, North Carolina, a pier at Wanchese, North Carolina and a site in Hyde County, North Carolina.

Some of the seized properties included a Cessna aircraft, a beach cottage at Nags Head, a truck, the cash proceeds from the sale of six vessels and all interest held in seven companies alleged to have been a part of the conspiracy. These would be seized if certain defendants were convicted.

Nine of the twelve were charged with racketeering. Three of them were locals, from Kill Devil Hills, Colington Harbor and Wanchese, North Carolina, all locations on the Outer Banks.

In July of 1984, there was another big bust, just a few miles away in another North Carolina coastal town called Sneads Ferry. It involved eight residents and one sailor, who were stationed aboard the USS Dwight D. Eisenhower when the indictments were issued. This bust involved 85,000 pounds of marijuana, a $68 million dollar drug operation. Sneads Ferry fishing trawlers picked up the marijuana from a Colombian ship in February 1981, transported it to a warehouse in Sneads Ferry, and then trucked it to a New Bern warehouse for distribution. All of these coastal fishermen know each other.

It is a small, small world out there for the drug dealers in that big Atlantic ocean.

Also in the fall of 1984, a local old wooden trawler went down off the New Jersey coast. There were nine crewmen on board and the vessel was owned by the Daniels family who owned Wanchese Fish Company based out of Hampton, Virginia. The men were never found.

Shirley wondered if that old wooden trawler owned by the Wanchese family was covered by insurance.

In December, she really got concerned when she read, "A Nags Head seafood dealer and three other local men were arrested following a federal indictment alleging that they helped smuggle 69,000 pounds of marijuana into Wanchese in 1981." She knew the Nags Head seafood dealer real well, had known him since she was a little girl but what really concerned her was that his seafood market was just down the road a couple of miles from theirs. They were all good friends. The Nags Head seafood dealer was an Austin and related to the Dare County Sheriff. This bust was tied into the earlier one in March. It was an ongoing investigation by the same Organized Crime Drug Enforcement Task Force for the Eastern District of Virginia. The paper indicated that the Task Force wasn't finished yet, they anticipated future indictments.

Shirley was sick in her stomach with all of these big drug busts that went back to the time when Jeffrey was missing and the possibility that he could have gotten involved. What kind of can of worms did her son step into? Every day she wondered "What really happened that day offshore, when the fisherman all gave the Coast Guard searchers a different story?"

Chapter Eight

The Year 1985

In January of 1985, H. P. Williams, the District Attorney for the first prosecutorial district of North Carolina, which included the Outer Banks and Elizabeth City where his main office was, returned a bill of indictments against these people. The district attorney was from the Outer Banks and related to many of the locals who were getting into drug trouble. The indictment, returned on January 14, followed a two and one-half year investigation by the Organized Crime Drug Enforcement Task Force for the Eastern District of Virginia. This task force was created in 1982 by President Reagan and the Attorney General to disrupt narcotics trafficking by organized criminal groups.

The organized crime investigation in this case was conducted by a Lieutenant Robert Eck of the Dare County Sheriff's Department along with others from the FBI, Norfolk, Virginia Police Department, the Virginia State Police and the North Carolina State Bureau of Investigation. Eck was not a local boy. He had been a Highway Patrolman in Massachusetts before coming to Dare County. His brother-in-law, Jock MacKenzie talked him into moving to the Outer Banks. Shirley later found out that the last boat to approach her son and talk to them was owned by Lt. Eck's brother in law, Jock MacKenzie. Jock had married a local Outer Banks girl.

Jock MacKenzie owned the boat, The Easy Ryder, but Edgar Styron, Jr. was piloting it that fateful day of November 13 when they were the very last people to see her son Jeffrey. Edgar Styron, Jr. was also the same man on the porch with Franklin Wall that fateful day, November 13, who had to go to Avon with Harry and his briefcase and couldn't take the time to tell the Coast Guard where they last saw the boys.

Many of Edgar's family were in the Coast Guard and one of them was at the helm of Jeffrey's search out of Hatteras. All the locals appear to be related either by blood or by marriage.

The river runs very, very deep on the Outer Banks of North Carolina and especially in Avon.

Shirley's father died on July 7th of 1985. After the funeral, Bud informed her that he was moving back to Ligonier. He had a contract on the Nunemaker retail business in Nags Head at the time. He asked her if she would handle the closing for him. She thought the weight of the world had dropped on her that day. She cried the entire weekend.

On Monday, she went to the beach and found out that Nunemakers was in danger of going into foreclosure. That was news to her. She had absolutely no knowledge that the fish house was in danger of foreclosure. Evidently the potential purchasers were aware of the many problems because they breached a solid contract   John Morrison the Mays' attorney wouldn't do a damn thing about it. He was not one to rock local Outer Banks boats or as a matter of fact, anyone's boat. She pushed him to make the buyers of the Nunemaker Fish Market honor the contract. Her efforts were useless.

Her new partner, the General, was more experienced about foreclosures and legal actions than she was so he immediately tried to find the problem. When they went to the Seaboard Savings and Loan to ask about the fish house loan, they were told that Tom White of the Kellogg Firm in Manteo had called the S&L to inform them of the pending foreclosure. The General immediately called Tom White and requested that he hold up on sending the foreclosure letter because he was helping Ms. Mays bring all the late payments up to date. The General knew all of these people and knew exactly how they did business.

At this same time, she was still trying desperately, with the help of John Morrison, to get Neimay discovery. She had been trying continuously to get information so they could take over the management of the partnership. Tom White wouldn't release the Neimay settlement sheets, Ray White wouldn't release the Neimay cancelled checks and Jack Adams, the accountant wouldn't release the Neimay books which rightfully belonged to the partners.

She was having a hard time getting any information. Little did she know at the time that this same group of guys were closing the remaining Neimay properties fast as they could, without the knowledge or signatures of the Mays and frantically paying off George Neighbors' debts at Planters Bank that had nothing to do with the Neimay partnership. At the same time, Tom White was also initiating foreclosure on them at the fish house. Tom White was also the attorney for Nags Head. He seemed to be everybody's attorney at that time and he was definitely playing legal hardball. Conflicts of interest were not a matter of concern for him. It appeared to be a way of life. Bud signed over any further proceeds from the partnership to Shirley when he left the area and moved back to Ligonier.

The legal ball on the Outer Banks of North Carolina was now in her court.

In the state of North Carolina, if the general partner dies, a limited partnership automatically dissolves and the limited partner can take over. All she was trying to do was get the partnership information that was legally theirs so the proper legal action could take place. Even the accountant Jack Adams was in business with George on a different development adjacent to the Neimay properties. They were obviously doing their best as a team to break Shirley Mays financially and eliminate a problem for all of them.

That did not happen, at least not at that time. The General advised her how to handle the Neimay problem. He first secured the loans involving the fish house so she would owe him instead of the bank. He then advised her to sue the lawyers, accountants and bankers involved with the Neimay real estate scam. She talked to John Morrison and he advised her to just sue George Neighbors' estate, the executor of the estate and the real estate company that the general partner had formed just because of this partnership. John advised Shirley that a conspiracy would be too difficult to explain to a jury, especially one in Dare County

In March of 1985, she initiated the lawsuit following his advice. The lawsuit was filed in Bud's name because his name was listed as the limited partner, but legally it had been transferred to her. The big one sided Dare County judicial fight was about to begin. She wanted a jury in the beginning but John advised that it would be better to explain it to a judge. She was advised by him that she could ask for one later. John forgot to tell her that later the request for a jury would be at the discretion of the judge. She learned that the hard way and later was denied a jury.

Shirley's biggest problem was that her can of worms was full of the same people. The people who controlled her also controlled the banks, also controlled the books and also controlled the judicial system in Dare County. She was in a rat's nest and she knew it. So did the General who had become her Outer Banks mentor. And the General knew most of these people much better than she did. He was looking forward to the battle. He loved war games. She had always been told by her mother, "When you have a drastic situation, the Lord sends you a drastic answer." And her mother Fannie was always right.

The Lord had sent her the General.

Chapter Nine

The Year 1986

The Virginian Pilot, February 28, 1986. "A federal investigation that traced a $270 million dollar North Carolina marijuana smuggling conspiracy over a six-year period has resulted in indictments against 28 people" reported the North Carolina U. S. Attorney. "We had long thought that northeastern North Carolina was a major gateway for the marijuana smuggling industry, but we did not realize what a gateway it was until we conducted this investigation and we learned what this one group was doing." He continued, "The indictments involve nine shipments of marijuana totaling 385,000 pounds between 1978 and 1984. We learned that this group of conspirators had attempted nine shipments into Dare and Hyde counties and the total street value of the marijuana which they attempted to bring in was in excess of $270 million. The Dare county shipments were primarily unloaded at the Oregon Inlet Fishing Center. The U. S. Attorney said he believes North Carolina has become a major port for marijuana entering the United States.

On at least six occasions, the major drug runs were unloaded at the Oregon Inlet Fishing Center. It was taken from several different fishing boats and loaded onto rented trucks or vans at the docks. The use of Oregon Inlet Fishing Center where, annually, thousands of sport fishermen avail themselves of the some 33 charter boats stationed there, came as a big surprise to the National Park Superintendent and the Coast Guard Group Commander, who said he often used the center as "safe harbor" for his patrol boats, which are normally docked across the inlet at the Coast Guard Station. The Group Commander said, "Drug traffickers have a great deal of nerve. Their operation patterns are seldom logical. We try to keep a high profile in the Oregon Inlet area but I believe that nine out of ten drug boats could get through."

The U. S. Attorney said, "The North Carolina operation is very important but very fluid, with people moving in and out as they are needed."

A Washington, D. C. Drug Enforcement Agency spokesman said in an interview that "big money flashed in some of the fishing centers in the Carolinas is often all that is needed to recruit local involvement in the illegal drug transportation business. Sometimes a $5,000 to $10,000 offer for one night's work looks pretty good to even a smart businessman who is having a bad year. Dealing strictly in cash requires a "laundering" method of the case, which then is returned to the economy in a number of ways – especially easy in an area developing as rapidly as Dare County. Real estate, construction, even buying a car or a boat," he said, "can be done with cash without suspicion. Sometimes the cash can be divided up among a number of individuals who can purchase cashiers checks at banks, all under the minimum reporting level of $10,000. Then the checks can go to other bank accounts, all very neat," he added.

In the spring of 1986, a waterspout went directly over the Mays' Coast Guard Station in Kitty Hawk. Eric Kreiger, Jeffrey's buddy from Ligonier and his wife Susan were visiting when Shirley received a phone call from Rosemary Jones, a friend of hers. Rosemary informed Shirley of the waterspout coming her way. She told them that the radio was announcing that it was heading in the direction of the Kitty Hawk Coast Guard Station. They ran to the dining room door, which faced south, and saw it coming. It had picked up wallboard, lumber and other debris and was coming straight at them. She had been through a lot of hurricanes but had never seen anything like this it in her life.

Eric quickly hustled them into the central hall of the four downstairs bedrooms and threw a mattress over them. The waterspout sounded like a train going over their heads. As soon as they thought it was safe, they ran to the front door facing the ocean and saw it turn around. It looked as if it was coming back straight at them. It lost its strength before hitting land but for a few more minutes, it was frightening.

Her phone started ringing. Friends were checking to see if she was OK because the Station had been mentioned over the local radio station as being in the direct path of the waterspout. Rosemary came over to compare notes. Shirley noticed Eric staring out the window looking north, but thought nothing about it. Then he quickly got up and went to the big porch facing the ocean. As soon as the company left, he said, "Shirl come here fast!" She did and Eric pointed to two guys, with heavy beards and heavy clothes, walking back across the street and getting into a pickup with a dog in the back.

"That's the little guy, that's him!" She didn't immediately know what he was talking about but he continued, "Shirl, that's Jeffrey, that's him!" Eric was about 6'2" and Jeffrey was only 5'10' and Eric sometimes affectionately called him little guy. He was excited and adamant. "I know his wave, I'm positive it is him." She didn't want to upset Eric. The two heavily bearded guys were walking away when she got on the porch so she didn't get as good a look at them as he did.

"Let's take a ride and see if we can see the truck." Shirley said as they were running to the car. She told Eric what had happened a few days before at the Station. She needed some clay for the driveway so she called Outer Banks Construction, the local paving people in Kitty Hawk. She was shocked when the truck drove up. It was Dale Winslow driving, Ted's friend who was rumored to have left Elizabeth City right after the search and to have possibly been involved with whatever happened to the boys. Dale grew up like a brother to Ted in Elizabeth City just like Eric grew up with Jeffrey in Pennsylvania. She had heard that Dale had left town and followed a route to Alaska as if he were tracking the boys. She had also heard that he came back and married Ted's younger sister, Rachael, and had taken her to Alaska to live. A lot of people were surprised at that marriage because there was a big difference in age. They had grown up like sister and brother.

Shirley said to Dale as he was fixing her drive, "I didn't know you were back from Alaska. What do you hear from Ted and Jeffrey?" Dale never flinched. He was extremely composed as if he were waiting for years for the question when he answered, "Ms. Mays, if Ted was alive, I would have heard from him." Shirley didn't believe Dale Winslow then and she doesn't believe him now. She asked about Rachael and inquired as to where they were living. He said, "First Flight Village." He never mentioned Alaska nor showed any emotion at all when she did.

She and Eric headed south after the waterspout incident. "Let's go to First Flight Village and look for Dale's house." It was a big subdivision with lots of crooks and crannies. Although she had never been in that subdivision before, somehow she directed him right to the house. They parked and walked straight up to the front door. Eric knocked heavily and Dale said, "Come in." They walked in and Dale was lying on the sofa, looking in the opposite direction. He never got up and never looked their way. Eric sputtered out, "I just saw the guys. What do you know about it?" Dale was just as composed as he was a few days earlier in the driveway, almost as if he was programmed. "I don't know what you mean."

About that time, Shirley asked Dale if Rachael was there. She knew Ted's little sister Rachael from the search and liked her a lot. She was a sweet, beautiful girl and she had no reason not to like her. Rachael walked out from the bedroom. "Hi, Ms Mays! How are you?" They hugged and had very little to say because Eric was teed off and wanted to get out of there. He knew Dale wasn't going to talk and he wanted to leave before he grabbed him around the neck and hit him.

They drove around awhile to get rid of their frustrations and then headed back to the Station. Eric was positive he saw the boys that day and nothing was going to ever change his mind.

Shirley seemed to always just get pieces of her big puzzle, a few at a time, on a need to know basis. It was a very, very big puzzle to her and she kept good notes to go with those small pieces. She always thought when the Lord wanted her to know where Jeffrey was, he would give her an exact address.

Her faith remained solid.

Chapter Ten

The Year 1987

In 1989, Shirley was approached by an undercover man, a friend, who gave her a few letters that were dated 1987. He asked her to keep them confidential because they could get him in trouble.

- The first one read "7-14-87 SP Wytheville, Va. To Highway Patrol Headquarters Raleigh. Relay to all North Carolina Law Enforcement agencies. Approximately 8 years ago a white male (name unknown) was facing drug charges in North Carolina. Prior to the trial, the accused was believed to have drowned in a boating accident. The body was never recovered. Any agency having circumstances as described please contact Virginia State Police, Special Agent J. D. Widener, Wytheville, Va."

- The second letter was dated 7-21-87 and was addressed to a Captain W. O. Leary in the Elizabeth City Police Department. It read, "This is to confirm the conversation between you and Special Agent J. D. Widener on July 14, 1987, at which time the following information was provided: The following information was received from a concerned citizen who wishes to remain anonymous. The information was received third hand. Approximately eight years ago in North Carolina two subjects went out on a boat. One of the subjects was facing drug related charges at the time. The two subjects arranged for the boat to appear to be taking on water. A passing boat stopped and asked if they needed assistance. The two advised they were taking on water but they could handle it. Later the two disappeared and were presumed drowned. The bodies were never recovered. A memorial service was held for the two. One of the subjects is living in Kodiak, Alaska, where his brother is in the Coast Guard. The subject has contacted his sister who lives in Southwest Virginia. Please be assured of our desire to cooperate in all matters of mutual concern. Signed by S. C. Delp, Special Agent in Charge, Bureau of Criminal Investigation, Wytheville, Virginia.

- The third letter Shirley was given was dated August 3, 1987 and it was addressed to Lt. Martin Phillips, Group Commander, U. S. Coast Guard, Group Cape Hatteras, Buxton, N. C. It read, "Dear Lt. Phillips: I have attached a copy of a letter I received from Captain Leary of the Elizabeth City Police Department. Ted Wall is the person referred to as facing drug charges. I checked with Captain Leary and he advised me that he had charged Wall with Driving while impaired and at the same time confiscated some white powder on suspicion that it was a controlled substance. This substance was submitted to the SBI Laboratory and it was determined that the powder was not a controlled substance; however, Wall was not aware that the results of the tests were negative. Wall's brother, Theodore Franklin Wall is the man that is supposed to be stationed in Alaska. This is all the information I have. If we can be of any further assistance, please feel free to contact me". It was signed by Dare County Chief Deputy Rodney Midgett.

She did not receive the attached letter of Captain Leary from the Elizabeth City police department. Apparently it was missing from the police records.

- The fourth letter she was given was dated September 24, 1987. It was a reply to the Dare County Chief Deputy and it read: "Dear Rodney: This is in response to your letter of 3 Aug 87 regarding Ted Wall and Jeff Mays. Coast Guard records do not indicate a Theodore Franklin Wall in the Coast Guard. It is possible that the subject was previously in the Coast Guard, stationed in Alaska and subsequently discharged. Should future leads develop or if we can assist in any other matter, please feel free to call." It was signed by J. E. Tunstall, Lieutenant, U. S.Coast Guard by direction of the Group Commander.

Jeffrey had been missing since 1980 and these letters were dated 1987 and given to Shirley confidentially in 1989. Captain Leary or nobody else in the Elizabeth City Police Department had ever mentioned any of this to the Mays. Shirley and Bud divorced in 1987. The overwhelming stress of their lives caught up with them. She was still caught up in this nightmare. It never seemed to let up. She felt trapped. The bad memories now outweighed the wonderful memories of growing up in Elizabeth City.

Chapter Eleven

The Year 1988

A lot of the drug activity moved south to the Port City of Wilmington, North Carolina in 1988. There was too much "heat" at the Outer Banks.

Chapter Twelve

The Year 1989

It was quoted in the North Carolina papers, "If drugs were part of legal commerce, cocaine would carry a foreign label and marijuana would bear the North Carolina state seal." Illegal drugs had become a regular but virtually unstoppable part of the North Carolina economy.

Marijuana was the No 1 cash crop in the state and rough estimates said cocaine accounted for about $180 million in sales in 1989. While marijuana became largely a domestic product, cocaine was smuggled into North Carolina.

The jagged coastline peppered with inlets and bays always had been a haven for illicit activity on the seas. During the pirate days, North Carolina was supposed to be the ideal place for smuggling because it gave them a place to attack and there were so many places to hide. The state is a "smuggling paradise" because of the shape and isolated nature of much of its shoreline.

The profile of a drug boat in the early eighties was a 200 to 300 foot long ship packed with tons of marijuana. In 1989, they were producing smaller, sleeker boats with flattened bags of white powder whose value would multiply as much as 10 times before distribution.

One day, somewhere in this 1989 timeframe, Shirley looked out at her 100 by 300 foot dock where she had six boat slips and saw some people trespassing. Her office was in the back of the John Deere building facing the river so the trespassers were difficult to miss. She had heard that a celebrity from Las Vegas was moving to town. His developer friend in Virginia Beach had bought him a place out by the private little airport, adjacent to the Coast Guard Station – sight unseen – at an auction, on the phone. Nothing was strange to her anymore so what was this celebrity doing trespassing on her property? She opened her door and loudly said, "You are trespassing." Wayne Newton was with his pilot, a big guy and his girlfriend. He looked sheepish and pulled his hat down over his eyes like celebrities do. She walked over to them. "This is my property and I live there" pointing to her big three story brick house next door. She had heard that a lot of big money, maybe drug money, was looking around town with the thought of buying up prime downtown properties. She wondered if this big well known Vegas resident had an eye on her prime waterfront property.

The press always associated him with the Mafia in Vegas and she had a strange feeling that he was looking out over her gorgeous view, visualizing a gambling boat offshore and thinking that all of this might one day be his. Very shortly after his trespassing, she received a call from the Virginian Pilot, a paper that most locals in her hometown read, and they informed her that the celebrity who had bought a house near the Coast Guard base and private airstrip was leaving Elizabeth City. The press asked her, "What do you think about that?"

Newton's friend, the developer who bought the local house over the phone at an auction suggested to the Virginian Pilot that they call Shirley Mays for a quote. She said, "It is certainly his loss. This is a beautiful little town, a wonderful place to live." She wondered why she was the only local quoted in the press. And she wandered if she really thought her hometown was beautiful anymore. She also wondered how much investigation the Vegas Mafia had done on her.

Chapter Thirteen

The Year 1990

1990 was a year of pure hell for Shirley Mays. The intimidation and harassment she received from everywhere was almost more than she could bear.

- May. A druggie trespassed at her Coast Guard Station at the Outer Banks and wanted to know if she was there "all alone." She had him arrested and was told by the Kitty Hawk police that he has caused trouble with the Nags Head police and had pulled a State Highway Patrolman out of his car. In spite of that, the district attorney's office covered for him, made sure she was not in court the day of the trial and dropped the druggie's charges. She had been in court earlier but an Assistant DA postponed the trial in her presence. She then wrote a certified letter to the DA asking to be notified of the date of the trial. The certified letter was totally ignored. Who targeted her besides the district attorney? The druggie was represented by Russell Twiford, a prominent local lawyer.
- June 15. She made a formal complaint to City Hall in Elizabeth City for the lack of law enforcement on the waterfront. It turned on her.
- July 12. She had a break-in in her shopping center deli in Elizabeth City. She was told by the investigating officer "not to take it personal." That officer had just been suspended by the State Department of Justice because he couldn't pass his gun test.

- July 27. She contacted the FBI in Charlotte, North Carolina about the drug trafficking in the public parks in Elizabeth City next to her house.
- July 28. She was stopped by the N. C. Highway Patrol when she wasn't speeding. An Assistant District Attorney didn't like the way it "smelled" so he shelved the charges.
- Aug. 7. Elizabeth City Manager instituted a set of rules that Shirley Mays was not to get any more public information without a request in writing. The rule didn't apply to the other citizens. Shirley Mays was concerned as to how the Community Development Funds were being accounted for. That requested paperwork later disappeared from City Hall.

On October 24, 1990, the City Manager abruptly resigned, just before being fired.

On October 28, 1990, Mike Midgett from Elizabeth City was convicted on three federal narcotics felonies. Shirley knew him well. Ted Wall had been a close friend of Mike's. She heard the rumor that Ted was involved with Mike selling drugs in Elizabeth City. She and many others in town heard that Mike Midgett had been set up by Captain Olie Leary of the local police. She was told by William Allen, the local FBI special agent that Midgett would serve 15 years with no possibility of parole. He was accompanied to Raleigh by Elizabeth City police officers and released immediately. Something strange happened after he was taken to the courts in Raleigh, North Carolina. Either Mike "rolled over" or he threatened to tell all he knew about the local police and he knew a lot.

Chapter Fourteen

The Year 1991

In February of 1991, Shirley Mays lost the Neimay Lawsuit which had been deliberately dragged out for seven years in the Dare County courts. It was a judicial joke and everyone knew it. The local boys in Dare County, the lawyers, bankers and accountants, had managed to bring in the judge of their choice, a retired guy from outside the area whose nickname was "Shoot from the Hip George Fountain." Shoot from the hip George Fountain did and by doing so, managed to free all the white collar criminals involved. During the three day trial, she had mentioned the drug activity involved that ran through their partnership account and when she mentioned Lunsford Crew's name, Shoot from the Hip said, "I know Lunsford Crew. His father is a friend of mine."

Lunsford's father was a lawyer from a nearby town. Shirley had shot herself in the foot without even aiming. These lawyers and bankers and accountants and a few of the judges were like buzzards and they definitely stuck together.

She notified the FBI in Charlotte and tried to get them involved with the real estate fraud taking place on the Outer Banks. Some of the same local professional people involved with her lawsuit, especially Tom White, was deeply involved in the Great Atlantic Saving Bank scandal which was just a few blocks away from the Dare County courthouse.

She tried to explain all of this to the legal people in the Real Estate Commission but they seemed to think that the way the Outer Banks lawyers conducted their business was OK with them. They made her think that she was the problem. She later learned that the Real Estate Commission lawyer to whom she was reporting admitted that he was in law school with one of the Outer Banks lawyers who was causing problems for the Mays by closing Neimay properties behind their backs. He even wrote her a long four page letter and copied the Dare County lawyer, who had attended law school with him . That should have alerted all of them that the coast was clear according to the Legal Department of the Real Estate Commission. She considered it very unethical for the RE Commision lawyer to have copied his buddy on such a confidential letter.

The organized crime family in Dare County was powerful and out of control. It appeared nothing could stop them.

On June 29, 1991, the headlines of the Virginian Pilot read, "D.A.'s brother guilty of drug charges." The paper said the sentencing on felony drug charges in Dare County Superior Court drew a tight-lipped reaction from the District Attorney. "I will not comment on that," he said. "I'm not going to let you hang my brother out to dry just because he's my brother," he added.

Shirley read that the district attorney's brother name was Harry and he was from Avon. She had to wonder if he knew Edgar Styron, Jr., and by chance happened to be that "Harry from Avon with the briefcase" that Franklin Wall saw that day while he was desperately trying to get the search started for the boys. Her son's search was delayed because of Harry and that briefcase trip to Avon.

This was the same district attorney who had "shut down" her investigation with the SBI when she tried to bring them in against Tom White. The DA had said to the SBI in a letter dated 6-26-87 "It is my opinion that at this time there does not appear to be any criminal violation by any individuals who are now living. For this reason, I am requesting that your file be closed."

This was the same district attorney whose office had arranged, without her in court, to let the druggie, represented by Russell Twiford, who threatened her life go absolutely free with no charges.

She had a lot of problems with this district attorney. She wondered which side of the law he was on and she knew, without a doubt, that what goes around comes around. It is a universal law and just a matter of timing.

On August 3, she wrote John Morrison, her attorney in regards to the speeding ticket she received when that Highway Patrolman pulled her off the road for nothing. "In District Court you told me twice that the Assistant DA asked you if we would accept lowering the charged limits. I said no because I am not guilty. When the appeal was scheduled, you said the Assistant DA suggested it be tabled because he didn't like the way it smelled, your words John not mine. You said the next time it came up the DA's office suggested a "prayer for judgment continued" which would put it on the shelf for a year and if I didn't commit murder or rape, it would probably get dropped. I am sure you have no reason to believe that my losing the seven year Neimay lawsuit in Dare County would influence the district attorney in any way about the "unshelfing" of this two year old speeding charge."

She wondered, "Is this why that same district attorney is giving Lunsford Crew, the captain who piloted that mother ship a "prayer for judgment continued as late as 1988?" If he didn't commit murder or rape, would his drug smuggling case get dropped?

It was beginning to look like the DA's office, or at least some of them, might be on somebody's payroll other than that of the State of North Carolina.

On August 4, 1991, Marty Bergman, Investigator from CBS 60 Minutes called her to ask about her story. Gus, a developer friend of hers from Long Island, New York was a friend of Marty Bergman. Gus had a lot of land in Hyde County that the environmental people wouldn't let him develop so he called Marty to tell him his story.

Bergman told Gus his story wasn't quite "ready" yet, so Gus asked Marty to call Shirley Mays and ask about her story.

She told Marty everything about her missing son off the Coast of Cape Hatteras; about her not being able to develop her Elizabeth City waterfront property because of the extreme environmentalists; about her seven year real estate accounting white collar crime at the Outer Banks of North Carolina and the organized crime in general to which she and others in the area were being exposed. Marty was very interested and he asked her to send some background documentation. He mentioned that it almost sounded like three different episodes. Marty Bergman left CBS before he could follow up on her stories because they wouldn't air the whistle blowing tobacco story he had been working on for so long. Disney ended up doing the movie The Insider, which was the tobacco story Bergman was working on.

On August 8, 1991, the senior resident Superior Court judge in Northeastern North Carolina retired with three years left in his term. He had been very fair to Shirley in her discovery period with the lawsuit. After trying unsuccessfully for several years to get the estate records, he ruled in favor of the Mays. That was when she found two estate accounts from Planter National Bank and only one was being reported to the government. Ray White, Tom White, and Jack Adams were well aware of the deliberate hiding of an estate account that wasn't being reported. The hidden information involved monies from a development that George had with Jack Adams, the accountant and is still hanging in the air in that open 1983 estate file in the Clerk's office in Manteo, North Carolina.

On August 11, 1991, the Elizabeth City Police Chief who had been serving for 44 years was asked to step down by the State Department of Justice. Chief was disappointed because he was shooting for his 50 year pin. He received a letter from the state Criminal Justice Department's Training and Standards Division. Appears a routine audit of the records showed he was no longer certified to arrest or carry a gun. He was one of her Mom and Dad's best friends. Chief was a very nice person but he should have stepped down years earlier. No one should serve 50 years in any public job, especially that of police chief. Serving that long kills any opportunities for young officers serving under him. Actually the Elizabeth City Police Chief and the Dare County Sheriff were known as politicians not law enforcers. Most little southern towns had the same problem. They were the unspoken "governors" of their towns. They ruled the roost. Drug activity flourished in many small southern towns during these "governor" years.

On August 17, 1991, Shirley resigned as Vice Chairman of the Board of Trustees at the local University, with three years left. She had been a Governor's appointee. She refused to be a part of the political corruption between the University and the City.

One of the local radios called and invited her to go on the air. "About what?" "Anything you want." "OK, I want to talk about the judicial system, the victims it creates and about the local district attorney."

On September 17, 1991, she called the Attorney General of the State of North Carolina. "How do you get rid of a district attorney?" They had never been asked before. Three days later, she received the statute 7A-66-Removal of district attorneys.

She went on the air to relate what had happened to her. The radio station phones started lighting up. Victims were calling in. They too were upset with the DA. Without knowing it, she had opened a Pandora's Box. She immediately began forming a victim's group that very day on the radio. She was told by someone at the radio station that the DA was there about ten minutes after she got off the air. He wanted a tape of the entire conversation.

She received many phone calls from victims and people who just wanted to talk about the problems of the judicial system but one call she decided to follow up on was from Dare County. She drove to Dare County and met with a man who said he was an ex-police officer. He wanted to give her some court papers showing that it was wrong how the DA got his car back after his brother Harry was charged with drug dealing. He also wanted her to know that many good attorneys and law enforcement people supported her but they couldn't come out publically because of their jobs. She took the court information from him, gave it to the press but it didn't fly. These were prominent people and the local press didn't usually step on their toes. That practice of the press was an advantage for the wrongdoers.

In October, the Governor of North Carolina was going to appoint someone to replace the senior resident judge, who had retired three years early. Shirley worked very closely with this Governor. The rumor was that Tom White would get the seat. She wrote the governor saying, "Please, please, please do not appoint Tom White to be a judge. I'm trying to put him in prison." Tom White did not get the appointment.

On October 29, 1991, only about eight short months after being freed from the Neimay trial, Tom White, acting in the capacity of the township attorney for Nags Head, North Carolina was involved in a quitclaim deed for The Nature Conservancy that ended up creating legislation that affected properties throughout the United States.

The Great Atlantic Savings Bank asset involved was called the Nags Head Woods. It was a subsidiary venture in which the S&L was part owner. Tom appeared to be a party to legislation that created the law requiring the FDIC/RTC to consider a property's ecological value and to give conservation groups the first opportunity to make an offer to buy. That meant that any non-profit, no matter who it was or how quickly it was formed, would have first grab at a lot of valuable land all over the nation, but immediately coastal land in Dare County. The legislation passed and ended up involving thousands of assets from over 747 defunct S&Ls which were registered by the FDIC as environmental impaired.

The quitclaim deed to the land for The Nature Conservancy was drawn by Randy Meares, Esq., signed by William C. Thomas, Director of RTC at Atlanta, Georgia and sent to Tom White who was the Nags Head attorney at the time. The Nags Head asset was far from clear. It created a big fight for some locals, even ones related to each other.

There were many liens against the Nags Head Woods at the time of the drawing of the quitclaim deed. There was a lawsuit, an issue for foreclosure. which the Dare County Sheriff ignored, and hardball fighting in general, Outer Banks style.

The parties involved with the Nags Head Woods were real seasoned hardball players and they intended to win one for Nature Conservancy and in turn, for them. Nature Conservancy is a big international outfit and Tom White was sure they would have their eyes on many more of the properties throughout the country, especially one in Kitty Hawk, right down the road from Nags Head.

The Kitty Hawk Woods properties created several indictments for that little local S&L right downtown in Manteo, North Carolina.

At that exact same time in October, there was a national scandal brewing with the BCCI, the Bank of Credit and Commerce International. It was reported that some of the world's most powerful drug dealers quietly withdrew millions of dollars from their BCCI accounts just days before a surprise arrest by federal agents. Although they denied it, the Bank of America owned 20% of the BCCI.

The Bank of America in Kitty Hawk, North Carolina, which was once NationsBank, was the institution that acquired the defunct Great Atlantic Savings Bank FSB in Manteo, North Carolina back in 1991 at the same time of the Neimay Lawsuit. The Kitty Hawk NationsBank branch was involved at the beginning of the mishandling of the acquired properties. Bank of America is presently (2009) involved in a development lawsuit that is almost identical to the ones that brought the S&Ls down in the early 90s and in this particular case, it is the same Kitty Hawk branch. It appears that banking has not changed much in the last twenty years at the Outer Banks.

It was reported in the press in 1991 that the BCCI's connections to politicians and intelligence agencies prevented federal investigators from going after its top executives.

Shirley thought, "If the Outer Banks area was deeply involved in international drug dealing as reported in the press, why wouldn't the local drug dealers be involved with international banking?"

The next biggest event, after losing her Neimay Lawsuit in February of 1991, was a huge storm that was referred to as 'the perfect storm.' It occurred in October and it was called the Halloween Storm. She lost most of her porches on their historic Coast Guard Station and knew that she was not financially able to replace them.

Her mentor, the General died within two weeks of that storm.

On November 29, 1991, Shirley wrote the Commander of the Fifth Coast Guard District in Portsmouth, Virginia to formally request the SAR (Search and Rescue) file of Jeffrey's search "I have reason to believe there was an investigation and I would like to request a copy of the report and any other information pertaining to the search." They responded immediately with an assigned case number 91-AFO-066. The Captain, who was the District Legal Officer said, "We have forwarded your request to the Commander, Coast Guard Group Hatteras and they will endeavor to respond to your request as soon as possible."

She worked very closely with the Coast Guard trying to get a copy of Jeffrey's search until April 8, 1992, at which time they had to tell her that everything involved with that search was missing. They could find the search before it and the search after it but everything that had anything to do with Jeffrey's search was missing.

Chapter Fifteen

The Year 1992

January of 1992. "This state is a damned armed camp," said the director of the North Carolina SBI. "If things continue, we'll be living in one of the top 10 most-dangerous states by the end of the decade."

She had been trying desperately to tell that to local, state and federal law enforcement since November 13, 1980, twelve years ago. Elizabeth City was almost totally out of control with drugs.

March 1, she read an article in the local paper about a couple of young boys from the Outer Banks who had just been released from the Dominican Republic prison. One of the names was Ron Austin from Avon and she just thought she would like to talk to him. She called her friend Jimmy Austin, the seafood fish dealer, who had been caught in that big drug raid in 1984 to ask if he knew this young man. She liked Jimmy a lot and knew that he would help her if he could. "Jimmy. are you related to that young man who just got out of the Dominican Republic Prison?" "Yes, Shirley, Ron is my cousin." "What are the chances of me talking to him?" "I'll arrange it for you." She thanked him and hung up.

Jimmy also told her that he was in Hatteras on the day that Jeffrey was missing. He said that a trawler was caught that same day with four Americans aboard.

She did not know that.

He said if Jeffrey's boat had blown up, it would go to the water line and even if it sank, something would float. He said he had been on boats all of his life and there would be some sign of debris or bodies. She knew that Jimmy would like to help her but he was scared. He said he never squealed on anyone. He called her back on June 5 to say that his cousin Ron would talk with her. He gave her his phone number so they could make their own arrangements.

On June 19, Shirley and Eric engineered the move of the Station from the oceanfront to his new lot, about ¼ mile south and on the west side of the beach road. It wasn't as visible anymore but it was a lot safer.

Soon after moving the Station, she made a trip to Avon for a prearranged meeting with Ron Austin. Ron told her that he knew the boys, had coffee with them and other fishermen every morning at the Froggie Dog in Avon. He said Jeffrey was 21 and he was 19. He didn't know them real well but enough to speak. He told her that his cousin was Edgar Styron, Jr., the last to see Jeffrey on November 13, 1980. He said his brother-in-law was Harry Williams, the D. A.'s brother, who Shirley thought was Harry with the briefcase from Avon.

Those two relatives of his were responsible for holding up the search for Jeffrey.

Another brother-in-law from New Jersey owned the Froggy Dog where all the fishermen congregated for breakfast. Ron said that he had trouble in his marriage and the New Jersey brother-in-law sent him to Fort Myers, Florida to work on his trawler. Ron told her that they would make drug trips from Fort Myers to Mexico with no concern about getting caught. He said they were never checked by Customs or the Coast Guard until one day they got set up. They were stopped by Customs who found drugs and they were thrown in the Dominican Republic prison.

Very shortly after that, the press reported that the Ex-Sheriff from Fort Myers pleaded guilty to 4 cocaine charges.

Ron Austin, with tears in his eyes while talking to her, credited his mother and his sister for getting the two of them out of that foreign country. He said they told the government, "We have heard there are groups of 100 or more young American men being held in your prisons and being used as slave labor. We are working with Prime Time 20/20 to tell our story." Ron said, "That is why the government released us. They didn't want the bad publicity." He then told her, "But the guys in the Haiti prisons have it worse." She was very sad thinking that could be Jeffrey. Ron promised her that he would get in touch with *Carlos* and try to find out something about what happened to Jeffrey. Shirley thanked him and left. Her heart bled for that young man.

Several months later, while waiting to hear from him, she got the word that he had walked to the end of someone's pier and committed suicide. She didn't believe it then and doesn't believe it now and neither did his family. The Sheriff's office in Dare County never conducted an investigation or checked prints on the gun.

Strange events were happening to her in Elizabeth City. She was getting phone calls and visits from local people whom she knew were involved in drugs. They were offering to give her free help if she needed anything. It was frightening to her. At the same time, she was getting sick and tired of everything, especially the lack of progress with the development of her waterfront property because of the rigid costly requirements of CAMA and the other regulatory bodies. They just kept changing their rules and making her do another environmental impact study (EIS). She had already done three with each one costing at least $10,000. She was tired of the local politicians who aspired to "take" her property for public or for themselves, without paying for it. She was sick to death of the druggies who surrounded both sides of her house and celebrities like Wayne Newton who aspired to buy up the prime waterfront in town.

All they had to do was wait her out. The government had plenty of money and resources to do that. The environmentalists, plus local governments can stop you from any progress if they choose. Shirley was just hanging on a lot longer than they thought she could.

When she received a call from First Citizens Bank informing her that they were going to bring in a geologist to do a Phase I environmental study on her properties, she made a decision to sell and leave town. She had become very disgusted with First Citizens. It had been her grandfather's bank, her father's bank and then hers after she moved back to North Carolina. She didn't trust many of the board members. One was the county attorney, one was a State Representative and one owned the local shipyard. Her father's best friend was on the board and gave her advice. The shipyard owner was very much against everything she tried to do. Shirley was well aware that the bank was eyeing her property. She was so disgusted that she refused to do business with the local bank anymore. At her request, someone from the regional office of First Citizens Bank in Raleigh, North Carolina was assigned her account.

On the day before First Citizen Bank's geologist was scheduled to see her, she called three local developers. Her price was set and the first one to the table would get her property. Bill Rich, the first one of the three Shirley called, put the deal together first and they closed at 2:00 am in the early morning. To her knowledge, no one but Bill Rich was aware of the deal.

The next day, First Citizens' regional banker flew in with the geologist who was chosen to do the dirty deed. Robb Porter did most of the work for First Citizens through Ward and Smith law firm out of New Bern, North Carolina. Robb became very impressed with Shirley's environmental documentation. He needed someone of her talents to do investigative title work for him and also someone to help him run his business. He saw a lot of her research and could easily see that she was very good at investigating troubled properties. He also was well aware that environmental restrictions on private properties were going to be a real issue in the future. He was a genius at geology but lousy at running a business. He actually was just working to support his real habit which was stunt flying.

When he arrived on her deck, he was wearing a Harley Davidson leather jacket, a very sneaky smile and was carrying a manila file folder. He strutted down her alleyway between the two buildings like a peacock. If he were not a wrestler, he had surely missed his calling. She later found out he had been a wrestler and a very good one at that.

He did most of the environmental work for First Citizen Bank who had acquired a lot of S&L properties. He knew the bank was trying to get the nerve to foreclose on her. After meeting her, he asked her, in front of the regional banker, "Will you have lunch with me? I'd like you to work with me but I can't afford you." She looked at him disgustingly and said "No thank you." The regional banker was a little mouse of a guy, had a bad cold and let Robb do most of the talking. He then announced to both of them that he had to meet with Ron Turlington, the local manager of First Citizens Bank where she had all of her accounts. He suggested they go to lunch together and he would meet them afterwards.

Reluctantly, Shirley agreed to go to lunch with this arrogant stunt flying Harley Davidson hot shot geologist because she wanted to tell him how much she despised extreme environmentalists and the local, state and federal regulatory bodies that had caused her so much financial anguish over the years. At lunch, he told her he had already been warned about her and he showed her his notes in his manila file folder which said "Proceed with caution because this woman hates environmental agencies." He then said to her, "Actually I don't like them either, especially the ones I have to work with in Raleigh."

After hearing that remark, she changed her mind and accepted the consulting job with Robb Porter so fast it made his head spin. She needed to get out of town and buy some time until the closing with Bill Rich and she had to make sure her one of a kind CAMA permit from that environmental agency in Raleigh got properly transferred. Robb was a paranoid kind of person so he immediately suspected that she had an agenda and thought he might have made a mistake hiring her. This looked like it was going to be a very interesting combination of talents.

She found out later that the little mousy regional banker parachuted for a hobby so he was in awe of this hot shot stunt pilot First Citizens had hired. She believed that the regional banker eased up on the pressure he planned to put on her mainly because of her now working with Robb Porter. She also doubted that the regional banker was aware of the magnitude of the local game plan involving her and her waterfront properties.

This was the beginning of a rocky but very strong friendship between Shirley Mays and Robb Porter which lasted for many memorable years. She knew immediately after meeting him, beyond a shadow of a doubt that if she ever had to go to war, she would want this man by her side. He was truly one of a kind. She suspected he felt the same about her.

She considered Bill Rich a personal friend. She was pleased he thought he could put the deal together fast. Bill thought it was going to be a simply and fast closing until local politicians reared their ugly heads with a different agenda. He later told Cruising Magazine. "I've wanted that property since I was 17 years old."

She knew she was going to have a difficult closing, with the town now fighting him instead of her. She also anticipated a very hard time getting her CAMA permits transferred   Thanks to the Governor of North Carolina she owned a deed to the land under her house, the water bottoms. It had been no small task acquiring that one of a kind deed.

The Republican Governor that she worked with so closely had changed the administrative law in the state to make the deed possible. He said her project was exactly what he wanted for his Coastal Initiative Program. He personally presented the application for the deed to the Council of State and got the vote. This was her biggest problem at the time because some elected officials of the opposite party in the state didn't want her project to move forward. If the permit were used, it would create lawsuits all over the state. She found that remark in a letter she discovered from the Corp of Engineers. She knew that they would be trying very diligently to stop the sale of her waterfront property and that permit from being transferred to Bill Rich.

She packed up and moved out of town so fast, everyone had to wonder what happened to her. She packed up the house, the shopping center, the Coast Guard Station in record time. She was very fortunate to have some wonderful people working for her. Ruth Bogues had been house cleaning for her and counseling her since she arrived in town. Ruth's mother Mary Riddick had worked for Shirley's Big Mama and family is family. Ruth's husband Leon Bogues also worked for her in the afternoon after finishing his city job. When she told them she was moving, they brought their children and grandchildren, 19 in all, to help her pack and move. With nineteen people plus saying to her "what's next, what's next," it was just a matter of being able to hang on and ride. They were all a good team, had been for years and she was going to miss them like mad. She was packing and crying and packing and crying. The frustration of being sandbagged by the local, state and federal system for so many years had taken its toll on her.

She rented a small condo on Lake Norman just two exits from where Robb had his business. The name of his business was Environmental Integrity and integrity was oozing out of the head of that geologist. Charlotte, North Carolina was two exits in the opposite direction. She needed a little R&R and this was certainly the place for it. There was a swimming pool right outside her door and a marina and restaurant in her front view which was only a short walk from her condo. She anticipated being there only a few months, at the most, while Bill Rich was getting the permit transferred and the closing accomplished.

Robb's business was in a mess. He was paranoid and didn't trust anyone and that now included her. His accountant knew that he was a money maker but knew nothing about the books so the accountant offered to back him and manage the business. Robb had a big old office and put Shirley right in there next to him so he could keep an eye on her. The first diagnosis she gave him was that he personally was the problem. She also said his accountant was not being fair and he needed to let him go.

She knew about accounting fraud after investigating it from 1983 to 1991. After the lawsuit was over, she considered herself an expert in accounting real estate white collar crime.

On Wall Street, they try to call it sloppy bookkeeping but if anyone gets caught, it is then referred to as white collar crime. She was very aware of what Robb's accountant was doing and planning to do with him. His accountant had a master plan to finance his environmental business and take over his books and his life. He needed to be released fast.

Shirley composed a letter to the accountant for Robb to sign. She knew what accounting laws he was breaking. Of course, the accountant threatened to sue but soon recognized his threat was not intimidating Robb or his new consultant. Robb got all of his records back. Shirley put them on the computer and hired a new accountant. She had only been there a couple of days. They were off to a good start.

He quickly moved her into an office of her own. One morning soon after that, he came into her office with his head down looking like someone had eaten the red off his apple. He said, "I think I'm in trouble." Shirley said, "What now?" He lived in a small development with other pilots and they had their own airstrip. His hanger was attached to his home. The end of the airstrip was Lake Norman so you had to come down quickly over the water for the landing. "I was landing yesterday and when I got out of my plane, this jerk was speeding right up the middle of the airstrip and blocked my plane. He was trespassing so I pinned him against the car and threatened him." "Oh my God Porter, did you hurt him?" "No, but he has filed charges against me."

Richard Duval, a lawyer from Ward and Smith in New Bern who was responsible for getting Robb most of his environmental work for First Citizens, really liked him and knew what a maverick and paranoid person he was. He and Shirley talked a lot on the phone about Robb and tried to keep him out of trouble. Her first thought was to call Richard so she could get the legal advice she needed to get Porter out of this really big mess he was in. The jerk who trespassed on the airstrip was a prominent doctor who lived on the water just before the touchdown spot. He said that Robb was always buzzing the house when landing and it was driving him crazy because he was sick with cancer.

That was a hard one for them because they felt sorry for the doctor but they got Porter out of his mess again, hoping he would soon grow up and learn his lessons in life. Shirley tried very hard to reduce Robb's stress without increasing hers. It didn't work. Every day was a challenge for both of them.

She taught Robb to recognize a lot of the dirty tricks that the government uses to trap you. She had a costly education on government dirty tricks and wanted to pass them on to anyone that she could. She taught him to always send certified mail but if you did hand carry the info, get a signature and time of delivery. Robb previously had developed problems with the state agencies but after developing the new habits, they told him he was a role model for them involving documentation.

They were the same agencies that she had tried very hard to work with for years. She thinks her reputation preceded her to Charlotte and they said it with tongue in check. Using her advice, at least Robb identified the less efficient state employees who always made him their scapegoats. He had no more trouble with them.

She was not aware that Robb was a walking one man militia when she joined him. He had a gun and knife collection that most armies would envy. He hated the government and knew that one day he would have to defend himself and his family. She always took his little sports car to the local post office until one day she opened the trunk and saw that it was full with ammunition. He had enough weapons to take down a battalion. He told her it was all registered but she decided to take the company pick up truck after that discovery just to be safe. Besides she didn't know how to shoot a gun and especially those automatic ones. She couldn't help that a list with a few names on it quickly crossed her mind! She tried not to discuss that situation with him anymore for fear she would learn more than she needed to know. He insisted on telling her about the gun that wasn't legal that he kept broken down in the vacuum cleaner. She didn't plan to ever offer to clean his house after that bit of knowledge. She'll never know whether he was kidding her about that or not.

Robb had several stunt planes and one was a Russian Jag. He was so carried away with the plane he decided to become a dealer and stock and sell Jag parts. He went to the bookstore and bought some books on Russia and how to speak the language. He started studying and very shortly thereafter made a plane reservation to Russia.

Upon arrival in Russia, he was met by some of the Jag company officials who were to be in charge of his visit. Robb had learned some Russian curse words and thought he would try out some of his manly actions to loosen them up. He was originally from West Virginia, deep in the mountains, so you can imagine the accent that came out of his mouth while he was attempting the Russian curse words. The Russians bent over laughing and said to each other, "We had better take him home with us so he doesn't get in trouble." His visit was memorable to all.

The next instructions she received from Robb was to be at the airstrip for his arrival. He and a Russian official were bringing in his newly purchased Jag that was being escorted by his pilot friend who was flying a Baron.

Life was never dull with Robb Porter.

On October 22 of 1992 while she was living on Lake Norman, the headlines in the North Carolina section of the Virginian Pilot read, "Four citizens seek ouster of the District Attorney." The first affidavit filed with the Superior Court Clerk was from Shirley Mays, an Elizabeth City waterfront developer. Her affidavit alleged that the district attorney:

- Failed to allow a State Bureau of Investigation probe of a Dare County estate dispute which could have uncovered criminal activity involving a white collar crime.
- Failed to perform his duty when she was the recipient of a threat on her life from a known drug person in Dare County.
- Failed to do his duty in prosecuting a breaking-and-entering case at her Elizabeth City shopping center on the waterfront.
- Failed to properly handle a case involving a trespasser on her Elizabeth City property.

Chapter Sixteen

The Year 1993

In January of 1993, the DA had his day in court and so did the victims. Shirley willingly drove to Elizabeth City from Charlotte for the big courthouse event. Even after hearing all of the many charges from the victims, the visiting judge decided there was not enough evidence for the DA to be put out of office. The victims group had been able to cause enough damage to his reputation that he easily lost the next election. He had been unchallenged for too many years.

Also in January, the Savings and Loan scandal from Dare County was beginning to hit the news. A big developer from Kitty Hawk could be sentenced to 20 years in prison and fined more than a million for his part in the S&L fraud in North Carolina and Georgia. She knew the local name. She and the General had sold their condo development to him and his brother. This was just the beginning of the indictments. He was the sixth of seven defendants to plead guilty to charges involving the Dare County thrift. An eighth defendant was found guilty during the trial. The indicted included the former chief executive officer of the Great Atlantic S&L and his roommate from California and Connecticut. Most of the local defendants were well known. The problem was they didn't get any of the lawyers or law firms responsible for the mishandling of some big coastal assets.

She stayed in close touch with Bill Rich after moving. He was having a difficult time getting her permit transferred. She asked him to let her handle it with CAMA because she didn't trust them. After all, she had spent almost ten years dealing with them. It was a good thing she insisted on it because they tried to change the legal language without his knowledge. It would have slipped past him but she quickly realized that CAMA was trying to kill her permit. It was finally properly transferred and it was time for a closing. The first scheduled closing was for May 23, 1993.

She made a trip back to Elizabeth City and started studying the legal documents before the actual closing. She was staying about fifty miles away at the Outer Banks with her friend Ann from Florida. She and Ann were analyzing the situation when they realized that Shirley was heading for a trap. Bill wanted to close on part of the property and close on the rest separately in a few weeks. She knew that would destroy the CAMA permit and she might not get the rest of the property closed. It looked like a setup to her. Not from Bill but someone or several someones who had their own private agenda.

The closing was scheduled for 1:00 p.m in Elizabeth City. It was 8:30 a.m and she was fifty miles away. This closing presented quite a dilemma because the bank was pushing her for money and making her feel desperate. Ann was adamant about Shirley not going through with the closing. She could see the danger of dividing the properties. She suggested they take a quick stroll on the beach.

She agreed because the sun and the surf always seemed to have a magic effect on clearing her mind. Ann's house was several miles away from where her Coast Guard Station had been located. To her knowledge, no one even knew she was in the area.

They hardly started walking in the sand heading for the pier when they passed a drunk who whispered in passing, "Hi Ms. Mays." She did not recognize him. Ann did not hear him. She stopped and said "Hi." Ann panicked and kept walking. Shirley never knew when she would receive a piece of Jeffrey's puzzle so she was always alert. The drunk staggered sideways and said, "You know who I am?" She said, "Aren't you a friend of Billy Winslow?" She knew that Billy, who had worked for her and was involved in drugs, might be a good name to throw out.

"Yes ma'am, at your service ma'am" and he saluted her. "What service are you in, military or law enforcement?" "Kenny Williams. Vietnam, ma'am! Demolition." She knew she had a nut on her hands but why was he there on that particular day. It was the day of the closing which took several months to schedule. How did he know she was there and how did he know her name?

Ann was standing at a safe distance and frantically pointing to her watch. She had not forgotten about the big closing and was scared of this strange, young, homeless looking drunk. Immediately, Shirley said to him "And Kenny, what do you know about my missing son Jeffrey." Kenny went crazy, jammed his beer bottle in the sand behind him and said, "I've got to piss. I need a beer." He started staggering towards the direction of the Avalon pier and she calmly said, "We live right across the street and we have a bathroom there. I'll send my friend to get a six pack."

She wasn't about to let Kenny Williams out of her sight. The puzzle involving Jeffrey was never far from her mind and this encounter on this particular day was very intriguing.

Ann was in a tight panic now. Shirley said "Ann, go get a six pack – NOW." Ann mumbled something about the closing and started heading towards the house. Ann's good friend Irene from Virginia Beach was also at her cottage. She was sitting on the front porch drinking coffee with her head stuck deep in an intriguing mystery book that she had not been able to put down. She was an introvert, always reading a book. Irene's mind was already fuzzy because her friend Ann had purchased two cotton ribbed spreads for the beds they were sleeping on the day before she and Shirley came. Fumes from chemicals in the dye had caused an allergic reaction for her and she was having difficulty breathing and had edema in face, legs and feet as a result. She knew she needed to leave to get back to Virginia Beach to see her allergist, but for several reasons would and could not leave before the girls returned from the beach and left for the closing in Elizabeth City.

About that time, Shirley managed to steer Kenny across the busy road without either of them getting hit by a passing car. Irene's first thought, upon seeing them, was that they had befriended and picked up a young, homeless beach bum. He was so unkempt. Ann appeared from nowhere and said nervously "I have to go get a six pack."

Shirley took Kenny straight to a picnic table and bench in the backyard. She fully intended to start the interrogation about her son. The major closing in Elizabeth City was the last thought in her mind. Irene, sitting on the porch peaking beyond the pages of her mystery book, did not know what to think. She had just been pulled out of one mystery to another that was happening in front of her eyes. Her deep concentration had been shattered like never before! What happened in that short half hour? Where in the world did they find this drunk? Why were they buying a six pack when they needed to be heading to the closing? Irene knew that truth was stranger than fiction and the events she was witnessing epitomized it.

Kenny had not forgotten that he had to piss. Shirley shouted out to Irene in a real calm voice, "Ireneeeeeeeeeeeeeeee, we're coming in to go to the bathroom." When they walked past her, it was like passing a statute. She didn't appear scared, just frozen in time. Shirley marched Kenny right down to the bathroom door and waited patiently outside for him to finish whatever he had to do. He was not going to get away from her. When he came out, his pants were falling to his knees. She helped him get him pants up and steered him right back outside to the same wooden bench in the sandy backyard. She never even saw Ann drive up, put the beer on the table or go inside. A ghost could have delivered the six pack for all she knew but one thing was certain for her, she wasn't letting go of this beer drinking demolition Vietnam veteran until she had performed a full drill on him involving her missing son.

Kenny popped open his first beer and started talking. He said he and his brother who was a biker had been on a trip across country and they stopped at a bar on Bourbon Street in downtown New Orleans. He said he saw Jeffrey sitting alone in a corner appearing to be in a state of shock when he saw them. He said he and Jeffrey knew each other from buying fish at the Daniels fish house in Wanchese. He said he had changed his name to Eric King, was married had two children, a boy and a girl and worked on an oil rig offshore. Kenny offered if Shirley wanted to send him to New Orleans, he could give Jeffrey a message. Jeffrey had been missing thirteen years at that time.

The only thing she knew for sure at that exact time was that this person who was telling her all of this stuff was not on the beach in front of that Outer Banks house on the day of the closing of her waterfront properties in Elizabeth City by mistake. She also knew that she wasn't finished with Kenny Williams.

Time was quickly passing by so she told him that she had to go to Elizabeth City on business but she would like to talk to him some more. He said he would go to Elizabeth City with her. She said, "Oh no, but I will take you home. Where do you live?" Luck had it that he lived halfway to Elizabeth City in Currituck County in a trailer park called Walnut Island. It was right on her direct route to the closing. She took him directly to his door, put him out, all but kissed him goodbye and said," I'll talk to you soon Kenny."

He had given her his phone number and allowed her to see where he lived so he must not be a figment of her imagination. Her mind was going crazy but one thing she was sure of was that she could not go through with the closing that day. Her friend Ann was exactly right. It was a setup. If someone was so concerned about that complicated closing in Elizabeth City, had gone to the trouble to find out where she was staying and had sent Kenny Williams to mess up her mind, then she needed to find out exactly who was calling the shots. She would suggest a dry closing only including both the John Deere building and the Cotton Mill where her house was and Bill Rich could give her *all* of the money at once as soon as he could get it. First Citizens Bank would have to wait for her money and the CAMA permit would stay in tack.

Ann was very happy about Shirley's decision and signed a breath of relief. She knew how stubborn her friend could be at times but she also knew Shirley usually came around to the right decision when pushed. She had definitely been pushed. She had asked Ann to sit in on the dry closing that day to watch the body language of all present and give her an opinion afterwards.

Bill Rich brought another person to the closing without her knowledge. It was someone that Shirley and Ann both knew while growing up. They both liked Buddy Fletcher but were surprised Bill had not mentioned that he would be at the closing. His name had never been mentioned when she and Bill verbally closed the deal. There were five people present; Bill, Buddy with his two checkbooks, Shirley, Ann and Tom Nash, their lawyer.

Shirley noticed there was one more person almost present. It was the third developer that she had called the night she decided to sell. Don Parks couldn't get to the table with the money before Bill. Strangely he was walking the hall outside the conference room where the closing was taking place. Evidently, Bill and Don had the same lawyer. They had once owned a real estate company together and after splitting up the business did not end up as best friends. When she walked into the conference room Don nodded to her and said, "If this falls through Shirley I'm right here for you."

Everything about this day was strange starting at 8:30 a.m. with a drunk on the beach fifty miles away talking about her son, a developer she hardly knew walking the halls, and her buyer bringing a new player to the table without her knowledge. She had experienced a lot of dreams and nightmares since her son became missing, but this day was really beginning to top it all. There appeared to be panic everywhere except with her and Ann. They were both real estate brokers and had their strategy all figured out. They were quite ready for the games to begin.

Ann talked to Bill and Buddy who was holding his two checkbooks in front of him with his right hand while Shirley talked to Tom Nash, their lawyer. She giggled to herself when she saw Ann pull out two of her checkbooks and place her right hand on them.

While Ann was keeping the two of them busy with small talk, Shirley quietly asked Tom Nash if it wouldn't be better to do a dry closing since Bill didn't have all of the money that day. Tom agreed. Then she turned to the rest of the table. "Bill, your attorney suggested that we do a dry closing and I agree." Bill and Buddy looked startled and Buddy said in shock, "I have my checkbooks right here and I am prepared to write you a check for half." Bill said, "I thought we were going to close today!" Shirley said, "A dry closing is a legal one but it would be cleaner to pass all the money at one time so we can do a dry closing on both properties right now and you can pay me as soon as the S&L comes through with your money."

They had no choice; it was her way or the highway. She was prepared to drop the deal if necessary if Bill couldn't produce the money at the time of closing. She was not about to lose her one of a kind CAMA permit and half of her property. She wasn't afraid of First Citizens Bank either. The dry closing was accomplished.

Sylvia and Webb Williams, good friend of hers in Kitty Hawk, were planning a celebration party. They had lived through her problems for many years. A few other people and a developer from Canada were attending the party so she decided not to inform any of them that the closing didn't take place and just go on with the celebration as planned. When they arrived back in Kitty Hawk after the strange happenings and the dry closing that day, she and Ann made small talk during the gathering and tried to avoid the truth. It was really awkward for her not to be up front with her best friends who wanted to celebrate with her but she had bigger things on her mind after meeting Kenny that morning.

Almost immediately, she was on her way to New Orleans to find Eric King. Kenny had given her that alias and told her Jeffrey worked on an oil rig. He gave her an area and the name of the retired Coast Guardsman who oversaw the oil rig. His name was John White. That's more direct information than she ever had involving her search for Jeffrey. Wild horses couldn't have stopped her from going to New Orleans immediately. She called her brother Ken in the Keys and he met her there. They staked out houses of all the people with the name of Eric King. There were five. They checked out the name of the retired Coast Guardsman. His name checked out to be true. Then she called her cousin Alan in Virginia who had recently retired from the FBI after working for the Director. He knew all about Jeffrey and unfortunately had lost his son about the same age in a car accident. He called an FBI friend in New Orleans and asked him for a favor. He said they would do what they could without opening a case. As a favor to him, the local New Orleans FBI found out the following information:

- Eric King was a contract employee with NOWCAM
- Exxon Platform GI-16
- Grand Isle, La.
- Supervisor – James William White
- NOWCAM – Bellechase, La. Bayou 25 miles south of La.

She had obtained enough facts to know that much of the information that Kenny had given her panned out with the New Orleans FBI. After giving her cousin the above information, they said the Mays would need to hire a private investigator. They recommended an ex FBI employee in the New Orleans area who was an attorney.

She was exhausted. After returning from New Orleans, she confided in her daughters. Her older daughter suggested that she and her husband hire the recommended PI. Shirley lost direct control of the New Orleans investigation at that time. Her daughter just wanted to help but didn't have all of the knowledge that her mother had after all these years so the pieces didn't come together for her. The girls were concerned about her and the extended family knew it. She headed back to Charlotte and to Robb.

Kenny called her immediately upon her arrival from New Orleans and said that Jimmy Shannon had kicked him out of his house. He said the bikers have Jeffrey and that he is safe and he will get in touch with her.

It appeared that Kenny was beginning to trust Shirley more than he did whoever was planning his itinerary. Sometimes he would cry over the phone and call her Mama. He always called her Sue Mae. She had no idea where he got that name for her but she was beginning to feel a bit fond of and very sorry for Kenny. He figured out he was being used. That made him mad. It made her mad also because she knew that none of them had the balls to do what they were asking of Kenny.

She drilled him until she found out who was giving him instructions. It was Jimmy Shannon, the same person, the same informer who had come to their business in Elizabeth City in 1981 immediately after the search who said the boys were in trouble with the Mafia and he could get them out of it for $100,000. She was beginning to put two and two together. Both Kenny and this local police informer lived in Currituck County very near each other. Kenny said Jimmy Shannon and his brother the biker, who was with him in New Orleans, were close friends. She had heard that the Mafia was deeply ingrained in Currituck County and so was drug dealing. She was told the informer worked with the Elizabeth City police. She was beginning to put many pieces of the puzzle together.

She continued to keep herself busy with Robb while waiting for Bill Rich to get his money from the local Elizabeth City S&L so the properties could change hands. No money, no deeds, no keys. Bill was on the spot. She finally got a call from him, "I've got the money!" "Are you sure Bill, because I'm not signing the deeds until you do? And I have a long drive." After being assured that he had the check in hand, she drove back to Elizabeth City to sign the deeds and take her money directly to First Citizens Bank. It was almost the end of July.

When she arrived at Tom Nash's office, Bill Rich was standing in the street in front of the building saving her a parking place. The two council people who had helped stall this deal for nine months rode by twice. She wanted to pat them down to see if they were armed but she figured the local police would protect the elected officials and arrest her for harassing them. The money passed hands, the deeds were signed and Bill asked her to come to his real estate office for a little celebration.

She did and while there she called First Citizens Bank and said she was bringing the money. The banker gave her the figures including the last nine months interest. She was a little short. He told her they couldn't take any unless she had all of it. Bill was shocked and couldn't believe that the bank would not take her money. This was real strange to him. She said, "Bill, don't you understand, First Citizens Bank and their Board of Directors don't want my money. They want my property. That's all they ever wanted."

She confided in him about Kenny Williams and said that she was supposed to meet him in Currituck at the 7-11 parking lot after the closing. She and Bill had talked in the past at length about Jeffrey and the drug situation in general so she felt comfortable confiding in him. She asked him if he would follow her and park where he could keep a watchful eye on her and be sure she was safe. He agreed to help her out.

While still in Bill's office she wrote a note to the banker which said, "Here is your money and the rest will be paid in 30 days." She asked him to follow her to the bank on the way to Currituck. She went through the drive-in window, with him close behind, and dropped in a check for a couple hundred thousand dollars and the note. She didn't wait for service. She just drove on to Currituck to meet Kenny. That was her top priority now that the deal was closed and the bank was almost paid off. They were half way to the 7-11 when Bill flashed his headlights. She pulled over to the side of the road. He said First Citizens Bank had just called him because they couldn't get her and that they thanked her for the check and 30 days would be fine with them.

Damn right it was fine. It had better be.

Banks are supposed to be in the business of making money and not acquiring real estate and to refuse a check that size would not look good for First Citizens Bank with the Banking Commissioner. She would make sure of that if they refused her check.

She met Kenny outside the 7-11 at the entrance of Walnut Island in Currituck. Of course he had been drinking. They sat in her car and talked for a few minutes. He appeared to be clamming up for some reason. He was not so talkative anymore. She thinks he was getting scared of something or somebody. He never asked for money but always asked her to buy him some cigarettes. She didn't get much out of him that meeting but she was determined to keep the contact. She left Kenny and drove off with Bill Rich in his black Mercedes close behind. Halfway back to Elizabeth City she stopped on the side of the road to thank Bill. She told him at that time that she was heading back to Charlotte. He told her to stay safe and he wished her good luck. She wished him good luck with the properties. She knew he was going to need it.

Bill Rich had just inherited all of her waterfront problems with the city. She knew that they, all of them, would not give up at this point. Government never gives up, neither does CAMA nor does the Mafia. Whatever plans they had for that property would be intact for many years into the future.

She always did a lot of reflecting when she was driving and she seemed to be doing a lot of both these past few months. She knew that she would be leaving Robb but she didn't know how to tell him. They had become very close. Robb was just a few years older than her son Jeffrey. She had no idea how he would stay out of trouble without her but she had no choice. She knew beyond a doubt that she had to move back to the Outer Banks and let everyone in that area know that she was looking for her son. She wanted more pieces to her puzzle. She also knew that First Citizens Bank had taken all of her hard earned money and she needed an income.

Reading the Charlotte paper the next morning, she came across an ad that said, "RTC Seminar. $35.00. She said to Robb, "I'm taking the day off and going to a seminar in Charlotte." Robb didn't question her because she was on a consulting contract with him and her time was her own. That was their understanding from the beginning. She had not told him at that time of her plans to return to the area of Jeffrey's disappearance.

She had a little bit of money left and actually went to the seminar because she heard about all of those S&Ls going broke and she had read that they had lots of good real estate to sell. She and Bud had always invested in real estate and they both had an eye for good real estate properties. Unfortunately, all of the good waterfront properties they had purchased together had been desired by the local governments so they had a hard time trying to develop them into better investments.

She thought, "This time, I shall not go near the water!"

Upon arrival at the Sheraton Hotel where the seminar was being held, she signed up and quickly realized that this was a government dog and pony show. They were looking for contractors and mainly minority ones. She quickly realized that she might not be able to purchase a piece of property but the lunch menu sounded good so the day might not be a complete failure. Listening to the government lawyers was irritating to her because she knew they had no clue what they were talking about when they brought up the environmental issues and how those issues might be detrimental to the properties the government had acquired from the defunct banks.

She raised her hand several times to make comments. She knew a lot more than they did because of her past experiences dealing with the local, state and federal agencies and especially from what she had learned from her geologist genius Robb Porter. During the chat session afterwards, she was approached by the legal speaker. "Why don't you become certified to work with us? We need minority women and you mentioned that you were a woman owned business." Working with the government had never been one of her desires because of the way she felt about all of them. But she took the paperwork anyway and bid them goodbye.

Little did she know at that time that going to that $35.00 seminar in Charlotte, North Carolina would change the rest of her life. And probably some of theirs too.

She got up the nerve to tell Robb she was leaving. She felt responsible for him now that he trusted her. He was heartbroken. "You are too old and nobody cares about you." "I know Porter and I love you too. But I have to go back and get some answers about Jeffrey." "If you will stay, I will pay you anything you want." "Robb, it isn't about money. Don't you know that by now?"

"Back in 1989, I was given some letters from an undercover cop that were from a special agent in Wytheville, West Virginia. The letters were dated 1987. Didn't you say you were from West Virginia?" "Yes, Wytheville, as a matter of fact and my uncle is a cop. What do you need?" "I need to talk to the special agent who wrote the letters."

Robb called his uncle who arranged for her to meet with the special agent. She went to Wytheville. The special agent wouldn't give her any information. "Do you have an open case?" "No." "Then you have to talk to the FBI." That was not good news for her because she had tried to talk to the FBI for several years but only encountered steel doors afterwards.

Robb assured her before leaving the Charlotte area that he would always be there for her, no matter when or where. She gave him the same assurance. They knew they were soul partners for life and thereafter.

She moved back to the Outer Banks of North Carolina in September of 1993. She bought a little condo at Sand Piper Quay, a development in Kitty Hawk very near where their beloved Coast Guard Station had been on the oceanfront. She had moved the Station, which was on the Historic Register, a couple of years earlier using a federal relocation program.

The regulatory agencies mostly including CAMA had put her in a financial bind everywhere. Kitty Hawk had wanted the Station for a welcome station for a long time but she managed to work with Congressman Jones, who was a close family friend, and get the deed transferred to Eric Kreiger from Ligonier, Pennsylvania. Jeffrey's buddy had grown up summers with him in that Station. He would want to make sure it was saved. It was her children's favorite place in all the world and she needed to save it anyway she could.

Her cousin David Seymour was available once again in her time of need. He had lived with her at the Coast Guard Station one summer and in the Elizabeth City waterfront home one year. David was always there in her times of emotional needs, which were many. He usually helped her move and this move was no different. He came to Lake Norman to help her move back to Kitty Hawk. Shirley had become like family to Robb, his wife Carla and Robbie and Lindsey, their two wonderful outstanding children. They were all there to help her move. There were not many dry eyes when Shirley and David drove off in the small U Haul truck. They drove east to the coast, unpacked and got her settled once again. The condo that she purchased at Sand Piper Quay in Kitty Hawk was small and cozy, just like the rented condo at Lake Norman.

She wasn't looking for R&R this move. She was looking for answers to help her find her son or whatever happened to him that fateful day 16 miles offshore on November 13, 1980.

Sand Piper Quay had an association. They had a manager to watch over the development. If anything went wrong, it would surely be reported to her by a neighbor. She knew she was in the right place at the right time. She could just feel it. Sometimes right feelings might not always be safe feelings and she was about to learn that first hand.

She wanted to talk to Kenny again. Maybe he would be more talkative than the last meeting. Dealing with him was like being on a sea saw; sometimes you're up, sometimes you're down and sometimes you just hit the ground real hard. Maybe he would meet with her again. He answered the phone "Hey Sue Mae!" like nothing had ever happened

She told him she had moved back to the area and wanted to meet him again, at the 7-11 if that was convenient with him. He agreed.

During this visit Kenny told her a story about what happened offshore that day on November 13, 1980 when Jeffrey went fishing and never returned. He said he was hired by the Daniels family from Wanchese to blow up one of their wooden boats. He said there were two fishing boats; the Margie and the Sealee. Kenny named everyone aboard the two vessels without hesitation. She recognized all of the names. He said he was below deck waiting for his signal to detonate, looking out the porthole when he saw a big yacht coming along side. He said the yacht had foreign identification. He said there were many black dudes aboard with guns, and 27,000 pounds of cocaine worth $4 to $7 million.

These are Kenny's facts, not Shirley's.

He said the Jamaican or Bermuda boat brought the cocaine and the Mafia in Hampton paid for it in cash from a suitcase. He said he then saw a V shaped boat like Jeffrey's Sea Ox coming to the area fast and a black dude was running it. He said Jeffrey was aboard and was put on the foreign boat. He said it was about 4:30 p.m in the afternoon on November 13.

He said the demolition plan was aborted and the boat he was on, the Margie, went back to Wanchese. Kenny even let her tape the conversation. She had reached out for the local law, the SBI, the FBI and many others for years and years but no one seemed to reach back or offer to help her find her son Jeffrey. She had no idea who would be interested in those taped details from Kenny other than her.

Chapter Seventeen

The Year 1994

On January 2, 1994 the local Daily Advance in Elizabeth City reported that "William Allen, the local FBI Agent retired. He was one month short of 29 years as an FBI agent. He decided to keep his home in Elizabeth City and become a private investigator so he could continue a professional relationship with one "of the best group of local law enforcement agencies" he had ever contacted. When Captain W. O. Leary of the Elizabeth City Police Department stood up to read a poem written during the lunch hour, Allen knew he was in trouble."

"I wanted an easy job, I ain't gonna lie; So I went with the government and worked with the FBI. I wanted to be a great crime fighter. It's exciting work doing reports on a typewriter. Then I went to work in the undercover scene. I spent two years dressed as a drag queen." The press reported, "While Leary probably ribbed Allen the most during the "roast", others kept sharing memories that were more fond. Allen reminded everyone this was not officially a retirement but a "changing of careers."

William Allen FBI agent was quoted in the press as saying, "I've found heaven and I'm not moving."

William Allen, FBI agent, lived in a nice waterfront home next door to Buddy Fletcher in Riverview Estates. Buddy had been one of the developers of that upscale neighborhood and had lived next door to Allen before he bought part of Shirley's downtown waterfront home and moved there.

After she moved to Kitty Hawk, she was contacted by one of the victims who had joined the group to get rid of the DA. The group continued having meetings while she was in Charlotte. The caller had joined the group while she was away. "Hey Shirley, this is Becky Smith, you might not remember me. I grew up in Elizabeth City around the corner from you." "Of course, I remember you Becky way back on your tricycle. I know many of your family." Becky's extended family members were very prominent and held high political offices, many on a state level. She told Shirley that she had started an escort service at the Outer Banks in the seventies. H. P. Williams, the local DA had helped her with the paperwork necessary to start the business.

She had been busted and she was sure the DA had been instrumental in the arrest and that was the reason for her joining the victims group. She said she was a threat to many prominent people because her girls had entertained prominent politicians, government officials and even some Department of Transportation employees. Becky said that they busted her for drugs but what they really wanted was her rolodex.

She told Shirley that she realized she was looking for her son, Jeffrey and if anyone could help her, she thought it would be the undercover cop who kicked in her door and busted her. After busting her, he used her as an informer because he realized she had been setup by the DA's office. The undercover cop told Becky that he turned the rolodex over to the DA's office but while sitting in court, waiting to testify against her, he thumbed through the confiscated rolodex and several prominent names were missing.

Becky had penciled in on the rolodex how many times she had sent girls and to whom. Many times the "clients" requested the same girl. She even made notes of what kind of "tricks" the clients liked. Wow! Shirley knew this was dynamite against the DA's office. That coveted rolodex could provide blackmail against a lot of big politicians and a few judicial officials. Becky was an excellent writer and did not hesitate to keep the Coastal Times editor informed of her political concerns by writing to them. She was truly a threat to many people, and many of them were best friends of her well known Mother and Father.

Northeaster North Carolina is an interesting area and Becky was just trying to bring her up to date. She said, "The undercover agent who busted her worked out of the Dare County Sheriff's office and was working with an Organized Crime Task Enforcement Team involving FBI, DEA, Customs, and other agencies at the time he arrested her. His name is Lt. Bob Eck. Bob was run out of Dare County under the false charges that he stole from the funds he had seized from drug dealers."

Becky said, " Bob was a good man who didn't do what they said and everyone knew it. Some officers in the local Dare County Sheriff's office just wanted him out of there because there were rumors floating around that he should run for Sheriff." After busting Becky, Lt. Eck had used her as an informer. Becky had enough information to contact his mother in Massachusetts and find out how to locate him. She gave Shirley his phone number and address as soon as she received it.

Shirley always liked Becky when they were growing up in Elizabeth City. She knew Becky was smart as a whip and was one of the straightest shooters she had ever met. Although she didn't approve of her choice of profession, she took her advice and called Bob Eck. Becky had already talked to him first so he was aware that she was Jeffrey Mays' mother. He was shocked for many reasons. He hated Dare County; in fact all of North Carolina, for what had happened to him. After getting kicked out of Dare County he bought a tractor trailer and just rode the roads for about five years. He had just parked his rig about two weeks before Becky called.

Shirley didn't believe in coincidences.

Bob Eck had trained the first drug dog in North Carolina so it was no surprise that he had a Rottweiler riding with him during his five year road trip. His Rottweiler was appropriately named "Munch" and only understood German commands.

She said to him on the telephone, "I'd like to fly to Tampa and interview you. Maybe, if things work out, you can come to Kitty Hawk and stay with me for the month of October. I want to walk the walk in this area, especially Hatteras and let them know I want answers. I'd like you to walk that walk with me." Bob Eck agreed to meet her anytime. She immediately scheduled a plane trip to Tampa. This was in July of 1994. She made a reservation at a local motel near his home. She asked for a "no smoking" room. She had her conference in that room. She had all of her voluminous research involving Jeffrey and she started presenting it. This was early in the morning. After taking her first breath around 2:00 p.m, she asked him if he would like some lunch. He readily agreed. They went to a nearby restaurant and he excused himself for a smoke. He was a chain smoker and in a near state of panic.

He only ordered milk. "Aren't you hungry? Why didn't you tell me you needed a smoke?" "Because you were blowing my mind with your research." Bob Eck made this remark on July 18, 1994. Shirley will never forget that date because that was her son Jeffrey's birthday.

She and Bob connected on that trip and she made arrangements for him to come to Kitty Hawk in October. He didn't need much time to prepare for his trip to the Outer Banks. He had lived there for fifteen years as an undercover cop and the area was ingrained in his brain. In fact, he had tried to forget most of it during his five years of riding the roads. He wasn't sure he was glad this woman had found him but he was intrigued by her information. She thinks he took the job because he wanted to show the area he wasn't afraid to go back. He had done nothing wrong. She liked his style and felt comfortable that she would get her money's worth by hiring him.

Bob Eck and Munch arrived in Kitty Hawk at Shirley's condo in October of 1994. After spending time with him in Tampa, she agreed with Becky that he was honest and a good cop. He was also tall, trim and handsome, a real TNT (tough and tender) kind of guy. He was a role model Navy Seal. She felt safe in his presence but Robb Porter wanted to make that decision for himself so he immediately flew to Kitty Hawk to check out this cop. He didn't like many cops either. Porter was a good judge of people. He was also TNT and anybody that touched Shirley Mays' life touched his.

Robb and Bob got along famously which pleased her because both of them were very valuable to her. She wanted a team that she could trust. Porter had already passed the test. Bob Eck was about to begin his. Porter asked a lot of questions. He found out that Bob had been a Navy Seal and had been in Vietnam on two separate tours. He had been a highway patrolman before he came to the Outer Banks with the Dare County Sheriff's department. Porter had been in the Marines until he hit a General's son and received an early discharge although he was sure it wasn't his fault.

They talked and drank for several hours. Beer for Porter and scotch and water for the Navy Seal and Shirley. When she couldn't keep her eyes open any longer she excused herself and went to Sylvia and Webb's house for the night knowing full well that the talking of the two outstanding men was in her best interest and far from over.

She left so they could get to know each other even if it took all night. She went to bed that night with the assurance that if she ever went to war, she wanted both of them right by her side. She too was a good judge of character and they both fit the bill perfectly. She was feeling very safe and everything was still feeling right.

She was ready to start her journey with Lt. Robert Eck, walking the walk, step by step, side by side on the Outer Banks of North Carolina from Kitty Hawk to Cape Hatteras.

She learned during his stay that Bob had been banned by his third wife from entering the County in which she lived and that he had not seen anyone in the Sheriff's office since leaving five years earlier. He had no desire to see any of them. She learned a lot about Bob Eck but the most interesting fact of all was that his ex-brother-in-law was Jock MacKenzie who owned The Easy Ryder that last approached her son's

Sea Ox on November 13, 16 miles offshore. Edgar Styron, Jr. was running the boat that day but Jock MacKenzie owned it. Bob was adamant that Jock was a trust fund baby and didn't know how to run the boat. Bob said that Jock just happened to be there that day and didn't know anything.

Shirley thought to herself immediately, "Houston, we've got a problem."

She thought, how could anyone as smart as this Navy Seal think that the last person seeing her son 16 miles offshore didn't know a thing about that day even though it had created one of the largest Coast Guard searches ever on the East Coast? That remark and Bob's insistence on it was the only problem they would ever have.

He told her that at the time of his "retirement", he and many other lawmen were working on flow charts that involved the drug activities of politicians, law enforcement officers, local commercial fishermen, boat builders and some Coast Guardsmen. They were just getting ready to really hit the real estate guys. It was his belief that someone in the Sheriff's office had worked hard to discredit him. This was confirmed by other sources. She always did her own background search.

They spent time in Hatteras, Elizabeth City, Raleigh, Hyde County, Sneeds Ferry and elsewhere. One night in Sneeds Ferry, Bob said to her, "Damn, you're going to get us killed Mays." She said, "Hope not Eck." She had no idea at the time how big Sneeds Ferry fit into the overall international drug smuggling of the area.

She took him to the Attorney General's Environmental Division in Raleigh and the Environmental Section of Marine Fisheries in Morehead: with two copiers, several reams of paper and of course had a lawyer send each of the agencies a letter in advance saying she was coming. Bob could now add environmental consultant and bodyguard to his law enforcement resume.

They visited Jock MacKenzie, his ex-brother-in –law in Hatteras. Bob's first wife was Jock's sister Heather. Heather and Bob had grown up around the corner from each other in Massachusetts. Jock had moved to North Carolina first, many years ago, married a local Hatteras girl and persuaded Heather and Bob to leave Massachusetts and move to the Outer Banks. That's how Bob got to the area. Bob's wife had a problem with drugs so they divorced. Heather went back to Massachusetts and then Eck married a local girl. They divorced and she was the one who had him banned from North Carolina. Shirley had always heard about Navy Seals and how they were intriguing individuals. She was learning just how intriguing this particular one was.

In fact, this Navy Seal undercover cop had his own story.

Many people were shocked to see Bob back in the area, especially some of the people he had busted. They all seemed to like him and were excited to see him. He told Shirley he was always fair, even when arresting people. She believed him. She wanted to call Bert Austin, the Dare County Sheriff, who was like family to her, and tell him Bob Eck was there working with her but he thought that was going a little too far and wouldn't allow it. Before leaving the area he reconsidered and made a phone call himself to tell the Sheriff that he was in the area helping Shirley Mays look for answers about her son. That was a good move for Bob because he was going to need that Sheriff later on.

She wanted to meet with Kenny Williams in person while Bob was there with her. She called him with Bob listening on another phone. "My Daddy said you are setting me up." She assured him she wasn't and scheduled a meeting at their 7-11 parking lot. She and Bob went as scheduled but Kenny, for the first time, didn't show up. Shirley wondered how Kenny knew exactly when to meet her and when not to. Was she being watched? It had been real strange that summer when she got back from meeting Bob in Tampa and she received a call from Kenny, who was very drunk or drugged. "Sue Mae, if you send me to Tampa, I'll find your boy but if you don't, they are going to put you in a bag and take you to him."

Damn, how did Kenny know she had been to Tampa? He never ceased to amaze her. He was almost as intriguing as her Navy Seal.

October of 1994 came and went.

In December, she headed back to Florida to visit family and friends. On a whim, she decided to get in touch with a man from Missing Persons who heard about her case and wanted to get involved. She had put him off for five years because he sounded so macho. She thought he wanted into the case for the personal publicity. She knew he would be shocked to hear from her because she had not shown any interest in all those years.

His name was Dick Ruffino. He had just retired from Missing Persons organization. He was from New Jersey but had just moved to Florida a few days before her visit. Shirley had learned his address from friends in Whiteville, North Carolina who also had a missing son. They had dealt with Dick Ruffino extensively over the years and were very complimentary of him. She went directly to the town where she heard he had just moved and called him from a nearby restaurant. He was shocked and asked if he could meet her there. She agreed. During that meeting, she decided she liked him enough to work with him. She invited him to come to Kitty Hawk.

She intended to walk the walk with several people until she got some answers. She scheduled him for the first of the year 1995.

Dick Ruffino, Missing Persons, did his homework. He asked for a package about Jeffrey and family. He wanted pictures and information about close friends and family. Shirley sent him more information than he had requested. Dick had visited his good friend the Sheriff in Columbia, South Carolina who made him a special agent just for this case. He had the proper people in DC enhance Jeffrey's picture to see what he might look like at the present. He was definitely trying to do his job because he wanted badly to solve this case. He had performed a Missing Person's search for a friend of Ronald Regan and prided himself on high profile cases. He was ready to get started.

It was a most interesting fall and winter and Shirley felt like she knew more than she ever had. She was getting many more pieces to her puzzle.

She spent Thanksgiving of 1994 in Seattle with her youngest daughter, Christmas in Florida with her oldest daughter and New Year's Eve with her brother Ken in Key West.

She had not seen Ken since they had traveled to New Orleans to look for Jeffrey. She needed to see him so they could compare notes. On a whim she decided to fill out that paperwork that she received from the RTC seminar in Charlotte before driving to Florida in December. She actually never thought she would have any desire to do work involving the government but she had nothing to lose so she filled out the paperwork and sent it in.

She brought in the New Year with her brother and was now thinking about heading back north. She decided to check her answering service at her condo before leaving. She had a message from Gemini Asset Managers, a minority government contractor in Springfield, Va., wanting to know if she would submit an environmental subcontract bid involving vacant land in Duck, North Carolina. Evidently she had been approved by the government or the FDIC because they were the ones who formed the RTC to manage and sell all of those many properties that the taxpayers now owned.

Over a thousand S&L Banks had gone defunct and the FDIC/RTC was responsible for managing the assets which now belonged to the taxpayers who bailed out the banks. It was the biggest financial disaster the country had ever experienced. It was a huge bailout.

The property in question was in Duck, North Carolina, a few miles north of her condo in Kitty Hawk. She knew the area and was positive that there were no environmental issues because it was now and had always been only sand, sand and more sand. There were no filling stations or businesses which could cause environmental problems so this

Phase I contract should be a piece of cake. She called the Springfield contractor and asked for an extension until she could get back to North Carolina. She told him she was in Key West. He seemed glad to accommodate her with whatever time she needed because they wanted a local environmental contractor.

That bid was how Shirley found out that she had been certified to perform environmental and real estate consulting and to sell and investigate all kinds of real estate for the RTC and the FDIC. Maybe she would do a little business with the government after all. This was right up the alley for her and Robb.

Chapter Eighteen

The Year 1995

It appeared that 1995 might be a prosperous New Year for her. She hoped so. She needed a littler prosperity.

She left the Keys and headed back north. She called Robb on the way and told him to send her a proposal for a Phase I. They had performed many of them together. She could do this one alone but wanted to be sure she dotted her i's and crossed her t's for her first government job. She brought in her soul mate, the best geologist she knew. This would be fun for them working together again. She sent the bid, which included Robb's proposal to her, to the Springfield contractor and it was quickly accepted. She had never known the government to act this fast before but actually it wasn't the government. It was a private minority contractor hired by the RTC as an asset manager to handle some of their defunct properties. When she became certified as a minority contractor, she had no knowledge of just how big this financial disaster was for the taxpayers. She only knew that she was over qualified for the bid she had just taken. How could she and Robb possibly get in trouble with this environmental subcontract dealing with raw land? After all, they had tackled huge environmental problems involving Superfund properties while she worked with him in Charlotte. This looked to be a slam dunker! She was wrong again.

She always did her investigative title work first and then performed the site check. She knew that if you didn't have clear title, you sure as heck shouldn't be developing the land. She headed off to the Dare

County courthouse where it seemed she had spent hundreds of hours researching deeds for the Neimay Lawsuit.

Shirley felt very much like an expert in white collar crime after they had sandbagged her in court. It had been an eight year education for her from 1983 to 1991. She was told that her reputation preceded her in the legal circles because of the Neimay case. She had been gone from the area for awhile but she was sure the Dare County boys would remember her. She certainly remembered them.

She came across many problems while searching the title for the raw land in Duck. Dottie Frye, the Register of Deeds was a friend of hers so they were talking while she was doing her research. "Dottie, are you familiar with a property in Duck at the corner of Scarborough Road?" She and Dottie had known each other a long time and they both knew the area very well. "Looks like they have a lot of problems." She had not noticed that there was a prominent local lawyer in there doing a search of his own.

Dottie glanced at some of her paperwork. "Good God Shirley, are you doing work for those RTC people?" "Yes, why?" "They have been in town causing a lot of trouble for many locals."

She knew nothing about the local Great Atlantic S&L at that time and had no idea what Dottie was talking about. Dottie said, "I don't know about that property but why don't you ask a lawyer" and she winked and looked towards the local lawyer doing his own search. Shirley turned around and recognized the lawyer, who had been one of the many involved in the Neimay lawsuit mess in which she had been involved. In fact, it was the one who had been copied on the letter she received from the Real Estate Commission lawyer.

"Crouse, are you familiar with the Duck property I'm talking about." He said, "I'm their attorney but they have not started building. They only have the pilings in." That was interesting information to her because her contract stated that it was raw land. She was yet to do a site check.

There should be no pilings at all because her contract was involved with a $200,000 loan from the Great Atlantic S&L. Her bid said it was raw land. The land was collateral for the loan and the loan had not been paid off or rather the FDIC/RTC who acquired the loan after the Great Atlantic S&L went down wasn't aware of the payoff. There should be no pilings.

Shirley Mays smelled a problem and Dottie and Crouse smelled it at the same time.

She drove straight to Duck which was about a 25 minute drive from downtown Manteo. She pulled up to the address. "Oh my God!" What she saw was not vacant land but construction in progress. There were many pilings and a huge sign that said a large shopping center was in progress. And their attorney didn't know that? She was going to have to sell Crouse that same Brooklyn Bridge.

That simple piece of raw land which she and Robb had a simple Phase I environmental contract on turned into a huge nightmare for someone right at that moment. She had thought that working for the government wasn't going to be that easy but now it was confirmed.

The sign said a Corporation from Virginia was building a large shopping center. The loan actually belonged to the taxpayers because they had to pick up the bill for all those defunct S&Ls including the local one in Manteo, North Carolina. She knew immediately that her obligation was to call the contractor in Springfield, Virginia who in turn had an obligation to her for a subcontract to perform a Phase I on a piece of raw land and let him know they had a problem. She went back to her small, safe Sand Piper Quay condo and made the call.

The project manager with Gemini Asset Managers who issued her the contract said he made a trip to the Outer Banks and the asset was raw land during that trip. He appeared not to know what was happening. But he asked her if he could call her back on a conference call. He called back in a very short time and several others were asking her questions. She wondered how many lawyers were listening. "I think you have a problem. Someone is building a large shopping center on a piece of land that has a $200,000 lien against it." "Can you send us that paperwork that you got at the courthouse?" "It'll be in the mail in about an hour." This was in mid January, 1995.

On January 25, 1995, the local paper's headlines read, "50-Member Task Force Launches Drug Sweeps." With an unusual disregard for secrecy, local and state law enforcement officials held a press conference late Thursday to announce one of the biggest drug sweeps ever held in Northeastern North Carolina – **BEFORE** it happened.

She knew that the Keystone Cops were back in action but this time they had a new leader. He was the Director of the ALE division of the N. C. Department of Crime Control and Public Safety and of course the local Elizabeth City Police Force. The new Police Chief in Elizabeth City told the news and television reporters, "we're going to send a message to law breakers that it will no longer be comfortable for them in Elizabeth City."

And he told them this *BEFORE* the raid.

He preserved a degree of secrecy by immediately putting the reporters and photographers in a special vehicle that followed the raids.

While Bob Eck was in Kitty Hawk with Shirley during the month of October, he had suggested they go to Elizabeth City and take the new district attorney out to lunch. Bob knew him and liked him. Shirley suggested they also take the new Police Chief who she knew from growing up. While walking to the restaurant, the new Chief asked Shirley if she could get him a job. Evidently the pressure was building up at that time, a few months before this ridiculous showtime drug raid.

She knew the Keystone Cops in Elizabeth City had arrested some very small players, mostly African Americans, the ones that went through the revolving doors every other week so the police could keep up their statistics of drug arrests. It was a law enforcement joke and she knew it. Most of the public probably knew it too.

She had more accurate information now. She had been informed by Lt. Bob Eck, who had been on the OCDETF that Roland Dale, the ex-Hyde County Sheriff, who had been appointed Director of ALE, had been a real problem for their task force. He said before every drug bust in Hyde County, they had to notify him and when they arrived, the drug folks were gone, every time. He said there were many ditches in Hyde County with body parts in them and even law enforcement hesitated to venture into the county.

He said the biggest problem the Organized Crime Task Force had was dealing with the local law in Northeastern North Carolina. It appeared to be rotten to the core and not concerned about being exposed.

Some bigger, more legitimate drug busts were more successful south, near Wilmington, in the small town of Dunn, North Carolina. A potato farmer from Dunn was stopped on Interstate 10 going through Louisiana. That routine stop ended up bringing down the potato farmer and 19 others, including prominent businessmen from his area. His network was running drugs from Mexico into Arizona where they were hidden in motor homes and trucks and smuggled into North Carolina. The article related, 'The profits bought beachfront properties and other luxuries."

Dick Ruffino arrived with great flair late afternoon February 14th. He was a little guy but talked big. He wanted to meet with Burt Austin, the local Sheriff so he called him at 9:00 p.m. "This is Dick Ruffino, special agent on the Jeffrey Mays case and I would like to meet with you at soon as possible." Shirley thought that he sounded like a real big shot. She was surprised at the tone of his voice. What she did not know at that time was that his buddy, the Sheriff from South Carolina, had made him a special agent just for this case, and had called Bert Austin, the Sheriff that day. "My agent is coming down to see you and

I wanted you to know that we have all the planes, men and money we need to back him up."

The Sheriff was at home in Hatteras when Ruffino called him late that night. Burt said he would meet Ruffino the next morning in front of The Dunes, a local popular restaurant in Nags Head at 9:00 a.m. She was surprised at the reaction of Burt Austin who agreed to such a quick meeting. She thought he would be taken by surprise by this big talking special agent.

Burt Austin, Dare County Sheriff and Clarence Owens, Police Chief of Elizabeth City were both dear friends of hers and of her parents. She liked both men and knew they were well aware of how Jeffrey's disappearance had affected his family.

Ruffino met with Burt and then told Shirley he would like to go to Hatteras. He never shared any conversation with her that he might have had with the Sheriff. He now wanted to meet with Jock MacKenzie, one of the two guys who last saw Jeffrey on November 13. She called Jock. She had met him with Bob Eck in October so she felt comfortable calling him. He agreed to meet with them. She made an appointment for the next day.

They went to Hatteras and upon arrival at Jock's, Ruffino said, "Would you mind staying in the car? I think he will say more if you're not there." She readily agreed because her goal was to get answers about Jeffrey and she didn't care who got them. After about an hour, Ruffino came out and Jock walked out to the car with him. Jock said hello to Shirley and then really started talking. He asked her to come in. He said he had not been able to sleep since she called him. He had been up since about 4:00 a.m. He told them that he had bought his boat, The Easy Ryder, from a man at Pirate's Cove. Jock couldn't remember who. He thinks he paid cash. Edgar had told him about the boat. He said Edgar offered him $5000 a day for use of boat. Jock said he refused.

Shirley wondered if Edgar paid him on November 13.

Jock said Edgar was a jerk. He said he had to go to Massachusetts because his mother was sick so he sold his boat to Edgar for cash and it was paid to him in packets of zip locked bags. Jock said Edgar still owed him money.

Jock said that Edgar told him, shortly after the search started, that the boys were OK.

Jock said that Edgar often goes to some island with the owner of the boat he runs. The boat is named Pure Magic. He also often goes to Wilmington and Florida. He said Edgar and S. S. (unknown person) were in high school together and got in an accident going over 100 miles an hour. Edgar was messed up. He limps, is scarred and has back trouble. Jock said   S. S. knows all. He is legit and runs the head boats in Hatteras. Both of them are about 44 or 45.

He said his wife Kathy is a Gaskins and they have one daughter. Her mother and dad live right down the road at their bed and breakfast inn and he keeps his boat in back of their house.

Kathy came into the room about that time and joined in the conversation. She told them about Don Burrus, a local boy. Kathy used to go with Don in high school. Don was caught coming off a plane in Miami with a briefcase full of money. This happened about the same time the boys were missing. Don married a girl whose father was in the Mafia. The Mafia killed them both in execution style and buried them in Virginia. Their bodies were discovered. The Mafia came down and threatened Don's parents if they talked. She said the family might talk now but she wasn't sure. Don's father was dead and his mother worked at the local grocery.

She said Edgar's friend Johnny Davis is in Bermuda and stays there all the time.

"Didn't Kenny say it was a boat from Bermuda with 27,000 pounds of cocaine that met the boat he was on that day?" It appeared to her that they really wanted her to have that information. Ruffino appeared shocked because he learned very little before Jock invited Shirley into the house. So much for Jock not talking in front of her. She had many more pieces of the puzzle now and that was her bottom line.

She gave Ruffino a tour of the area including the Coast Guard Search and Rescue Center where they had spent so much time during the search for the boys. They then headed back north to her condo in Sand Piper Quay which was about an hour's drive from Hatteras.

When Dick arrived the night before, they made phone calls to Jeffrey's buddy Eric Krieger in Pennsylvania, Bud's friend Eddie Miller at the Outer Banks and Bob Eck, the undercover cop and Navy Seal from Tampa. Ruffino appeared to be doing his homework. That night while they were relaxing in Shirley's condo and going over the day's events, she said, "Dick, do you ever work with psychics?" "Yes, all the time. Sometimes they help and sometimes they don't." She said," I have a friend in Rochester, NY whose best friend is a psychic who works with the police in finding missing people. Would you like to talk with her?" "Sure." Shirley called Judy the physic in Rochester, told her about the special agent and asked if she thought she could help him. She had met Judy only one time when she went to Rochester and had not seen or talked to her in a few years. "Yes, please put him on the phone." Shirley gave the phone to Ruffino and grabbed an extension.

Judy started talking as if it were a planned presentation. "I see two trucks, in a chase. One of them has dogs in the back. One truck is black and one black and white. The black one is trying to run the other one off the road. I see condos, all attached with many people, moving in and moving out in a hurry. I see a truck with the license "Delaware. I see a black jeep and someone keeps rolling the blinds in it up and down."

Shirley thought maybe Jeffrey was in the truck being chased. Judy continued to talk but Shirley's mind trailed off. All she could visualize was her son not being safe and being somewhere in Alaska in trouble being chased by a truck either black or maybe black and white.

She was staying at Sylvia and Webb's house again, and Dick Ruffino was staying in her little condo. They talked a little bit longer that night and then she excused herself. It had been a long busy day and she was mentally and physically exhausted.

The next morning, Dick Ruffino was like a different person. He appeared scared. He said he had never been involved in a case like this with such big drug implications. He left and Shirley had the strong feeling that she had seen the last of the hot shot special agent who for five years couldn't wait to get involved with this case. Evidently he got more than he bargained for.

She heard a commotion across the street from her about midnight. That was the same day that Dick Ruffino left. She looked out and saw a man running into the back of a condo. It was a very strange incident and she had trouble sleeping the rest of the night.

Events started happening very quickly the next day. Headlines in the local paper stated that a man and his three children had burned up in a van at the Wright Brothers Memorial which was only a few short miles down the road from her condo in Sand Piper Quay. It was a big mysterious event for the area that brought in the SBI and the FBI. They were not disclosing a name or much other information about the people. The article said the man had run from his van into the woods leaving the children inside the van. The van caught on fire. The children burned up. And then the man shot himself before they could apprehend him.

He was from Delaware. Not much more was stated in the paper. It scared Shirley because he could be about the age of Jeffrey. She called the Kill Devil Hills Police Chief and met him in the K-Mart parking lot. He knew who she was and he assured her that it was a banker about 36 years old from Delaware and not her son Jeffrey. She wasn't sure she was completely satisfied with his explanation. Too many unexplained strange things were happening too fast. She felt he was holding back on the true story. She hoped not.

The next day, Rosemary, one of her best friends, who lived a few miles away in Nags Head called and said her father had just died. She made a cake to take her because that is what people in the South do immediately after hearing of a death in the family. They take food as if somehow that will make everything alright. When she came back home, she experienced another very strange problem. She had water all over her hall leading to one of the bedrooms without a trace of where it came from. She checked the water heater and it was dry all around. There was no sign of water or a water leak.

She called her Navy Seal in Tampa. "What do you think happened Eck?" "Be careful of electrocution Mays." She stood on a chair and called Sylvia whose brother was a plumber. She then called her brother who said he would be there as soon as possible. He also suggested someone who could remove water from the rug. They both arrived at the same time. She was in the kitchen while the two men were checking out the water in her hall and she heard them say, "This is real weird." She went down the hall. "What is real weird?" She was still reeling from the special agent, the burning of the van and the death of Rosemary's father.

The guy who came to suck the water out of the rug spotted one of her research book. "What do you know about that RTC group?" "I am doing some work for them, why?" "They have screwed me out of a piece of land in the Kitty Hawk Woods that I had mortgaged with the local Great Atlantic Savings Bank. I don't trust them."

Shirley's mind flipped back to the courthouse where Dottie Frye had said, "Do you work for those RTC people?" She was beginning to wonder into what she had stepped. Looked like a big barrel of it. She asked the guy who was getting rid of the water if he could come back the next day and talk to her about his RTC problem. He said he would and then he and the plumber both left at the same time. Shirley had the strong feeling that both of those men who just walked out of her wet condo knew more than she did about what was going on in the area at that time.

Events got weirder the next day. She looked out her window and saw a black jeep in front of her condo with the blinds pulled down. She didn't put it together right at first. Just then the Sand Piper Quay condo manager's husband marched right in, without her permission and she said, "What's up Doug?" He had come to look at the water situation and asked her why she didn't call them. He obviously was mad which put great doubt into her mind as to why?

"Because I wanted my own plumber." Doug acted irritated, stomped out and went upstairs. She realized that someone new was moving in right above her. She got the distinct feeling that it was someone from the black jeep. She immediately marched upstairs to say hello and get a look at them and by doing so threw everyone into somewhat of a tizzy. "Hi, I'm your downstairs neighbor." The man immediately turned to the wall so she couldn't see his face.

She thought to herself "What in the hell is going on?"

Doug told her that the local jailer's daughter was moving in. She said OK and left. All that day, she spotted people across the street moving in and out, in and out, and going to the dumpster which was at the end of their street. She wondered what they were throwing away. She got up the next morning real early, before the dump truck came and climbed in the dumpster. She saw lots of good cans of food that had never been opened and some First Union bank statements in their original unopened envelopes. She took the bank statements and ran fast as she could as the dump truck was approaching. She hoped no one recognized her in her pajamas.

While opening the bank statements, she noticed the condos across the street from her. There was still a lot of activity going on. There were people moving in and out and all of them appeared to be in a panic. There was a black truck with a dog in the back. There was another vehicle with Delaware license plate.

When she and Dick Ruffino were talking to the Rochester psychic, she imagined the activity Judy was explaining as being in Alaska because those letters from the special agent in West Virginia had said one of the boys was in Alaska.

"Good God everything Judy told us is happening right here across the street before my eyes in Sand Piper Quay. It didn't happen in Alaska. It is happening here and now."

She studied the bank statements. They were statements from a real estate company. They had checks to Kenny Williams with a Currituck address. No wonder Kenny knew everything she was doing. Her every move was being watched right across the street from her. She must have been watched during the month Bob Eck and Munch were with her and the time Dick Ruffino was there. That is how Kenny knew she went to Tampa. And that is why Kenny said he was being set up and didn't show up at a 7-11 meeting they had planned. She was being watched all the time from a condo that was directly across from her. Surely, they had her phone tapped and her condo bugged also.

Who was watching her and why?

She packed a few things and got the hell out of there in about fifteen minutes. She wasn't too far behind Dick Ruffino. She called Bob Eck in Tampa, told him what was happening. "I've only felt fear twice in my life and I am experiencing it now." What should I do? "Take a left, a left and a left and they will be in front of you?" "Eck, you are well aware that we only have two roads, a beach road and a bypass." "Then drive like the devil is after you and get the hell out of there Mays."

She took a quick right out of Sand Piper Quay and passed the dumpster she had just climbed out of. She drove at a rapid speed and knew in her heart that she wouldn't be back. At least she would not be back to live in Sand Piper Quay. She drove to the cutoff in Currituck where you had to decide if you were going to Elizabeth City, North Carolina or Virginia Beach, Virginia. Her car went to Virginia Beach to the home of friends of her brother Ken. They knew her and loved her brother. They were well aware of her son Jeffrey's disappearance so she didn't have to explain anything. She knocked on their door. "I need a safe place to sleep so I can make some decisions." "First bedroom on the right and call us if you need anything." She had not seen them for several years but some people never change and they were that type of people. She felt comfortable and safe temporarily but indeed had to make some big decisions.

The next morning she got up early, without having slept all night, had a cup of coffee and quickly told them what was happening. She had decided at some point in the last few hours that Carolina Beach, a suburb of Wilmington, North Carolina would be her next stop. Why? For several reasons. She had heard a rumor that if the boys headed south that day offshore in the direction of Wilmington that they probably came in at Southport, an inlet near Wilmington. Someone had mentioned Snow's Cut.

Shirley was in search of Snow's Cut for years and she found one right at Carolina Beach. She had friends there and felt that she would be safe. Besides this area was the birthplace of her oldest daughter and she had spent two of the best years of her life close by at Wrightsville Beach.

She had about a five or six hour drive from Virginia Beach to Wilmington. She had a small suitcase and a few other items that she grabbed while running out the door of her past home, the Sand Piper Quay condo. Fortunately she had remembered to grab her RTC paperwork because Gemini Asset Managers owed her money and she intended to collect it.

She arrived at Carolina Beach and stopped at a phone booth to call her friend Carol from Rochester, NY. Carol was staying with a friend of hers from Rochester who had just moved to Carolina Beach. Carol was also house hunting. She had met Carol in a very unusual way. A few years earlier, she had been traveling the East Coast looking for a place to develop and build her a barber shop and she somehow ended up in Elizabeth City at the door of Shirley Mays' waterfront home. Shirley was not at home at the time so Carol left a note on the door which said, "If you are ever interested in selling your property, please contact me at ----------, Rochester, NY".

She was not interested in selling her Elizabeth City properties at that time so she called Carol to thank her but say she had no thoughts of selling. They stayed in touch after that. Years later, Carol told Shirley that before she left Rochester to look for a property on the East Coast, she was having lunch with her friend Judy, the psychic, and Judy drew a sketch for Carol showing two buildings and said, "The woman who lives there has a missing son."

That was in the late eighties.

Carol decided to move from Rochester to the Wilmington area at the same time that Shirley fled from Kitty Hawk in March of 1995. Shirley called Carol. "Guess what? I'm in Carolina Beach. How do I get to you"? "Come on. I'm staying with my best friend Denise who just moved here and we have room for you also." Shirley arrived on a Saturday night and spent the evening catching up with Carol's latest episodes. On Sunday morning, she met with a local real estate agent and bought a little duplex house, with a huge front porch and an excellent view of the ocean. This move felt right thank goodness. She moved into her new beach house on her birthday, March 18, 1995. She felt safe once again.

Carol told her that she and her boyfriend from Rochester had bought a piece of property at Snow's Cut. It was right on the Intra-Coastal Waterway at Carolina Beach. They were having problems and needed some advice from a local attorney. Shirley called a local friend of hers who had also grown up in her hometown of Elizabeth City but had lived in the Wilmington area for over twenty years. She was a real estate broker. She asked her if she could recommend an attorney who had a reputation for being real tough. Her real estate friend told her who her company used. It was a third generation well know law firm. Shirley said "Give me the name of an SOB who can win in court." Her friend did; his name was Gary Shipman.

She made a quick and unannounced trip back to Kitty Hawk and once again, her cousin David moved her out of that condo in record time. She didn't feel the need to inform David of the danger they might be in. He might not have believed it anyway.

She was hoping that the Swat Team across the street from her was working at their real estate office and not on guard at the time. She wanted to catch everyone off guard. She felt like she was in enemy territory but at least she was moving fast.

She called a real estate friend in the area she trusted. "Sell my condo. I need the money for a replacement." Doug, the Sand Piper Quay manager's husband got very irritated with Shirley once again when he heard about this because he usually controlled the resale of condos in that development. Doug's actions were very puzzling to her.

She settled into her cute little duplex at Carolina Beach, once again with a clear view of the Atlantic Ocean and once again trying to figure out, "How did I get to where I am?" That question was getting as big as Jeffrey's puzzle and seemed to almost have as many parts to it.

She had started working with the FDIC and/or RTC in January and this was only March and she was already in trouble. She started gathering information about the S&L defunct banks and realized that it really was the biggest financial scandal that the United States had ever experienced. Some very good investigative journalists had reported the damages as high as $1.4 trillion. She had a hard time saying that figure, much less understanding how much it was! All she knew was that some minority contractor named Gemini Asset Managers in Springfield, Virginia had hired her to do a Phase I environmental subcontract on a raw piece of land in Duck, North Carolina and they owed her $1,800. She could not finish the contract because of all the liabilities that she had uncovered. She was not about to bring Robb Porter with all of his ammunition into the picture. He never flew without it. He might take a shot at them just because of what they had done to her.

Shirley called the project manager at Gemni. "I've moved. I've done all I can and I would like for you to send my check to my new address." He said he would have to check with his boss. He called back. "We are sorry but we can't pay you because you didn't finish the Phase I." "And I am not going to finish; there is too much liability. I don't dare bring a geologist in. Don't you people realize that the taxpayer is losing all the way around? They own the loan and therefore the land. The loan has never been satisfied and a huge project is being built."

She told them "It appears to me that the government might have to buy this loan back."

She used comparables and sent them her very best broker's opinion of the property. She put in writing about the liability and the taxpayer's loss and sent it on its way to Springfield. Her last sentence said, "I strongly suggest you send my check, by return mail, to my new address." She had her check for $1,800 within a day or two of their receipt of her certified letter. She thought, "That is the end of them and probably my efforts to work with the government." She was wrong on both accounts.

She had set up an office in her Carolina Beach home. Her fax hummed one day with several bids from Graimark Realty Advisors, another minority asset manager out of Detroit, Michigan. The bids involved commercial properties in the Research Triangle area of Raleigh, North Carolina. "Wow. These aren't bad properties. I can probably make phone calls and sell them." She had worked with developers from several states who respected her real estate opinions.

She drove to the Raleigh area, a couple of hours west of Wilmington, to investigate the properties. She always did her title work first, before accepting bids. This was a habit for her because of all the liabilities that the regulatory bodies had put on her own personal properties and those of private property owners everywhere in the nation. She might recognize it before other realtors because she had been such a victim of the regulatory system. She had paid a very big price for her regulatory education.

She was at the Durham Courthouse, asking a question of the Registrar of Deeds, when a local lawyer who appeared to be doing research said to her, "If you're looking for an RTC property forget it. You can't find them."

Another strange remark about the RTC.

Shirley could find the information she needed because she was standing there with an RTC bid in her hand and it gave her information that the local lawyer didn't have. Investigating troubled properties was what she had been doing since 1983. It was beginning to look like many of the RTC properties might be "extremely troubled." For some reason she did not go to the site that day. It was probably because of her belief that clear titles were the driving force of a piece of property. The Research Triangle was a large well known area and it was getting late. It was about time for the courthouse to close. She felt that she had enough information to send Graimark Realty Advisors some decent bids. She thought the bids would be good competitive ones.

She heard back from Graimark in record time and was awarded exclusive contracts to sell four very good properties. Two of them were commercial properties in north Raleigh. One was a gorgeous horse farm in north Durham and the other was a sad looking piece of property, several acres, in a little town called Spring Hope, south of Raleigh. She was dealing with Graimark's office in Richmond, Virginia. They were headquartered in Detroit, with offices in Richmond and Philadelphia. She checked on their ownership this time and found that the Corporation was owned by a CPA from Chicago and a lawyer from Philadelphia.

"Don't let your mind even go there," she thought, but it raced ahead on its own to the Neimay Lawsuit, the seven year accounting fraud lawsuit in Dare County involving accountants and lawyers and Robb's crooked accountant.

"This is ridiculous of me to think this way. I am lucky these professional people have the education to know how to dot their i's and cross their t's. I am of good fortune to be working with a minority accountant and lawyer."

She headed back to the Raleigh area and put her personal signs up on two of the properties. The next day she got a call about the sad looking acreage in Spring Hope. "I saw your sign and I am interested in the farm you have in Spring Hope. I work at a local college and I could meet you wherever you wish." They agreed on a restaurant in north Raleigh. She drove back to Raleigh the very next day to meet with this young lady whom she had talked to on the phone. She was a beautiful black girl, very soft spoken who apologized for bothering her. "No bother . How can I help you?" The young lady's name was Joyce. "I have to tell you the truth. I am very familiar with that farm." Shirley told her she was very glad because it is best to work with knowledgeable buyers. This young lady appeared to be very educated. "My grandfather lost the farm years ago. The banker and his attorney were so nice to my grandfather that they loaned him the money he needed right out of their own pocket."

Shirley was beginning to fume but didn't want to show it.

"My cousins and I got together and we are pooling our money so we can buy back our family farm." She said "You'll get that farm. You can count on it." "We had no idea what to do or where to begin until we saw your sign." Shirley said, "Let's write a contract and we'll start there. Trust me, I will do everything possible for you and your cousins to get your family farm back."

She stopped by Spring Hope on her way back to Wilmington that same day. She went to the local governmental offices and asked for the environmental department. She researched their records and found an environmental impact on that farm. She walked the farm which was just a few miles away and failed to see their concerns. She knew she had another environmental abuse on her hands. Thank God for her past experience in dealing with those type problems. An ordinary realtor wouldn't even have noticed the pending danger. She made several phone calls to developers she knew and quickly secured the other contracts with qualified buyers and 10% escrow checks for Graimark Realty

Advisors but all the while her heart was involved with getting the family farm closed for Joyce and her cousins.

She called her Graimark contact in Richmond, Virginia and inquired about the environmental impact on the Spring Hope family farm. The project manager talked in circles as if the environmental issues might be a problem. Shirley was accustomed to people doing that. It is called legalese when the lawyers do it but BS when others try to confuse the issues. Actually it is called BS from all of them.

She was a straight shooter and just called a spade a spade so for this Graimark project manager to talk in circles made no sense at all to her. Evidently she was asking too many environmental questions because the project manager seemed to be getting rather irritated with her. She didn't care. She wanted direct answers for her buyers.

Shirley played hardball with Graimark. She had been thrown into the games people like this were playing for many years. You had to learn to play and either win or lose. She wasn't about to lose this family farm that belonged to Joyce and her cousins. They would get that farm if she had to blow up Graimark and the RTC. Maybe she would have to call in Robb on this contract after all.

While she was busy with the closing of the Spring Hope farm, Graimark, with no warning at all breached all of her other contracts. How could they do that? After all, she had sent them escrow checks to secure the contracts. These properties legally belonged to the taxpayers and the RTC had a fiduciary responsible to honor her contracts. She thought to herself, "First things first. Secure the family farm for the cousins and then deal with the Detroit CPA and the Philadelphia lawyer."

The closing attorney in Raleigh, at her request, sent her the HUD papers before the closing date for the Spring Hope property. That was proper and it was her right as the closing broker to have them. She worried that they were charging Joyce and her cousins too much for closing costs but she didn't know what she could do about it. The charges from two mortgage brokers were excessive. She had the HUD closing documents but didn't find out until much later after the final closing that the HUD documents had been changed after having been sent to her and four mortgage companies' charges had been added before closing. She would have known that the buyers were being sandbagged if they had sent her the final HUD closing papers. She was already concerned that Joyce and her cousins might lose the farm because of the two mortgage brokers. They ended up dealing with four. She didn't like what she was experiencing with the RTC.

Chapter Nineteen

The Year 1996

Many of Shirley's friends who cared deeply for her suggested that she should write a book about Jeffrey and maybe some people would come forward after all of these years with information that would help her in her search. She had taken the advice of her friends and had been working on the book off and on for a few months. It was just too complicated, too confusing; she couldn't seem to get it to flow. Dr. Bill Morgenroth was a dear friend who always gave her excellent advice. She looked to him as her Senior Advisor. Bill was a twin and his twin brother Dr. Bobby Morgenroth lived in Chapel Hill. Bobby was a professor of literature at the University of North Carolina. Bill made arrangements for his brother to meet with her in Chapel Hill and bring some other qualified parties to the meeting. He could give her some real good feedback on how her book was progressing.

She drove to Chapel Hill. After meeting with the literary group and leaving each of them a draft she decided to stop by Kitty Hawk and visit with her dear friends, Sylvia, Webb, Rosemary and Bill before going back to Carolina Beach. It was truly a tight group and they were always there for her. They had lived through many good and bad times together.

Sylvia usually saved some of the local papers for her so she could keep up with the Kitty Hawk news and this time was no different. She was thumbing through the papers and up popped a November 15, 1995 edition with a front page picture of a fishing vessel. It was a big local

Wanchese vessel named Mister Big that had been kicked out of Alaska. It grabbed her attention immediately and she thought it would make a good cover for her book. She enjoyed a few days with them and headed back to Carolina Beach with her stack of papers, keeping the picture of the Mister Big on top of the stack.

She knew the photographer so when she arrived back at Carolina Beach she called to ask him for a copy of the Mister Big picture that he took when the vessel passed under the Oregon Inland Bridge on its way back to Wanchese. He answered the phone. "Hey Shirley, where are you living now and what are you up to?" "Carolina Beach" He said, "What can I do for you?" He had given her pictures in the past of her Coast Guard Station so when she asked for the one with the Alaska vessel she didn't anticipate a problem. "What do you want with that?" "I'm writing a book about my missing son and it would make a good front cover. Do I have your permission to use it?" He proudly said yes, just to give his paper the credit. She assured him she would gladly do that.

All of a sudden, she knew she was on a speaker phone so she asked her photographer friend, "Who is listening to our conversation?" "My editor." The editor then broke in and said, "I'd like to interview you about your book." She didn't know the editor and told him she wasn't ready to be interviewed but she would let him know when. She was a little surprised at the response of the editor. It appeared weird and sneaky to her.

The photographer was going to send the picture right away but somehow that didn't happen. She called him again in a few weeks. "I put it right in my outgoing box that day Shirley. I sent it but I'll go right down to the camera shop and send you another one from there."

She found out later that the editor, whose office was in Nags Head was a friend of Tom White, their ex-Neimay attorney and the attorney for Nags Head. Her mother Fannie always told her, "Birds of a feather flock together." Possibly the editor knew something she didn't. She had to wonder why the editor may not want her to get that particular picture of Mister Big.

She received the second picture in record time. It had been sent from the camera shop. While she was looking at the 8X10 color pictures, something jumped out at her. "Wait a minute! That looks like Jeffrey on the deck!" She hurried for her magnifying glass while looking seriously at the deck of the Mister Big. "That is my son. I know his stance. What is he doing on that local fishing vessel from Wanchese that just got kicked out of Alaska?"

She was having some electrical work in her kitchen done by a young man who lived at Carolina Beach. He had helped her several times before. He was from Virginia and had told her that his mother had close friends at the Outer Banks. She took him there a lot to fish. He named many of her friends and Shirley knew most of them. "Quite a crowd" Shirley thought. Several were Kitty Hawk folks that had migrated there from Virginia Beach back in the mid seventies. One was Doug, the husband of the Sand Piper Quay association manager. It was getting to be a small world out there for her.

The day she received the photograph of the Mister Big was one of those electrical repair days. In her excitement of receiving the picture, she almost forgot about the young man in the kitchen. He walked over and took a look at the photograph. "Would you mind if I borrow that picture to show one of my friends? I'll bring it right back." Shirley agreed but only if he hurried back with it. Her mind went into high gear.

When the young electrician returned with the picture, she asked, "Who did you show that picture to?" He gave her his friend's name and she exclaimed, "He is one of my son's best friends. I never met him but he was a good friend of Jeffrey's at East Carolina University. He called many times during the search. Do you think he will talk to me?" "I'm sure he will." Jeffrey's friend was now a fisherman. He and his brother owned the largest fishing fleet at Carolina Beach. It was located right at Snow's Cut. Actually, it was directly west of her duplex so she could go up to her crow's nest and see the fishing vessels docked outside the Blackburn Fish Company.

She called the photographer back and asked if she could get the negative of the Mister Big. He sounded like an entirely different person. He said the editor had rules and he couldn't send it. He said many people like lawyers, law enforcement even Marine Fisheries folks come in asking for things like that. He didn't send it but Shirley thought he was trying to send her a big message. She got it.

She was trying to decide when would be the best time to approach Britt Blackburn. Her brother Ken was coming up from the Keys soon so she might wait for him to go with her. Ken arrived a couple of weeks later. Shirley filled him in and the car couldn't start fast enough for Ken. They drove the short distance down the beach road, around the large party boats, and into the Blackburn Fish House property. She introduced herself and asked for Britt Blackburn. By luck she was talking to him. "I'm Britt, Ms. Mays. How are you?" She told him why she was there and wondered if he could tell her anything about Jeffrey that might help her.

He was extremely polite. "I went to the Outer Banks to visit Jeffrey in October just before he was missing. He showed me his beach house that you and Mr. Mays gave him. He was real excited. He had just moved in. Jeff was very excited about the fish business that his Dad had bought for him." Britt said that he was married now and has a little boy. He could imagine how she felt. He appeared sincerely sorry for her and wanted to help her any way he could. But somehow Britt didn't seem sad like he probably would have if he thought his friend was dead.

A couple of days later, she and Ken went back because she remembered some questions she wanted to ask Britt. He was on the phone talking in one room so she peeped in the next room and saw his older brother, Joe. She introduced herself. "I'm Jeffrey's mother and I wanted to warn Britt that if he gets in touch with Jeffrey to be very careful because he may be in big trouble." The older brother sat behind his desk in a state of shock listening to her. He was so shocked all he could do was stutter.

Actually, she had done some investigating into this fish house after leaving Britt a couple of days earlier and found out that they mostly sell their fish to the Daniels family from Wanchese. That would be the same family who owned the Mister Big that got kicked out of Alaska for raping the natural resources. The Mister Big picture was the negative she was trying to get from the photographer. The Daniels family also owned the Margie, the boat that Kenny Williams said he was aboard that afternoon of November 13 when he last saw Jeffrey. She had wanted to meet Britt's older brother Joe and disarm him. Britt afforded her that opportunity by being on the phone when they arrived. Once again, she had accomplished her purpose. She felt confident that Joe might know more than his younger brother. Her message went out to somebody. She was confident of that.

She decided to make another visit to one of Jeffrey's East Carolina University friends who lived in Dunn, North Carolina. Jeffrey, Britt Blackburn and Don Wellons from Dunn who she was about to visit appeared to be tight buddies at East Carolina right before Jeffrey disappeared. Dunn was about two hours from Carolina Beach. She made this trip alone. Don Wellon's father had a very big real estate company and a property management company and a construction company and other businesses in Dunn. He appeared to be the biggest deal in town. She investigated him before going to Dunn and found out that he owned property all over the nation. He had many HUD affordable houses, like many of the assets from the S&Ls.

Don was out of town the day she arrived. She left him a long note telling him that she would like to meet with him. He had called their home many times during the search. She was told that he had his own airplane even when he was in college. She waited and waited. No word from him. She contacted his office again and left a message. No response. She never heard from Don Wellons. She couldn't understand it because he had seemed so concerned during the search. After the search, one of the rumors was that Jeffrey had a friend who picked them up in Collington, an area near the Wright Brothers Monument not far from Kitty Hawk.

This was very confusing and she wasn't sure where it would fit into the puzzle. It just seemed strange that Don Wellons didn't get back in touch with her.

She couldn't get the picture of Mister Big that had been kicked out of Alaska out of her mind and the fact that it was owned by the Daniels family of Wanchese.

She and Eric had been discussing Kenny Williams and Eric decided he would write a letter for Kenny to give to Jeffrey. What did they have to lose? Nothing! The decision to do that was made back in November, about the time of that article and the picture of the Mister Big that Shirley didn't get until January. Eric composed the letter with information from their past that only the two of them would understand. She gave it to Kenny with instructions to get it to Jeffrey by any means possible.

Ironically his letter was dated November 13, 1995. The picture of the Daniels vessel being kicked out of Alaska was in the paper dated November 15, 1995. She didn't even receive it until January of 1996.

Eric had received a call at his residence in Maryland from the Kitty Hawk police on November 16, 1995, informing him of a break-in at the Station. They said it had to be a friendly burglar because nothing was disturbed. Whoever broke in kicked the upstairs door right at the necessary spot then went in and turned on all of the lights, the water faucets, and did everything but leave a thank you note. The Station had been winterized so when Eric came down to open up in the spring, the place lit up like a Christmas tree and sounded like a waterfall.

The Mays Coast Guard Station break-in happened the day after the Mister Big went under the Oregon Inlet Bridge on its way to the Wanchese Fishing Company in Wanchese, North Carolina on November 15, 1995.

When Eric reported the break in to Shirley, he was told by her that Jeffrey had this same MO when he was at East Carolina. She would get so mad at him because sometimes he would go to the beach and forget his house key. He would just pop the upstairs door open at just the right spot. He would act just like the friendly burglar. He would sometimes take a shower and just leave. Sometimes the only clue she had that Jeffrey had been there was a used towel hanging in the clean bathroom. She had Billy Winslow as fulltime help so he would fix the door in a flash. Billy really liked Jeffrey so he always tried to make an excuse for him.

She had long ago discounted coincidences so when Eric told her about this break-in, she chalked it up to one more piece of the puzzle. One thing she knew for sure was that the timing of events was not hers. She had absolutely no control over it. But the timing of the Lord is perfect and when he wanted her to know where Jeffrey was or what happened to him he would give her an address and a city. She believed that with all of her heart.

She moved into her Carolina Beach condo on her birthday, March 18, 1995. Now it was her birthday again, March 18 in 1996. It had been a very fast year and she was mad again.

This time she decided to investigate the RTC people themselves, whoever they were, and their minority contractor Graimark Realty Advisors, the asset manager who breached her contracts. She called the FDIC and inquired about their public records. She was told to call their Freedom of Information (FOIA) contact. She did and made a friendship that lasted for years.

She told her FOIA contact she was certified to work with the FDIC and/or the RTC and that she was working with Graimark Realty Advisors, a minority firm. She informed him that she too was a minority contractor. She gave him her corporate name and the name of the asset managers who breached her contracts. He faxed her a document that set her on fire. He did a "Detail by Contractor" report and found five checks in the official FDIC/RTC real estate database which were made out to her. One was the $1,800 that she forced from Gemini Asset Managers for the Duck, North Carolina Phase I environmental contract and the other four she had not received. The other four checks amounted to almost $60,000.

She had never received any money from those exclusive contracts because they had been breached before she could get the properties closed. She thought, "Good gosh, if I didn't get four out of five checks, how many other thousands of those checks are not correct?" She knew she had a big situation on her hands and all of those people who had bad mouthed that RTC group must be right. What in the world was she going to do with this knowledge?

She researched whistleblowing and came up with The Taxpayers Against Fraud webpage. She then scheduled a trip to Washington, DC and met with the Director of Taxpayers Against Fraud which was the False Claims Act Legal Center. The Director had worked with the Senate in getting the False Claim Act updated in 1986. It was the first amendment since the Civil War and this young lady who was the Director had worked with Senator Grassley to get it passed. If anyone knew what whistleblowing was all about it should be Senator Charles Grassley (R-IA) and this young lady. She was very knowledgeable. She advised Shirley of the statutes. She gave her some cases to study and told her to stay in touch if she needed help. She was told that the first thing required was to take the discovery to someone in the government before filing.

She returned to Wilmington knowing that she needed more research before making that first serious move to file the claim. She was fulltime investigating and receiving paperwork from her new contact at FOIA, when one day she received a big package. She had requested information about the horse farm in north Durham. She was trying to learn who received it after her contract was breached and also trying to find out what happened to that $200,000 loan from the Great Atlantic Savings Bank in Manteo involving that Duck property. To her knowledge, the loan had never been satisfied.

She will never forget that night. She was usual early to bed but that particular night she was busy studying her new discovery and at exactly the hour of midnight her phone rang. She had a young tenant and her baby downstairs in her Carolina Beach duplex. The young mother sounded frantic. "Shirley, look out the window. I just called the police."

She had been studying the documents all day and she had just that moment, at the stroke of midnight, discovered that her horse farm in Durham had been put into a $7.2 billion dollar securitized mortgage backed pool. She had it sold for $189,000. She could have sold it for at least $250,000 but the RTC wouldn't let her go beyond their appraisal of $189,000. She was looking at an official FDIC document that showed the farm sold for $4,769.78 with closing costs of $1,885.62 on September 27, 1995. It showed that it was sold for 1.53% of the asset. She was already in shock with the discovery when the phone rang. "What now dear Lord?'

What she saw was so unreal that she thought she was back at Sand Piper Quay. She saw two cars, with six black men in each one, put on their emergency lights, get out and just kept marching around their cars. "What in the heck were they doing and why were they here?" She was having a hard time focusing on anything when she reached for the phone and dialed 911. The operator answered and said, "Are they still there?" "They are driving off right now." "Did they hurt anything or anyone?" "Not yet." "We'll look into it." She isn't sure they ever did. The police never came by to check it out. Her new "safe house feeling" was already beginning to fade. She was very concerned that the Carolina Beach local police might have the same attitude as those in Elizabeth City and not really caring about what was going on around her

She worked on her discovery night and day. It was beginning to take on a huge picture. She wasn't sure anyone was going to believe her. If anyone, it would be her Congressman Walter B. Jones. His father, Congressman Walter B. Jones, Sr. had been the Congressman before him and was very much like a member of the Seymour family. He had been supportive of the Coast Guard search for Jeffrey from beginning to end.

Before Shirley could call and make an appointment with Congressman Walter B. Jones she received a phone call. She couldn't believe this call.

A man who identified himself as being from Alabama, working for a man in Tennessee, said to her, "Ms. Mays, my employer in Tennessee bought a securitized pool of properties from an auction in Kansas City and it contained an unpaid note for $200,000 from the defunct Great Atlantic Savings Bank in Manteo, North Carolina. He has just been forwarded your broker opinion report on a property in Duck, North Carolina and he wonders if you could help us identify the property."

"This is too much," thought Shirley. She had been trying to find out something about this $200,000 note since she was run out of Kitty Hawk while trying to make a left, a left and a left. It was the loan collateralized by the Duck property that she and Robb had a contact on.

She composed herself. "You bet I will help you. Tell your employer that he is backed up with a multi-million dollar shopping center on the property. Tell him not to worry about it being a junk loan." He said, "We are thinking about taking it to Federal Court. We might call a lawyer in that area." "Please don't call one at random. Most of the lawyers are involved." She then gave him the name of an attorney he could trust.

The Alabama man called the lawyer she recommended. She immediately received a call from him. "Shirley, I doubt if these people will want to pay what this research will cost." He was very familiar with the S&L scandals and knew it was a can of worms. "Don't worry. I will send you all the court documents you will need." She pulled her original Duck property title search out of her research and sent it overnight to him. He took the case for the buyer of that securitized pool and she was later told the issue had been settled out of court. I doubt that her lawyer friend even had to go to the courthouse. The case never ever reached the judge. She was pretty sure it wouldn't when she recommended the him.

Of course it was settled out of federal court because it was a stick of dynamite. It was one of those S&L properties, among hundreds of thousands that the FDIC and/or the RTC had guaranteed to be prudent and proper. She was discovering that most of them were not. If discovered by the purchaser of these pools that they were not prudent and proper, the taxpayers would have to buy all of them back.

Congress failed the people on the S&L disaster by not doing something about the problems. Where was Congress now? She fully intended to ask her Congressman as soon as she met with him.

She was getting smarter about this whole FDIC/RTC government mess. Somebody needed to know this besides her Congressman. All of the taxpayers in the country needed to know it. They were losing badly not once but twice in the example of this $200,000 loan from the Great Atlantic Savings Bank. The loan had been included in a securitized pool at auction even though Gemini Asset Managers should have known that it was never paid off. How big could this mess be? It was impossible to put a final figure on the damages for the taxpayers.

Shirley called the Congressman at his Greenville, North Carolina office and made an appointment. This was her first legal requirement before filing her qui tam case and she wanted to follow the statutes step by step.

The Congressman asked of the Seymour family and how they were doing. Then he wanted to talk about Jeffrey. He knew all about the search because his Dad had been the biggest support system of all for the Mays family. His Dad had been Chairman of the Committee that oversaw the Coast Guard and he was a powerful political force in the House of Representatives. When she was doing community work, whether it involved her hometown or the state, Walter, Sr. was always there for her. They believed in each other. He always told people,

"Shirley Mays is like an old dog with a bone. She doesn't put it down until she is finished." They respected each other because they were both "can do" people. You can be sure she wasn't finished with this bone involving her son.

After they caught up on family, the Congressman asked, "How can I help you Shirley?" She said, "I'm going to file a qui tam case but the statute says I must take it to the government first. I came to you because I don't trust much about the government but I trust you." Then she started discussing her FDIC/RTC discovery. The Congressman said to her, "I don't understand anything you said Shirley, but let's just say I believe what you said and what you are going to say, what can I do?"

She didn't know what to suggest. "I need to send you to see my Chief of Staff in DC. I have to have someone put it together for us and he is my top man." He also suggested the FBI but she said absolutely not.

She trusted the Congressman but she had doubts about his Chief of Staff. Everyone with any political knowledge at all knows the chiefs of staff try to run the government and she knew they were doing a lousy job of it. The Congressman was a dedicated servant, like his father before him, so he stayed in the field as much as possible. He had to trust someone and he had chosen this young man.

The meeting did not go well for her in DC. She felt strongly that she was betrayed by the Congressman's Chief of Staff. She thought she knew him from somewhere. In the meeting, she thought he had mentioned working for the North Carolina Republican Governor at one time. She had worked very closely with that Republican Governor who had changed his administrative law to help her secure her one of a kind CAMA permit in Elizabeth City. He was one of the few Republican Governors in North Carolina. He was an educator, not a politician, so he naively kept some Democrat staff workers when he took office.

She remembered telling the Governor one time after a visit to Elizabeth City, that his staff was undermining him. He was very upset with her for saying anything like that. Two weeks after her warning, he went public with his disgust of an investigation being put on him by the present Attorney General, a prominent Democrat, who was running against him in the next election. The big political players in North Carolina have their own set of hardball rules and the Republican Governor had learned that the hard way.

Shirley thinks her reputation preceded her once again and the Congressman's Chief of Staff knew all about her. When she left the meeting, his eyes were glazed over and she was not happy. She was later told by the Congressman that his Chief of Staff had done RTC research for Ken Starr when they were trying to impeach President Clinton over the Arkansas Whitewater deal. She knew more than Glenn Downs, his Chief of Staff about the RTC even at that early stage and that is more than likely why his eyes glazed over. She believes that any significant RTC research would implicate the Republicans as well as President Clinton so maybe that is why Ken Starr switched to Monica Lewinski and her blue dress instead of pursuing the Whitewater scandal.

She had created her first in-house problem by meeting with the Chief of Staff but she knew, beyond the shadow of a doubt that the Congressman would not do anything to hurt her on purpose. She would stake her life on that.

She immediately reported to the Congressman that she was disappointed in the meeting with his Chief of Staff. He then personally scheduled a meeting with the general counsel of the Chairman of the Banking Commission. The Congressman was on the Banking Committee. Her discovery was all about banking and that is as high as he could get her in the House of Representatives. Shirley knew this would be an important meeting so she called in some of her team. They were always suited up and ready for action when she called. She called Ann in Florida and Robb Porter in Charlotte and said "I need y'all." She picked Ann up at the Norfolk airport to drive with her to DC. Robb, of course, was planning to fly. He didn't drive anywhere even if he was only going fifteen miles in any direction. They arrived in

DC first and got a motel right at the airport so they could meet Robb when he arrived.

That night, Robb and Ann helped Shirley with her presentation. She valued their opinions and always wanted their feedback. The next day, all three of them caught the Metro right down to the Cannon Building. They felt like country come to town on the Metro because it was confusing and fast and they were not sure which way they were going. She was concerned that they might be a little late for the meeting. It wasn't her style to ever be late for a meeting especially one as important as this and even the thought of it upset her. When they got off the Metro, they looked up at the highest escalator she had ever seen. The problem was that it wasn't working. That meant they would have to climb the stairs. Shirley was positive that Ann would never make it as slow as she was so she and Robb started running taking the steps two at a time. She looked back at her dear friend Ann, who had come all the way from Florida, to be with her and she said, "I hope you don't get lost Ann but we can't wait for you."

She and Robb ran several blocks, found the building just in time and stopped to take a breath. They looked behind them and Ann was standing there. To this day, Shirley doesn't know how she did it. Somehow, Ann never ceased to amaze her.

She was glad they made it on time because the Congressman had taken some of his precious time to be there with her. He wanted to be sure she had a comfort level. He stayed for about half an hour and then excused himself to go back to his building for an urgent meeting. Wynn Yerby was the general counsel for Spencer Bachus who headed the Banking Committee at that time. He asked a lot of good questions which made her hopeful that he might be able to help. "Can you prove that the fraud is systemic?" Shirley had no clue was he was talking about. She had about a month's discovery and that was voluminous. She was mostly concerned about the checks totaled over $60,000 that the FDIC said she got and she didn't. She left the meeting feeling confidant that they would do what they could for the Congressman, if not for her.

Walter is a well respected Congressman who doesn't mind claiming to be a Christian. He is as honest as they come and everyone in DC knows it. He was doing his best for her. She is honest also and felt she had to inform this young general counsel that she was going to file a whistle blower's qui tam case against the FDIC/RTC Asset Managers. Wynn Yerby said he would be in touch.

On the drive home, Shirley and Ann were trying to tie things together. They were both real estate brokers, in different states, but aware of the rules and regulations of appraisals, surveys, closing, etc. She was driving her car about 75 mph on the freeway, trying hard to keep up with the DC traffic during rush-hour, when Ann said, "Pull over, I'm sick."

She almost wrecked several cars while trying to reach the shoulder of the road. She was in the far left lane when Ann very quietly told her about her trauma. She made it safely to the far right side without pulling any other cars with her. Poor Ann threw up, without getting a drop on her. "I'm sorry Shirley. I've developed a migraine headache." "Why not Ann? We have earned one." She was sure hoping her soul mate, flying overhead, didn't have a migraine while heading home. Where would he pull over? Chances are Robb Porter would find a place.

When they reached Norfolk, Ann wanted to go to the airport to rent a car. She planned to stay in the area for a couple more weeks and it was more convenient to get one at the Norfolk airport than Elizabeth City. Elizabeth City didn't have the conveniences of a big city like Norfolk. They were both going to Elizabeth City so they left the airport following one another. There were two different routes to get there and somehow, in the dark of the night, they turned on different ones. It was getting late, about 11:00 p.m. They had really wanted to stay together for safety. They both checked behind them and no one was there. They figured they had split the routes.

Shirley was driving a 450 SEL Mercedes with the doors locked. She always felt like she was safely in an armored tank when she drove the car that she had driven for the last eighteen years. All of a sudden, the car stopped dead in its tracks. It was 11:30 at night. She had no power at all so the most she could do was steer hard into the nearest driveway. She was alone on deserted country roads and there were not many houses. She walked up the long driveway and knocked on the door. The lights came on and a man said, "Yes?" She told him what had happened, where she lived, and that she needed to get her car towed. She told him her name and that her mother was a Seymour from Camden. He was a farmer, just like two of her uncles, and knew both of them well. He was delighted to help her. He looked under the hood and found the alternator belt was gone. "That will stop you in a hurry." She was difficult to stop but he was right; that alternator belt did it in a hurry.

He took her straight to her cousin David's house and made sure the wrecker took her car to the nearby Shell Station. David had planned dinner for her and had it ready since 8:00 p.m. He always planned a celebration after her big meetings. She had called and said she would be there much earlier but then all those things started happening.

After checking with Ann to be sure she arrived safely at her destination, she and David sat down with a welcomed glass of her favorite red wine and ate a three course meal which ended at midnight. It paid to have a well known family that night and it paid to have a cousin who was a fabulous chef. It had been a very long day but a most interesting one from beginning to end.

Shirley headed back to Wilmington the next day. This was in April of 1996.

Her brother Ken came from the Keys to visit her at Carolina Beach for the 4th of July week-end. She had been thinking about the guys that pulled up in two cars at midnight a few months earlier and it concerned her not only for her safety but that of her discovery. Knowing that her brother was coming, she thought maybe this would be the time to move her office out of her house into a secure building somewhere else. She found a wonderful spot downtown Wilmington in the Cotton Exchange at the Executive Office Center. The building had security at both doors. She felt sure her case was going to get bigger and she needed to have her discovery in a secure spot. When Ken arrived, they moved her paperwork first and still had time to celebrate the 4th of July.

She wrote her own qui tam case with the help of the Director of TAF and the sample cases she had been given by her. The Director did suggest that it might help if she got a local North Carolina attorney to help her file it in U. S. District Court. The next step she had to take, according to the statutes, was to file a complaint at the location of the properties and back it up with as much supporting evidence as possible. She was told to file the complaint in Raleigh but duplicate everything in Washington, DC. A qui tam case is filed by a plaintiff who is referred to as *THE RELATOR* and the United States of America on behalf of the taxpayers against the defendants. In this case, Shirley was suing 65 corporations who were FDIC/RTC Asset Managers and holding companies of big banks and over a dozen FDIC officials. This was overwhelming for her but she felt strongly that she had the discovery to prove her case.

The North Carolina attorney she chose to help her file was in the Wilmington area where she lived. It was the same SOB attorney she had recommended to Carol when they had problems with the Snow's Cut property. He won for Carol in court. Shirley had gone to court that day and had been very impressed with his dancing ability in front of the judge. Gary Shipman was a class action attorney who had won most of his cases. She arranged a preliminary meeting with him to question whether he had any qui tam experience. He said he tried once, for a farmer, but after four months, it didn't go anywhere. This was not what she wanted to hear so she decided not to let go of her case. She wanted her name on the case as The Relator and not his. He did a very good job of helping her fine tune the case and then gave her the instructions how to file it. She insisted on walking it through the process in Raleigh.

She had dealt with many attorneys, accountants and bankers. Most of those she knew dealt behind the scenes with each other. No one knew when they made mistakes because they usually covered for each other. There might be some good lawyers, accountants and bankers but the bad ones almost break their arms scratching each other's backs. This case was too important to her. She was going to walk it through the process herself. She took the instructions Gary Shipman gave her, put them in her notebook and headed for the Federal Courthouse in Raleigh, North Carolina, the state's capital.

The Federal Building was very intimidating. The first people she met didn't smile or act friendly when she went through the security checkpoint. If you weren't wearing a badge, you feel like a criminal just being there. You felt like you might be invading their sacred ground. Maybe it was different when attorneys pass through but Shirley didn't feel comfortable that July day when she was on such an important mission. She asked directions to the Clerk of Court's office where complaints are filed. After taking the elevator to the proper floor, she stopped in the ladies room to gather her composure. On the way out, she looked in the mirror and said, "You can do it. You are a taxpayer and they work for you."

A lady named Ann Caviness, who identified herself as an Assistant Clerk of Court, was very friendly and helpful. She had the only smiling face in the entire building. She told Shirley this was the first qui tam case that she knew of being filed in North Carolina. She sent her to the US Attorney's office because they are under the jurisdiction of the Department of Justice and she felt sure that was her first step. Rudy Renfer, the Civil Chief in the North Carolina US Attorney's office was not friendly and definitely not smiling. He not only was not friendly but he gave her wrong information. He said he would need a summons. It appeared to her that Rudy Renfer didn't know the difference between a plaintiff and a defendant in a qui tam case and he was the Civil Chief?

"Why did he want a summons? Summons are for defendants." She went back to the Assistant Clerk who called in her boss, the Clerk of Court, who was a lawyer. She told him about the Civil Chief's refusal to accept her information. The Clerk was very stiff and said for her to check with her attorney. She had a strong feeling that the Clerk returned to his office and made a phone call to Rudy Renfer right down the hall. It was obvious to both of them that the DOJ didn't need a summons. She wasn't suing the Department of Justice; she was asking them to join her in this qui tam case.

It appeared blatantly clear to her that day that neither her attorney, Gary Shipman in Wilmington nor Civil Chief Rudy Renfer of the North Carolina US Attorneys knew exactly what a qui tam case was or what to do about it. The only helpful person she met that day was the Assistant Clerk of Court Ann Caviness.

She returned to Wilmington and reported to her attorney that his instructions didn't work. He encouraged her to do a summons in lieu of. She knew that would not be correct and it would give Civil Chief Rudy Renfer a way out. That's the way those lawyers work. "No, that isn't correct and it will give them an additional 60 days to answer the complaint." By that time, she was concerned that unfortunately she might know a lot more about qui tam cases than her Wilmington attorney. After that encounter, her Wilmington attorney made himself scarce in her case and she then worked only with Patty Jensen, his paralegal. That was good for her because Patty was a very smart young lady. Together they figured out what to do. She signed her case formally on July 18th Jeffrey's birthday and got her case filed on July 24 right downtown in the federal courthouse in Wilmington.

She needed a break badly after finally getting the case filed so she went to Seattle, Washington to visit her youngest daughter. While there, she received a phone call from Wynn Yerby's office. It was the young legal assistant who had been in the meeting with them in DC. "Ms Mays, we got in touch with the FDIC about your information and I need to ask you some questions if you don't mind." She said, "I don't mind at all but first I must tell you I just filed my case and I sued a dozen FDIC people. I'd be glad to answer your questions if you still wish." He said he would fax them to her.

She never heard from him again. Her case was filed under seal and that probably legally stopped him from working with her.

Unfortunately, her qui tam case would be running parallel to a big Conoco environmental case that was headlines at the time in North Carolina. Even more unfortunate, her case was assigned to W. Earl Britt, the same Senior U. S. District Judge who was handling the infamous case for Conoco. He was covering up for a big oil spill. The spill was in a suburb of Wilmington. If he would do that for the big oil companies, what in the world would he do for the big banks right in his back yard at Charlotte, North Carolina? It is a good thing that she wasn't aware of all of this at the time it was happening. She might have given up and not filed her qui tam case.

The Morning Star, the local Wilmington paper owned by The New York Times was following the Conoco case very closely. There were many outstanding Conoco cases all over the nation and they were afraid that this Wilmington one might set a precedent. One potential case was a billion dollar one in California. This was the first trial in the nation to explore the dangers of an octane enhancer called MTBE, methyl tertiary-butyl ether. The spill affected many people living in a trailer park, on the outskirts of Wilmington, near the Conoco refinery. After the court decision, the trailer park residents were all driving around in Cadillacs but they were dying! They were not allowed to talk about how they got their Cadillacs because District Judge W. Earl Britt ordered that their case stay "In Camera and Under Seal" in order to protect Conoco.

A local Morning Star reporter and the Raleigh bureau chief had gone to the Federal Courthouse, the one where Shirley had just had such a bad experience, and asked to see the Conoco file even though it was In Camera and Under Seal. Ann Caviness was helping the reporters that day. She gave them the file they were allowed to see. All of the important In Camera paperwork was taken out first. It appeared some of the papers were loose, by mistake, so they wrote a story on what they had read.

They wrote that 178 Wrightsboro trailer park residents had received a $36 million settlement from the Conoco oil company. This fine outstanding judge who now had Shirley's future in his hands was furious and he decided to fine the Raleigh bureau chief of the Morning Star more than $600,000 to be paid to the Conoco oil company because they published an article that was supposed to be Under Seal.

Secrecy, when enforced by a Federal Court, can be an expensive proposition and Judge W. Earl Britt intended to teach that paper, owned by the New York Times a lesson.

Did Judge Britt really intend to take on The New York Times and their big barrel of ink? Of course the New York Times Co. appealed because the judge's decision was dangerous, unprecedented and probably unconstitutional. He had demonstrated contempt for a free press and for an open judicial system. Two press freedom groups and nine media outlets including The Associated Press, the News & Observer, The Charlotte Observer, Dow Jones & Company, Inc. and the Washington Post joined the Morning Star's defense.

In July of the year 2000, the Morning Star wrote that the newspaper and the two reporters won a legal victory in the 4th U. S. Circuit Court of Appeals when judges threw out civil and criminal contempt convictions for coverage of a lawsuit over groundwater contamination by Conoco Inc. at Wrightsboro, a suburb of Wilmington, North Carolina. Ann Caviness, the very nice Assistant Clerk of Court, who was personally responsible for the oversight of her case and the Conoco case and who had been so helpful to her got canned. She was less than a year from retirement. After thirty years of loyalty to the courts, Judge W. Earl Britt fired her for allowing the paperwork to be loose in the folder. The judge needed a scapegoat and Ann Caviness was it.

Shirley had discovery in her qui tam case that documented the closings of over 400,000 properties throughout the United States. She could prove that many of the assets from the defunct S&Ls were targeted to have environmental problems just like the Conoco property outside of Wilmington, North Carolina.

There was a disgraceful environmental scandal in Destin, Florida involving The Nature Conservancy. She had been able to beat lottery odds by receiving REOMS, the FDIC/RTC real estate database. There were twenty Nature Conservancy assets that needed to be investigated.

She wondered exactly how Judge W. Earl Britt was going to handle her bank fraud case that was said to be the first qui tam case filed in the state of North Carolina.

She decided to go to St. Petersburg to visit Dr. Morgenroth. She could relax in his condo on the Tampa Bay, with water views on both sides of the building, and bring him up to date on her case at the same time. He was planning a trip to Norway with his companion but was glad to see her and get brought up to date on her case before leaving.

Dr. Morgenroth had quite a background. She always felt safe taking his advice. He had a PhD in Management. He was a graduate of the Universities of Michigan, Northwestern, Pittsburgh and Colorado in management, accounting, mathematics, languages, economics and sociology.

His government involvement included being a Federal Agent in San Francisco, working with the U. S. State Department and CIA in Burma, being involved in U. S. Naval Intelligence in Europe, the Middle East and Asia, being an intelligence trainer to the military in Korea and Viet Nam, and being a Naval Intelligence trainer, discipline trainer to Naval midshipmen and had served on submarines and destroyer escorts during World War II.

His teaching involved management courses at Ohio State, California, Kentucky, Colorado and South Carolina Universities. He had been a management consultant to over 40 businesses.

She wasn't very comfortable around Dr. Morgenroth when she first met him many years ago. A dear friend bought him to her Coast Guard Station and to her waterfront home in Elizabeth City. She was intimidated by his intelligence. She didn't realize at that time that he couldn't help it. He became a mentor to her and helped her put her qui tam case together.

While she was in St. Pete with Dr. Morgenroth on September 16, Fran, a major hurricane hit the East Coast. The eye of the storm zeroed in right where she lived at Carolina Beach. She was shocked because the eye of Hurricane Bertha had just hit them about two weeks earlier before she left for Florida. She had stored a lot of the discovery in her shed house directly back of her duplex so she was extremely appreciative that her brother Ken had helped her move her documentation to her new Cotton Exchange office on the Wilmington waterfront July 4th. After Bertha, she bought a new shed house and had it anchored deeply before leaving for St. Pete.

This time, Hurricane Fran destroyed her house and her new shed house. Everyone had been evacuated from Carolina Beach. The son of a neighbor elected to stay and ride the storm out so at least she could get him by phone for awhile so he could give her a visual report of the damages. Very few phones were working at that time and fortunately his was one of them.

She left St. Pete immediately and hurried back to survey her damages. The island was closed down and nobody including the homeowners were allowed to enter. National Guardsmen had been called in from several states to prevent vandalism. They set up a roadblock to stop everyone, including the homeowners. She camped out with friends for a couple of weeks before residents were allowed back on the island. The officials felt sorry for the victims of the storm during those two weeks so they arranged for a bus to take them on a tour to see their damages.

Carolina Beach was a small area so it didn't take long. The sight was devastating. The residents were allowed to get off the bus for a short while to check their belongings or what was left of them.

Shirley was devastated. The waterline in her downstairs apartment was 4 ½ feet up from the floor. She had lost everything downstairs. She sat down and cried when she realized that all of her Coast Guard Station pictures of her children growing up were in that downstairs closet. They were gone forever. The pictures of Jeffrey and her two daughters when they were young were her biggest loss.

She went upstairs where some of her other treasured pictures had survived. She was in deep thought when the phone rang. She thought she had been shot. She couldn't believe she had phone service because they had condemned her house and a big yellow ribbon was tied all around it. She answered the phone while sitting on the sofa and looking directly at the sky. The man on the other end said, "Ms. Mays, I have been trying to reach you for a couple of weeks. I am from the Department of Justice in Washington, DC. I have been assigned to your qui tam case. I would like to make arrangements to meet with you as soon as possible." She thought surely she was in the twilight zone and this was just another dream.

While she was collecting her thoughts she mistakenly said to him, "Well, I have an attorney in Wilmington." Before she could finish her sentence, he said "Please give me his number and I will make arrangements for the meeting."

She had made a major mistake but couldn't correct it right then. "Would October 25th be OK with you?" She knew that she could be ready by then so she agreed. All she had to do was find temporary housing, file with FEMA, deal with the SBA because she had continued to keep part of her office in the duplex, put together a presentation by herself and try to reconcile with the Wilmington attorney long enough to have a meeting at his office. She convinced herself that she had been put through bigger storms than this one. The date of that first DOJ contact was September 23, 1996.

The DOJ was working on a deadline and she knew it. They only had 60 days to meet with her after receiving the complaint by certified mail. If the Civil Chief had been successful in forcing her into a "summons in lieu of," they would have doubled their time before answering her complaint. She had offended her Wilmington attorney by not following his suggestions so this was going to be a tricky meeting. She would need to make it appear as if she and her attorney were on the same team.

She received a phone call about that same time from a young woman who had worked with her on the waterfront in Elizabeth City. They were good friends and stayed in close touch with one another. She had married and moved away from Elizabeth City to another small North Carolina coastal town and had become an industrial developer. She was working closely with Congressman Jones and she had been with him that day. She wanted her to know that the Congressman had said to her, "The Banking Committee's general counsel told him that his group thought Shirley had enough discovery for public hearings during the 105th Congress, with or without Justice – after the seal had been lifted." That sounded good to her. She was encouraged that the Banking Committee was concerned with her discovery. That was October 2, 1996.

She found some temporary housing with people she knew on the island. They owned a big butler building. It was one of those steel ones that look like they are never finished. They had a few apartments that they rented out to construction workers. They didn't have one available at the time so she talked them into letting her move into an old office that they were not using. The smoke smell was terrible. She didn't smoke but knew this deserted office was temporary and she wouldn't be there long. At least she would feel safe with all of those burly construction workers around her. She made friends easily and she intended to bring them on board immediately.

She got in touch with Gary Shipman who couldn't believe that the DOJ was coming to town and would be in his conference room. This would put a crown on his head. He couldn't wait to tell the army of attorneys he was working with on an asbestos class action case. That case was getting a lot of press nationwide but nothing like having Main Justice come to Wilmington, North Carolina to meet in his office. Momentarily, he forgot how upset he was with her and suggested a meeting with her before they came. She agreed to the meeting. When she arrived at his office she knew something had happened between the time of her phone call with him and now. He appeared very uncomfortable.

While they were in the conference room discussing their strategy his secretary walked in. "Mr. Shipman, you have a phone call. Would you like to take it in your office?" A very few minutes later, he returned to the conference room. "Shirley, the DOJ trial lawyer assigned to your case is on the phone and he would like to postpone the meeting. Would you agree?" She threw her paperwork down on the table. "NO, absolutely not." "Well, you know they can do it if they want to." That really teed her off and she shouted, "You tell them if they cancel this meeting to forget about me. I will be out of the country and never available to them again."

Gary transferred the call into the conference room at that time He appeared to be more afraid of Shirley than he was of the DOJ. They heard her in the background. "Well, can we put it off for just until November 1?" She reluctantly agreed. She was not very happy when she left Gary that day. She knew she had a coward on her hands and she wasn't really sure whose side he was on. She knew, without a doubt, that he was intimidated by the DOJ. She also thought that perhaps Rudy Renfer from Raleigh and Justin Castillo from Main Justice, DC might not be on the same train that Gary and Rudy were riding.

Her cell phone rang before she got back to her temporary housing in the smoking office. Gary said the DOJ just couldn't make it. She gave him instructions that unless they decided to come as scheduled don't ever bother her again. She was the most frustrated she had ever been, except during Jeffrey's search.

She called Robb, who hated the government as much as she did and said, "Gas up Porter. I'm on my way to your house. We're going to Washington, DC and meet with the press." She then called the Congressman to inform him of her actions. He was a Republican and wanted her to talk to Major Garrett with the Washington Times. She remembered one time that her FDIC FOIA friend had told her about Susan Schmidt of the Washington Post. His wife had worked on The Hill and knew Susan and thought she was an outstanding investigative journalist. She had been the one who was assigned to the S&L mess covering the Whitewater case involving the Clintons. She should be more familiar with her S&L discovery.

While she was driving to Robb's house, she was debating between the two papers. She didn't want to upset the Congressman who had been so good to her but she wanted her discovery to go to someone who understood it.

She arrived at Robb's house late that night. The plane was gassed and ready to go in case she wanted to go out with the cover of darkness. Porter would have liked that. They were planning their strategy. The next morning he was sure someone had tampered with her car. He said the hood had been opened. That would normally have upset Shirley but she knew Porter was paranoid and besides she had bigger fish to fry in DC. She needed to stay focused. He filed a flight plan and they were just before taking off when she decided to check her answering service in her smoky temporary butler building housing. Sure enough, there was the coward attorney saying, "The DOJ called back and they will be here as you wish for the meeting."

"They damn well better be or I'm telling my story to the press." Porter didn't agree with them aborting this trip but she wanted to work within the system if for no one else but the Congressman. He was not someone to rock a boat and she had chosen him for her Captain. She was going to try to stay loyal to him.

She didn't feel safe going back to the Wilmington area to prepare for this very important meeting with the government. She had all the info she needed in the back of her car. She carried it wherever she went. Once again she called Florida. "Ann, I need a safe house. Can you go to your cottage and hide out with me while I prepare for this big DOJ meeting?" Ann immediately agreed. "I have decided to sell my house so I need to go anyway. I will ask Irene if she will put a For Sale by Owner sign in the yard as soon as she gets there and prepare some spec sheets. Maybe she can set up appointments if there are any interested parties."

Shirley called Irene and asked her if she could paint the garage windows before she arrived so she could come at night and drive straight in without being seen. That might appear to be paranoid on her part but they remembered Kenny Williams appearing out of nowhere in front of Ann's house on the very day of her big closing in Elizabeth City; no one questioned her instincts anymore!

Before she arrived on the Outer Banks she called Irene to give her an update on her location. She asked her to open the garage door. She drove into the garage and the door was put down in seconds by Irene who almost got hit by the car. Shirley apologized for the near accident. "Nobody could have seen me in that short time. Thank you very much Irene for doing all of that on such short notice." They went upstairs confidant that they had accomplished their mission.

She knew that Ann was going to be several more days before she could get there. She was concerned as to how she could get her work done without offending Irene. There was no time to chat at this point and her discovery was too complicated to try to explain it. By nature, Irene was very inquisitive. She was born that way. She wanted so badly to help that Shirley explained a little to her and gave her some ledger sheets. She allowed Irene to copy some information that she needed transferred to another ledger sheet. Little did she realize that she would grasp it so quickly. Irene was shocked at the fraud. Shirley prayed that the DOJ would be as intelligent as Irene at the November 1 meeting.

She never moved her car and never left the house. Soon after her arrival, they looked out and saw a man coming up to the house. Shirley ran to the bedroom and hid. Irene opened the door. "I was wondering about the house and how much it is selling for?" She said, "I don't have much information yet. I can't even show you the house. If you will leave your number the owner will be her soon and I'll have her call you." The man didn't leave a name or number but said he would check back later. Shirley was in shock.

She thought she recognized the man when they first peeped out the window and saw him walking up but now she was sure. It was someone she knew. He was a very prominent developer from Elizabeth City. She had heard that he was involved with the Kitty Hawk Woods scandal involving assets from the Great Atlantic Savings Bank. A few of the people involved with that scandal had been indicted and sent to prison including the President of the Great Atlantic. The man who came to the door had not been indicted. His nephew, a local attorney had been involved in some unscrupulous closings for the Manteo S&L. She had a sick feeling that the developer had been looking for her. He looked real sad. She had always liked him so she thought maybe he was going to try to talk her out of meeting with the DOJ.

A very short time after he left another man came. He was not sad and she didn't recognize him. Again she hid and Irene answered the door. She gave the same story this time but before she could finish he asked,"How old is the owner?" Shirley thought, "What does it matter?" but Irene maintained her composure and said, "About my age."

He left a name but no phone number. She recognized his name from her Great Atlantic Savings Bank discovery. He was from Greenville, North Carolina and had also been involved with the Kitty Hawk Woods scandal.

There were many people still running scared from the FBI investigations of the local Great Atlantic scandals and two of them had just been up on Ann's Kill Devil Hills porch. Shirley knew they would make a major effort to keep her from attending the DOJ meeting in Wilmington in a few short days. She had much work to do. The stress was overwhelming just thinking about the preparation required for the meeting. It wasn't going to be an easy day for her.

Ann had hardly arrived from Florida when Shirley's gut was saying to her "Get out of here fast." She didn't know how to explain that to her as she had just had a long drive and Ann didn't move fast anyway. She wasn't sure she could keep up this time but she remembered the escalator in DC and never underestimated her after that.

She had driven her white pickup truck with the enclosed camper so she could bring a new mattress. Shirley didn't even try to figure out why she would do that with her selling the house and all. Ann didn't follow a logical pattern all the time; in fact most of the time. She had her own way of doing things and they usually turned out OK. I think she wanted to be sure Shirley was sleeping comfortable. Little did Ann realize that Shirley's head would never touch that mattress.

She decided that she and Ann both needed some rest so she wouldn't bring up her fearful thoughts until the next morning. That night, things were as normal as they could be with these three gals. The next morning, bright and early, before anyone could fix coffee, Shirley said, "We have to go to Wilmington, now!" Ann, in her slow and casual manner said, "We can't. I have to call someone to help me get the mattress out of the truck and I need to do a few things first." She insisted on the urgency so Ann called a local real estate guy she knew who said he would send someone right over. Two men came and while they were unpacking, Shirley was frantically packing her boxes of discovery. Before the men left the house, she called them into her bedroom. "Would you guys please put these boxes into that truck where you just got the mattress?"

Ann had backed in the night before. If anyone was watching they will be totally confused by now as to what was going on. She then informed Ann that she was leaving in two minutes and taking her truck. If she wanted to go with her, be ready.

There was no way possible that Ann could meet this demanding deadline. It usually took her at least one maybe two hours to get ready in the morning and that was on a fast day. She told Irene, "I'm taking Ann's truck and turning left. If she isn't with me, you take your car and turn right and I'll meet y'all at K-Mart's parking lot. If you aren't there in half an hour, I'm gone. I'll call y'all from Wilmington."

The meeting was the next day and she needed to get to her temporary quarters. Her butler building landlord had called on her answering service and informed her that he had an apartment open up but she would have to move immediately because he had a list of storm victims waiting for it. This was going to be tricky. Her DOJ meeting was at 3:30 pm the next day and she hadn't even left the Outer Banks yet. She needed to move into the new temporary quarters before the meeting. She was tired of the smoke in the abandoned office.

Shirley decided to bring in a heavy hitter for the move and the meeting so once again she called in Robb Porter. He had been concerned about not hearing from her since she left on the run from his house. He told her he was about to report her missing when she called. She brought him up to date. "Porter, I need you to help me move and then attend a meeting with me." Robb and Ann both had attended the meeting in DC with the general counsel of the Banking Committee so they didn't underestimate Shirley or any of her discovery. "I'll be there when you say. Can you pick me up at the private airport in Wilmington?" She knew the timing was going to be tight the day of the meeting. She just didn't know how tight.

Shirley got in Ann's truck, looked both ways and sped out of the drive taking a left, a left and a left down to the K-Mart parking area. Bob Eck would be proud of her because damned if it didn't work this time! She backed in, out near the road so she could see who was coming and if necessary get out of there fast and sure enough there he came. A druggie appeared while speeding and looking both ways. He had lost her. He flew out the back of the K-Mart parking lot desperately searching for her. She knew he was a druggie because she could now spot them a mile away.

Irene and Ann jumped into Irene's big black Oldsmobile with Ann in her pajamas, her picnic basket full of clothes and carrying that tote bag of a pocketbook that was her trademark. They took as hard a right as Irene was capable of even though the spotter was gone. They came driving into the K-Mart lot looking like they were on a Sunday afternoon drive, right behind the druggie. They had no idea where anyone was. It was a sight to be seen and even with all the stress, she doubled up on the seat laughing. They looked like little old ladies with big, no, huge straw hats, big gas guzzling car in downtown Miami going to a parade. Shirley thought to herself, "I'll take them to war anytime. Nobody will ever figure out their moves."

They parked in blind faith and had no idea what to do next. She looked around and didn't see the druggie right then so she drove quickly up to Irene's car. She said, "Get in Ann, fast. We're out of here." Once again, Ann had arrived on time in an impossible situation. Shirley would never figure that one out either. They were almost to Wilmington when she decided that they would be much safer in a motel and definitely healthier without the smoke in her temporary home.

They arrived at the Wilmington airport just as Robb was landing. She never worried about Robb's timing. He was always Johnny on the spot and she had no doubt that the duffle bag he was carried was fully loaded with whatever automatic weapons he thought he might need. He never went anywhere unarmed especially when traveling with her.

Ann dressed in Shirley's musty quarters while she and Robb started moving her few things around the corner of the building to a larger temporary spot. Ann was trying to dress and put little sticky tags on everything at the same time because she desperately wanted to help engineer the move. She was moving at a snail's pace and nothing seemed to faze her. Time became an issue. "I've got to go or I'll be late. Y'all stay and finish and then come sit outside the door of the conference room but don't say a word. I want them to wonder who you are." She gave them the address of the law office on 5th Street in downtown Wilmington. It was about a fifteen minutes drive from Carolina Beach. She prayed that they would find it.

The Department of Justice Meeting 11-1-96

She arrived at the attorney's office and Gary was no where to be found. His secretary told her to have a seat in the conference room and he would be right there. She would be winging this meeting because the preparation meeting they were going to have was abruptly aborted when the call came from the DOJ in DC to cancel the meeting. She had not seen Gary Shipman since that day and had no idea what to expect. All she knew was that it was going to be an interesting day and she was ready for this forced meeting.

All of the employees seemed to be hiding in their offices that day. She looked in the conference room and they had enough cokes, coffee, cups and glasses to choke a horse. Gary's wife had been kind enough to prepare the room but it looked like it was for a social event. Shirley had no idea who or how many were coming because she had not checked with Gary. She had been too busy the last few days preparing for the meeting. One thing was certain. This was no social meeting for her and she intended to let all of them know it.

A black woman walked into the deserted hallway next to the conference room. "Are you here for the DOJ meeting?" She was very pretty and extremely friendly. Shirley approached her and again asked," Are you here for the DOJ meeting?" "Yes." "Where are you from?" Shirley meant Raleigh or DC. She introduced herself as Fenita Morris. "I'm from Elizabeth City."

Shirley looked shocked. "So am I. Are you familiar with Elizabeth City State University?" She said, "I graduated from there." Shirley was very excited and said, "I was Vice-Chairman of the Board of Trustees for over five years. I was a Governor's appointee." She didn't tell her that the Governor was a Republican or that she was headlines in Elizabeth City when she resigned over the corruption between the town and the university. There were some things better left unsaid. She knew that she had been a very popular trustee with the Chancellor and his administration. She told Fenita to feel free to call them for a personal reference on her.

Fenita informed her that she had replaced Rudy Renfer who had been assigned to this case and she would be the contact from the Raleigh US Attorney's office. This was the best news she had received lately. She had complained to the Congressman about being undermined by Rudy Renfer so evidently somebody had arranged to have him taken off the case. She didn't care who was responsible for the action as long as

Rudy Renfer was gone. They had a few minutes to chat before anyone else showed up.

Gary was waiting for the trial attorney from DC before making a grand entrance. She had a strange feeling at the time that Gary had been working behind the scenes with Rudy Renfer to kill any DOJ meeting. Also that DC didn't know what Raleigh was doing so Justin Castillo, the trial attorney from DC might not be in on the undermining.

While they were alone in the conference room, Fenita confessed to her that she didn't understand the case at all. Shirley thanked her for being honest and said, "Don't worry. I will give you all the time you want and will meet with you anytime you wish. The case is very complicated." They had established a good repoire by the time Justin Castillo arrived. He was an exact opposite of Fenita. He was just what Gary wished for, an attorney who looked capable of trying to intimidate everyone. He introduced himself as Justin Castillo the trial attorney with the DOJ in DC who had been assigned to the case. He was stiff, not friendly, and wasn't about to be honest enough to admit he didn't understand the case. It was obvious throughout the meeting that he didn't. Justin Castillo was a perfect example of why you shouldn't judge a book by its cover.

Shirley began her presentation. All three parties were listening intensely. Her attorney had not discussed the presentation with her ahead of time and knew next to nothing about the case so he was listening most of all. He had been too busy with his class action suit and had turned her over to his paralegal for more than one reason. Fenita asked all the right questions which pleased Shirley. She really respected her for trying to understand. Justin Castillo had no clue what was being said and was certainly not going to attempt a question. He was very tall even while sitting down in his chair. One time he heaved his body up as high as possible over her head to ask Gary a question. She raised up in her chair as high as she could and thought, "If you think that intimidated me you missed your mark." Besides, Gary didn't have any answers. He was hearing most of this for the first time.

After about two hours, they took a ten minute break. When they opened the door, Robb and Ann were sitting upright in their hall chairs just as they were instructed. Ann looked like a Philadelphia lawyer and Robb like a bodyguard. Shirley introduced them to everyone but did not say why they were there. Everybody was playing their part that day. If she were the critic, right at that point, she would declare Ann and Robb the Oscar winners for best actress and actor. She was also grateful that no one was taking their heartbeats.

The big DOJ meeting lasted for over four hours. No one had a glass of water, a coke or coffee so the elaborate preparations by the attorney's wife had been for nothing. That was OK with Shirley. She didn't care what version of the story they told after leaving the meeting. The lawyers said, "We'll get back with you." All she knew was that she had forced a meeting with the DOJ. It was documented in a legal environment. She had her own witnesses and she was ready to get out of there. Everyone was.

She and Ann were totally exhausted. They took Robb to the airport and then drove half way back to the Outer Banks and stopped for the night. She called and asked Irene to please pack her car in the garage with the rest of her belongings because she was going to drive in and out within minutes. She didn't feel safe on the Outer Banks anymore. She wanted to get back to her new temporary quarters in Carolina Beach surrounded by her construction neighbors as soon as possible.

They checked again with Irene while driving to the Outer Banks the next morning. She told them some disturbing news. She had not told them sooner because she didn't want to upset the meeting. She said the evening of their departure, when she had decided to retire early and read in bed, she went into the kitchen to turn off the lights. She noticed a rather tall, slim man standing at the corner of the cut through street from the By-Pass road to the Beach Road. There was one house between Ann's house and the place where he was standing. He was just standing there smoking a cigarette, clearly visible under the street light. There was no doubt from the position he was standing that he was watching Ann's house. She said she felt unnerved and had a sense of unease. She went around the house checking that all doors and windows which would allow easy access were locked. She went about the usual preparations not showing any panic and after all the lights except the ones in her bedroom were turned off, she watched from a darkened room until he was no longer there. She did not actually see him walk away or leave in a vehicle. He just suddenly was not there anymore.

After starting the coffee the next morning on the day of the big DOJ meeting, she just walked down the stairs to the road to get the Virginian Pilot from the box at the end of the driveway and coming back, looked behind her car and saw *"THE MESSAGE."* On the concrete driveway directly behind her car was a circle, perhaps 6" in diameter composed of various sizes, shapes and colors of rocks. Inside the circle were three cigarette butts! Irene thought it was a message someone was sending saying they knew the three of them were there and knew that they were a circle of friends. Irene asked Shirley and Ann if they thought the three butts represented them.

That was too deep a thought for Shirley immediately after the high powered meeting with the DOJ. All she needed was to get to Ann's house, get her car and head back to Wilmington. She hadn't believed in coincidences for a long while but she was going to have to give a little more thought to Irene's story.

Shirley knew that she was going to have to deal with FEMA and the Small Business Administration after Hurricane Fran took her home and belongings. She dreaded what was facing her because, so far, her experiences with the government had not been pleasant. She had read that both of the agencies had set up headquarters at the local private airport where Robb lands. The storm victims were directed to go there to start the insurance process. Her thoughts were confusing and almost out of control when the same recurring thought came up again, "How in the world did I get to where I am?"

She was now recognized by the DOJ as being a full fledged whistleblower and she was learning fast that no one really likes a whistleblower, especially the government, because basically they don't want to hear the truth, don't want the public to hear it and sure as heck don't want to have to deal with it. They would then have to address the problems associated with the charges so it easier for them to *kill the messenger.* Besides, if the FDIC has such a huge fraud problem, as evident in her discovery, why didn't someone in government catch it?

The complaint is called a qui tam action, pronounced several different ways. It is known as the False Claims Act. Fact is few people are familiar with the terminology. Shirley had never heard of it before approaching the Taxpayers Against Fraud in DC. What she was now realizing a little too late was that a qui tam case was just a federal trap.

Anyone with knowledge of fraud against the taxpayers is encouraged to come forward and Congress will support you if you are the original source. Original source means an individual who has direct and independent knowledge of the information on which the allegations are based and has voluntarily provided the information to the government before filing an action. She was the original source and she had gone directly to her Congressman before filing her case. So far, she was right on target with the statutes.

The False Claims Act encourage a Relator, which is what you are called when you are the plaintiff, to move forward with their discovery even after filing the complaint. The information given to her by the TAF Director said, "The 1986 amendments to the False Claim Act (FCA) were designed as a whole to increase the participation of the relator in the investigation and resultant litigation. The legislative history suggests that the relator should not only be kept abreast of the government's efforts, but should also take an active role in deterring the government from neglecting evidence, causing undue delay, or dismissing a suit without legitimate reasons. In particular, Congress recognized the importance of increasing the relator's involvement as a way of providing sufficient incentives for the relator to come forward."

The False Claims Act also states that an extension is granted only "for good cause shown." Shirley was well aware that statute applied to both her as the relator and the DOJ while they were deciding whether to join her case or not. She knew that Rudy Renfer who had been taken off her case because of her complaints was scrambling to kill her case. She even suspected that Rudy had brought Gary Shipman on board in that effort. Gary was ignoring her after she insisted on putting her name and not his on her case. Attorneys like to deal with attorneys and there probably aren't any exceptions to that rule.

It would be imperative for the DOJ to have "good cause shown" before asking for another extension. She documented the meeting by writing Gary. The letter was dated November 8. She requested a follow up meeting with him and said, "I again would like to point out that I had absolutely no say so in the extension request after they canceled their first meeting. They have given me no "good cause shown" or any other legal reason except that the material is too sensitive for the relator to see. Rudy Renfer did not date his extension request and the judge's order was dated a month ahead of time. I realize that everyone thinks these issues are just "petty mistakes" but I must repeat for you and the DOJ, I have sued sixty-five people who are multi millionaires at the expense of the American taxpayers and a dozen FDIC people. I did not know and was not informed that Amresco, Inc., one my defendants, was a Nations Banks subsidiary until Fenita mentioned that she worked for them right before coming to the NC US Attorney's office. Would that not create a conflict of interest for her?"

Shirley then closed her letter by saying, "I am concerned for my personal safety and that of my family. I hope the two people from the DOJ with whom we met on November 1 in your Wilmington office do not take that lightly." She never received a phone call or response to that follow up letter of November 8 to Gary Shipman.

She fully intended to continue her investigation as soon as she could get FEMA insurance filed and get back into some decent housing. Her fraud discovery appeared to be growing by leaps and bounds. She couldn't decide where she would relocate. Unfortunately that was a decision she could not make until her FEMA claim was settled.

She arrived back at Carolina Beach and went into her new temporary apartment. Actually, it was pretty nice. It was clean, smoke free and located at the back of the butler building in a safer location. She felt she could more easily identify vehicles that might be a problem for her because of less traffic in the back.

She immediately checked her answering service and had a message from Dr. Morgenroth. She returned his call. Bill was just back from his Norway trip. "Shirley, Laura and I met the nicest chap and his wife before boarding our cruise ship and spent almost the entire two weeks with them. He said he was with the FBI, worked for Janet Reno and if he could ever be of help to me, just call." "What was his name?" "I don't know. I have misplaced the information but he was a very nice chap."

That was not a surprise to her because Dr. Morgenroth is a typical professor who is so brilliant that he always forgets little things like names of people and where he parks his car. She brought him up to date and said she would be down soon to visit.

She started her FEMA and SBA claims and couldn't believe the cumbersome paperwork. Both groups looked like trains out of control. She had to fill out the same paperwork over and over. They had several different appraisers on her property from as far away as Texas and Louisiana They were all contradicting each other. One group didn't know what the other group was doing, not unlike the DOJ. She applied for a small business loan to help her get through the process but it was so complicated that she quickly sent the $5000 advance back to them. She didn't have time for problems with the SBA. Finally, she was told that both the state and federal insurance checks were ready to be mailed. She received the federal check but not the one from her North Carolina insurance company. She was hoping to get out of her temporary housing. She finally got so disgusted that she marched into the main appraiser's office and demanded to see her folder.

Everything had disappeared.

They had nothing in her folder. She found out that FEMA had intercepted her state check and put it in their federal discretionary account. It was a tricky move on their part because the check required two signatures, hers and that of the bank that held her mortgage. Shirley called the North Carolina Insurance Commissioner and requested that they look into the matter. They did a wonderful job of doing an investigation and retrieving a copy of the check showing only one signature. Sadly, they couldn't do anymore because it was a federal matter. They informed her that she would have to go to federal court to get her state insurance money. The feds appeared to be surrounding her from all sides and it wasn't anywhere near a fair fight. The timing of the FEMA actions was too obvious not to be associated with her whistleblowing case.

She received a call from the Raleigh News & Observer, one of the most prestigious papers in the State. "Ms. Mays, we are doing an investigation on FEMA, the flood insurance people, and your name has been given to us. We are trying to get your records from FOIA at FEMA and they won't release them."

She said, "I don't care if you get my records, everything. What can I do to help?" They asked, "Would you sign a release for them?" "Absolutely. It would be my pleasure."

She then got a call from an attorney at FEMA who said, "Ms Mays, I'm sure you don't want us to release your private file information, do you?" "Absolutely, I have nothing to hide!" A few days after that, she received the file from FEMA, plus their internal memos. They refused to send it to the press. The internal memos said that the SBA Inspector General's office had requested a copy of her file. The internal memo said, "What should we do?" The answer was, "Send it but fully document what was sent." They sent all of this to her instead of the newspaper. She sent it directly to the newspaper. The young reporter who wrote the three page story on FEMA wrote her a personal note thanking her and saying if he could ever help her, just let him know.

She had a strange feeling that she had been targeted by FEMA and the SBA because she dared to blow the whistle on the FDIC. They knew she couldn't afford to take them to federal court. She was already in federal court with her whistle blowing case. She was living in temporary quarters and didn't even have a home. It's amazing what the government will do if they are trying to stop you from blowing the whistle on something that will reflect poorly on them. In this case, they kept her homeless.

She made a big decision that day. She decided to move from her temporary housing because she couldn't afford to buy a home without her insurance check. She rented an apartment downtown Wilmington directly across from her Cotton Exchange office and promised herself that she would work night and day to expose the S&L mess which was quickly becoming known as the biggest financial bailout the country had ever seen.

"The wheels of justice grind slowly but they do grind." She was counting on that and was going to dig in for a long fight, if necessary. Besides she knew what she was doing all the time while all the attorneys she was dealing with had no clue what the other one was doing. That proved to be prophetic.

Chapter Twenty

The Year 1997

Fenita Morris of the US Attorney's office in Raleigh asked for an extension at the same time Justin Castillo, the trial attorney from Main Justice asked for a second meeting. Once again "good cause" for the extension request was not given. The same notation was on the bottom of the motion stating that it was too sensitive for the relator to see.

Shirley released Gary Shipman for conflict of interest and wrote a certified letter and told Justin Castillo, the trial attorney assigned to her case that she was looking forward to the second meeting.

Gary Shipman wrote her a letter immediately after being released. "I regret that you chose to relieve us of further responsibility in this matter as I believe that we had been able to create a good working relationship with the trial attorney sent from the DOJ in DC. The assistance of the DOJ is going to be key. However, I had also been able to obtain commitments from the firms that I am working with in the stucco class action to assist in your case, so that, either way, we were prepared to move forward."

Gary had breached the court ordered "In Camera and Under Seal" statute by talking to the other attorneys and he had put it in writing to her.

She then received a Federal Express letter from Justin Castillo. "At this point, it does not appear that a meeting will be necessary, but I will be in contact with you soon regarding the United States' decision in this case." That was February 28, 1997

Lawyers' loyalty to each other prevailed even though Shirley was being undermined in a federal whistleblowing case. Evidently Gary Shipman's conflict of interest didn't matter to the DOJ. The lawyers were showing her who the bosses were. "Sounds like showdown time coming from the DOJ."

She could just see all of those attorneys in Raleigh and DC racing to their computers to be first to type the sandbag motion.

On March 10, 1997 Fenita Morris filed an Application For Extension Of Time For The United States To Determine Whether To Intervene In This Matter. It was stated in the application, "The United States seeks this extension because the *Federal Deposit Insurance Corporation* requires additional time in which to make its recommendation regarding intervention."

On March 17 Rudy Renfer who had been taken off the case, according to Fenita Morris, filed the United States' Notice of Election To Decline Intervention. It certainly appeared at that time to her that the DOJ, who had the jurisdiction over her case, relied on the FDIC where she had a dozen defendants, to make the recommendation whether to join her very important <u>qui</u> <u>tam</u> case.

"Never underestimate the power of the government, especially the Department of Justice when they want to kill the messenger."

She wrote a letter on April 21 to W. Earl Britt, the judge assigned to her case and hand carried it to the Federal Court in Raleigh to have it filed. Since it wasn't a proper motion Ann Caviness didn't know what to do with it. Shirley requested, "Just stamp file on it." She figured that should be legal enough to get it put into her "In Camera and Under Seal" file.

The filed letter documented all the statutes that had not been followed by the DOJ and Rudy Renfer and asked for a formal investigation into the actions of the DOJ and reminded the judge that the complaint was brought in good faith on behalf of the United States of America. She told the judge about Gary Shipman violating the "In Camera and Under Seal" restriction that had been officially put on her case, by talking to all of the other asbestos class action attorneys. This is the same judge who had covered up a big environmental oil spill for Conoco by keeping it "In Camera and Under Seal" and sued the New York Times $600,000 for finding out about it.

Her whistleblowing case was all about bank fraud. It appeared to her that Judge Britt might be out to protect the big banks just as he had tried to protect Conoco, the big oil company. She wanted to cover her judicial bases by writing him that letter. She wondered, "Where is the oversight for judges?"

Shirley was working night and day on her discovery because she was determined not to give up. She wanted an investigation into the obstruction of justice involving her case. Her little apartment directly across the street from her office was very convenient. There was good security at the front and back of both her apartment and her office. She felt safe working all hours of the day and night.

The woman who had an office next to her at the Cotton Exchange did a lot of volunteer work at the University of North Carolina at Wilmington. They became very friendly. They often took coffee breaks together and discussed their families. When she found about Shirley's son being missing, she said, "I have this wonderful friend who volunteers at the University and you should meet him. He is a forensic expert." She was immediately interested because she often wondered what Jeffrey might look like after being gone seventeen years. Her friend arranged a meeting for them. She and the forensic expert connected immediately. His name was Barry.

She soon realized that Barry's real job was subcontracting with the FBI and other intelligence agencies. She visited his house, saw his awards, his paintings and some of his forensic work. She was totally in awe of his talents. He confided in her that he had been in South American on a contract and was almost killed. His partner was assassinated. Barry had developed cancer from some chemical warfare that he had been exposed to at that time. He was seeing the best doctors in the country who were trying experimental medicine but he was very chalky looking at the time she met him.

It appeared to her that he was very ill because his skin was jaundiced. He said he would really like to help her find her son. It would be one of the most rewarding things he could do in life. He was surrounded by mercenaries and she couldn't figure out why but somehow she felt like she was bringing another team member on board. One thing was for sure. Even though he was a big mystery to her, she felt totally safe in his presence.

Shirley told Barry about her qui tam case and her efforts to get her discovery exposed. He said he could help her with her son but that her discovery was out of his arena. He suggested that a new FBI special agent had just been assigned to Wilmington. He said the FBI agent was a white-collar crime expert from Boston. He offered to introduce her to him. When she had visited her Congressman in April of 1996 before filing her case, he suggested that they bring in the FBI. She would not agree with the Congressman then because she didn't trust the FBI.

She didn't trust many people and rightfully so. She had been to the FBI before about the out of control drugs in Elizabeth City; she never heard back from them and saw no results from the FBI. She trusted Barry already after the first meeting with him so she thought maybe this was the right time to try once more to work with the FBI.

She told Barry that she never made a serious move involving this case without the Congressman's approval because they were both trying to work within the system. She asked him if he would call the Congressman and arrange the meeting.

She had to make another trip to St. Petersburg. Barry got in touch with her Congressman while she was in Florida with Dr. Morgenroth. The Congressman came to Wilmington and met with him and FBI Special Agent Paul Cox. The Congressman requested that Paul Cox meet with Shirley. The FBI meeting was formally and properly arranged this time by a member of Congress.

First meeting with FBI in Wilmington on 4-30-97.

When she returned from St. Pete, she had her first meeting with Special Agent Paul Cox. Barry was kind enough to come to her conference room and personally introduce them. He made sure Shirley was comfortable and then he left. The meeting lasted 3 ½ hours in which time she hardly touched the surface of her discovery. She gave Paul Cox a large 3" notebook involving the Nature Conservancy scandals on the Outer Banks involving the Nags Heads Woods and the Kitty Hawk Woods. They had both been FDIC/RTC properties from the Great Atlantic Savings Bank in Manteo, North Carolina. She figured this would give the FBI an example of the magnitude of her fraud. She had sued William C. Thomas, Director of the RTC in Atlanta, Georgia who had signed the quitclaim deed for the Nags Head Woods. He was in charge of several East Coast states. The 3" book she gave Paul Cox covered the court records from beginning to end as to how the asset was handled. She had taken on a biggie when she sued William C. Thomas and she didn't want the FBI to take it lightly. It certainly looked like bank fraud to her.

Wilmington's Morning Star reported at the time that the S&L bailout was enriching lawyers. They quoted the House Banking Committee Chairman as saying, "We seem to have a legal factory and it is not clear to me that there is as great legal oversight as maybe there could be." They named the 10 largest legal contractors who had already shared $218 million in legal fees and expense reimbursements from the RTC. The House Banking Committee held hearings without much cooperation from the FDIC, RTC or the Treasury Department. It also appeared that too many people in Congress may have been compromised. To investigate much further would really open a can of worms.

Shirley knew the House Banking Committee had not even touched the surface in exposing this huge financial bank crime. She was willing to meet with them again and explain her discovery, especially involving the Nature Conservancy scandals, but she was never asked. She had twenty Nature Conservancy purchases that should be investigated. The FBI meeting on April 30, 1997 was the first of many very important meetings for her.

As she looks back on her many meetings, she knows without a doubt that the inefficiencies of the government agencies were unforgiveable. It appears all of them tried to create chaos instead of trying to work with her to get to the bottom of her discovery. All of her meetings were held at the request of her Congressman.

Her team was outstanding and stood by her side for many years. Shirley didn't give the FBI much slack time after the April 30 meeting because she was concerned about some of the things happening to her in Wilmington. Computer Sciences Corporation, the government contractor who held the FEMA contract was one of her targets in her RTC discovery. She heard that one of them was in town asking about her. She then received a letter at her office from a funeral home in New Orleans that said, "The Mays family should have planned their funeral long ago." She wondered how they got Bud's full name connected with her Cotton Exchange office address. She and Bud had been divorced over ten years. He had absolutely no connection with her office in Wilmington. It could not have come from a mailing list.

With these events in mind and no feedback from the FBI about their meeting and the concern for her safety, she made the decision to go public. She called her friend Ann in Florida. "Come on up. We're going back to DC."

Shirley had chosen Susan Schmidt, a well known investigative journalist with the Washington Post because of the recommendation of her FDIC friend whose wife had worked with her. She also knew that Susan Schmidt probably had the best background knowledge of the RTC fiasco of anyone she could pick. She called her and the appointment was made for July 21, 1997.

During their meeting, Susan gave Shirley an article that she had written. She pulled it directly from her folder. The text started out saying, "The federal government is turning increasingly to Wall Street to unload the enormous loan portfolio it has inherited from the fallen savings and loans, a strategy that some experts say looks good now but could cost taxpayers billions of dollars over the next few years if it backfires."

That was exactly what she came to tell her. They were saying the same thing but Susan was way ahead of her with her knowledge. Shirley didn't have a story yet. They met for a couple of hours and Susan had to run because of a deadline.

The Washington Post headquarters in DC had tight security. When she and Ann arrived at the security desk, they were thoroughly identified, given a badge and told to wait for the party who was expecting them. They were not allowed out of that room. Susan had to come downstairs for them when they arrived. While escorting them back down after the meeting, Susan said to her, "I have never recommended an attorney before but you need to get in touch with these attorneys in Denver." "Thanks but no thanks Susan. I'm finished with attorneys of any kind. I just wanted to try to expose my discovery with you."

She had written their names and phone numbers down. The two of them were ex RTC professional liability attorneys. They became whistleblowers themselves and testified in front of Congress with other RTC whistleblowers. They quit the government, moved back to Denver and started a firm that did nothing but represent whistleblowers. "Thanks anyway and thanks for the meeting." Shirley wanted to be polite because she was grateful for the time Susan had given her. She took the note and left. She had no intentions of every calling the Denver attorneys.

She had to hurry back to Wilmington because her oldest daughter had called her and asked if she could go to their Florida home for a couple of months while she and her husband were on the West Coast. She had no idea what her mother was doing and her mother wasn't about to tell her. She was back in Wilmington just long enough to pack for her trip to Florida. Without being able to stop herself, she reached for the phone and called Denver. She identified herself as a whistleblower and told the attorney that his name was given to her by Susan Schmidt of the Washington Post. She informed him she was heading for Florida the next morning and would be gone a couple of months. He asked her to send him some info. She did and then left on schedule the next morning making only one stop at FedEx to send him the requested information.

Shirley crossed the downtown bridge at Wilmington, headed her car for Route 17 South and wondered once again, "How in the world did I get to where I am?"

When she arrived in Florida, no one was at her daughter's home with the exception of Isabelle, their most efficient housekeeper. Isabelle told Shirley that her bed was ready, groceries had been bought, and everything was in order for her. She informed her that she already had a fax. She quickly checked the fax before getting settled and saw that it was from the attorneys in Denver. The fax read, "Attached is a letter containing some questions for discussion. I will call you later this afternoon to arrange for a time when Jackie and I can both speak with you. We do not charge for this initial consultation. We are both under the gun this week but it is important to keep pushing forward in light of your August 14, 1997 deadline."

Shirley had forgotten about her August 14 deadline. It was the farthest thing from her mind. She had been saved by the Denver whistleblowing attorneys just in time.

Bruce Pederson, Jackie Taylor and Shirley Mays had their first conference call on August 5. They discussed all of the questions that they had faxed her earlier. They told her what they would need and suggested that she request it from her FDIC contact. She told them she would think about it. She really had not decided what she was going to do yet.

The next day, she wrote Bruce and Jackie a letter thanking them for the conference call. She told them she had slept on it and decided to definitely move forward with them and their suggestions. Shirley always made quick decisions when her gut said it was right. She called the DOJ in both Raleigh and DC, as they had suggested, told them she had new attorneys coming on board and got their permission for an extension. She then called DC, talked to her FDIC contact, and requested the information that Bruce had suggested she order. Her contact called back the day after she called and said a strange thing had happened. All of the printers for that specific information had shut down. They had sent for people to repair them.

(In her next meeting with the FBI in November, Shirley would find out that Paul Cox and the Congressman had been very busy writing the Chairman of the FDIC and others about her accusations. She wouldn't find this out until her friend Barry forced Special Agent Paul Cox back to her conference room. And she wouldn't find out everything they were doing, on her behalf, until the year 2000. Ricky Helfer, the Chairman of the FDIC resigned before she answered the Congressman's letter.)

It was not surprising that the FDIC computers all shut down with her hiring Bruce Pederson and Jackie Taylor and with the Congressman and the FBI sending them letters with direct questions about Shirley Mays' contracts at the same time.

Bruce and Jackie were ex-RTC senior attorneys in the Professional Liability Section of the RTC's Western Regional Office in Denver. They were in charge of closing all of the S&Ls west of Denver. They had testified before Congress on several occasions. They were well known whistleblowers.

Whoever might have been tampering with Shirley's orders at the FDIC had a lot of reason to be concerned.

She had only been at her daughter's house for a couple of weeks when she called from the West Coast and said, "Mom, we are doing a Nike commercial and the company needs some articles from our house. Is it alright with you if they send an agent from Miami to make a selection?" Of course it was OK.

At the time, Shirley was entertaining a childhood friend of hers from Elizabeth City who had lived in Miami for many years. Her friend Doris had driven up for a couple of days and they were having a ball catching up on the news of their crowd. The Nike agent's name was Nora. Shirley gave Nora some space while she and Doris sat on the huge U shaped porch drinking a nice glass of red wine. She wanted to entertain Doris in the manner in which they were accustomed. The two of them had spent many a summer day sitting on her big Coast Guard porch in Kitty Hawk looking out at the ocean while reminiscing about their childhood.

When Nora was finished, she thanked her for being so nice and allowing her to roam around with her cell in her hands, while she and the Nike agents in LA decided what articles to take and what not to touch because of the problem of not being able to replace them. She was going to fly the articles out personally to LA for the commercial and bring them back. Shirley invited her to sit with them and have a glass of wine before heading back to Miami. Nora agreed to just one.

While she was trying to figure out the connection between the two girls, Nora asked Doris, "Where do you live?" Doris said Miami. The agent said, "Where do you work?" She said, "I'm a chemistry teacher at a private school." When Doris mentioned the name of the school, Nora said, "Oh, my aunt has a farm next to that school." Doris was taken back a bit because she knew it was a peacock farm belonging to the present Attorney General Janet Reno. Doris asked her if Janet Reno was her aunt and Nora said yes.

Shirley was shocked but never mentioned anything about her <u>qui tam</u> case or that her Aunt Janie held her future in her hands. She and Doris had been talking about her whistleblowing case quite a bit that afternoon so both gals looked at each other in amazement. Nora said she and Aunt Janie spend a lot of time canoeing and had passed her daughter's house several times.

Nora left and called a few days later and said, "Shirley, I'm back from LA and can you believe Nike is going to pay me to bring the articles back? When will it be convenient for you?" She knew anytime would be convenient because she had made up her mind that she was going to tell Janet Reno's niece about her whistleblowing bank fraud case.

While they were talking on the day she returned the articles, Nora gave her some advice. She said, "Why don't you write my aunt a letter and just tell her, in your words, what your case is about. Be sure to outline your motives in the beginning because she gets a lot of mail and that is her first concern." She continued, "Don't mention meeting me. Just let her know your concerns." Nora then told her that her companion of many years went to DC with her aunt as her Chief of Staff.

Shirley did exactly as suggested by Nora. She never received a response from Nora's Aunt Janie but she did read a couple of months later where her Chief of Staff left government and went back to Miami. She never learned if Attorney General Janet Reno received her letter or not.

While she was still in Florida she had to request another extension from the DOJ. When she received the order from the United States Magistrate Judge in Raleigh who was someone new to her case, it stated, "With some reluctance, the court will allow this motion. The reluctance is generated by the fact that this action was filed more than a year ago and still has not been served on any defendant except the Attorney General."

Not only did Rudy Renfer not understand the difference between plaintiffs and defendants but neither did this US Magistrate Judge who reluctantly granted Shirley the extension. She wasn't suing Attorney General Janet Reno. She was asking the DOJ to join her case. She knew she was in real trouble because those government attorneys will never admit their ignorance. They will do anything to stop you. The order had given her until November 11, 1997 to add associate counsel and amend her pleadings. She was warned, however, by this order that the court may refuse any further requested extensions of time.

She checked again with the FDIC to see if the printer problem had been fixed. Her contact informed her that they had seven people there and they couldn't find the problem. She informed him emphatically, "If they don't get those damn printers fixed, I'm out of business."

She packed up and headed back to Wilmington on September 1, 1997. By October 22, she had signed an agreement and sent a retainer check to Denver. Shirley Mays was fighting mad.

When she arrived back in Wilmington, she went to see her forensic artist, to tell him how disappointed she was with Special Agent Paul Cox. She also called the Congressman's office and complained about the FDIC printers being down for over three weeks. Barry quickly scheduled a meeting for her with Paul Cox and the Congressman made a call to FDIC and immediately followed up with a letter to her telling her so. The printers were fixed in record time, magically, and the Congressman's Chief of Staff, who she didn't trust wrote her a note saying, "The FDIC called to say that they are sending the reports you requested by Fed Ex today. Because of the delay, they will be waiving the customary fee." She immediately replied to him that the quick decision they made was a very good move on their part. The fee waiver was secondary. It was disgraceful that it took a Congressional request to get public records.

Second FBI meeting on 11-3-97.

Shirley met with Paul Cox again on November 3, 1997. It was a forced meeting and very awkward. Barry sat in the corner watching while they sat at her 10 seat conference table, straight across from each other. "So what is happening?" Paul Cox pulled out a few letters and put them in front of her. "What are these?" Paul Cox said, "Didn't the Congressman send them to you?" "No, and he probably thought you did." Shirley just glimpsed at the paperwork and saw that the letters were from the Congressman to the FDIC. They talked a short time longer while she let him know just how disappointed she had been with the apparent lack of action on the part of the FBI. She stood up and thanked him for attending the meeting. As far as she was concerned, the meeting was over.

She sat at the conference table studying what Paul Cox had given her and it took her about a New York minute to figure it out. There was a lot of missing information in what he handed her. Did he really think she wouldn't immediately figure that out? It was the holes she was interesting in, not the letters she was given. What was the FBI up to and to whom was this nice young agent reporting? She had many questions after that meeting.

This was November of 1997 and it wasn't until February of 2000 that she was able to acquire the FBI letter holes. One day, while talking to the Congressman's office in DC, while his Chief of Staff was out, Shirley asked an employee whom she trusted to please check her folder. They started comparing notes and every time the person would hit an FBI hole that she was looking for, she said, "I need that one and that one and that one."

The letters were immediately sent to her and she sat down with her new information. It appeared the FBI had drafted the letters for the Congressman so he could send them under his letterhead. The Congressman was very prompt about helping her and he had no reason not to trust the FBI.

One of those holes that put everything in perspective for her was a personal memo from Special Agent Paul Cox to the Congressman. She doubted that FBI Special Agents usually put their names on memos but in this case Paul Cox did. She was sure of one thing. He never thought she would see the memo. At the conclusion of the memo, it read, "Based on the FDIC review, the minority contractor did not actually cut those checks to Ms. Mays and therefore no false reporting was made to the government." Paul Cox further stated to the Congressman in the same memo, "I think we have to remember those assets are coming from failed financial institutions and if the bank could have foreclosed on the property and sold for a high percentage of book value they would have."

It appeared that Special Agent Paul Cox believed someone in the FDIC enough to make serious remarks to the Congressman without even getting an opinion from her. Her case was all about the mishandling of the assets and falsified records. The memo sounded as if Paul Cox had made his decision without any more input from her.

He didn't sound like the same person who had drafted those intelligent letters. Shirley did not think that Paul Cox was making his own decisions. He couldn't be that naive and be called a white collar crime expert. Her FDIC defendants had once again trumped her and it appeared somebody higher up in the FBI helped them out.

A normal Congressman might have given up at this point but not Walter B. Jones. He knew Shirley Mays and the Seymour family well and was aware of her many accomplishments for the State and her community. He knew that she never started anything she didn't finish. His father had always believed in her and he would too.

- On *July 8, 1997* in spite of the memo advice from Paul Cox, the Congressman forged ahead with a letter to another party in the Office of Legislative Affairs that asked four dynamite questions. The questions had been presented in Paul Cox's memo, before his closing remarks supporting the FDIC. The questions were excellent. There is a very good chance that Paul Cox never saw the Congressman's letter to the Office of Legislative Affairs following up on those questions.

- On *August 4, 1997*, there was an answer to the July 8 letter. It was again from the Director of the Office of Legislative Affairs, not the person to whom the Congressman had addressed the letter. It stated, "The Division of Resolutions and Receivership of the FDIC has prepared the enclosed responses to the specific questions posed in your letter of July 8." Once again, Shirley's defendants had disrupted the request of the Congressman by telling lies. Susan Schmidt was dead right in her reporting of what happened with these assets but she was facing a formable FDIC army and so was Shirley Mays.

- The last document Paul Cox gave her that second meeting in November was a recorded deed from the Durham Courthouse. It showed her that he had made a trip and an effort to find the Durham horse farm property but just wasn't able accomplish his mission. He did find anther property with the same buyer who got the Durham horse farm. At least Paul had tried. He just didn't have the information that she had in searching those troubled RTC properties. He was just like that other lawyer in the Durham Courthouse who had said to her the day she was there, "If you are looking for an RTC property, forget it. You won't find it."

She was well aware after studying all of the letters sent to her from the Congressman's DC office that she was more knowledgeable than most when addressing the wrongdoing of the RTC. The FBI just didn't understand the magnitude of her discovery. There were over 400,000 properties and if necessary, she could find the court records on every single one. They couldn't find them because of the way they were indexed.

She received a letter from her Denver attorneys that said, "Greeting Shirley. Enclosed is a copy of the Motion we will file on Wednesday with the federal judge assigned to your case. It enters our appearance as your attorneys and request an extension of time in which to review and amend your pending complaint. We asked for an extension of 120 days, figuring that even half of that amount will be most useful. I expect that our newly retained local counsel will keep us posted".

The Denver attorneys had to engage a North Carolina counsel to file their motions. The Congressman had recommended a firm in Greensboro for her before she hired them so Shirley suggested that they call them for a recommendation. The counsel they recommended had clerked for Judge W. Earl Britt. He had clerked for the judge right out of law school. His name was Tom Manning and he appeared to be the judge's golden boy. When Tom hand-carried the motion from Bruce Pederson for a 120 days extension to Judge Britt it was granted the same day with just a notation on the motion showing it was allowed. Amazing what judges can and will do for lawyer friends. Bruce was impressed but she wasn't because she didn't respect the judge. She knew immediately that the DOJ wanted her in this judge's courtroom, at any cost. Shirley was in judicial trouble again and she knew it. Good ole' boy attorneys don't appreciate a challenge and especially when someone decides to blow the whistle on them. The motion had been walked at record speed through the judge's office on November 12, 1997.

On December 2, Justin Castillo called again to ask her the status of her case and to inform her that he was leaving government in two weeks for private practice. Justin had been originally assigned to her case from DC, had arranged the first meeting in Wilmington and asked for a second one. The second meeting was cancelled because the FDIC didn't think it was necessary. Justin said he loved the Wilmington area, especially Figure Eight Island and wished her luck on her case. He said her case would be reassigned soon to a new DOJ trial attorney. She got the distinct feeling that he knew what was going on within the DOJ and he didn't want to be a party to it. She had a different opinion of him after that call. That is why you can't judge a book by its cover.

Many people involved with this case were appearing to jump ship. Hands down it was beginning to look like Shirley and Congressman Jones had the most staying power.

She decided to fly her new attorneys to Wilmington instead of her going to Denver. She wanted them to see her surroundings, including all of her discovery, and for all of them to talk face to face on her turf. She especially wanted them to meet Special Agent Paul Cox. They asked her to have Tommy Manning meet them at the airport so they could have a short meeting. She called Tom and he was delighted.

Tom Manning didn't mention that he had heard of her or her Dare County Neimay lawsuit while he and Shirley were waiting at the airport. Somehow he seemed to know a great deal. She learned that he knew all of the attorneys who had been involved with her seven year lawsuit in Dare Co. He claimed all of them as very good friends especially Russell Twiford, a local lawyer from Elizabeth City and the Outer Banks. Russell had been deeply involved with the Nags Head Woods property. Shirley also knew Russell well.

She heard an announcement over the loud speaker that the plane her attorneys were aboard was late leaving Atlanta because of a thunderstorm and would be midnight arriving. She had more time with Tom Manning than she wanted, especially after finding out about his best friends. He told her that he was real excited that this Denver attorney might ask him to help with the case. Shirley looked at him in amazement. Didn't he realize that she would be the one making that decision? He said that he had three brothers who were all attorneys; one in DC who was a Republican, one who worked for Ross Perot, one a local judge and he himself was a Democrat. She thought she understood him to say, "And my father was general counsel for the North Carolina S&L Association." She immediately thought "Into what deep kind of stuff have we stepped"

When the plane arrived at midnight, her new attorneys stepped off. Bruce Pederson was walking in front of his partner Jackie Taylor who was very ill with a head cold. They were both exhausted from the long and troubled flight. Bruce said hello to Tom Manning and asked, "Could we talk later maybe on the way back? We are exhausted." Tom agreed and they went separate ways. As soon as they got into Shirley's car, she told them, "Don't ever tell that man anything. I don't trust him." They agreed they wouldn't. They never met with him, never talked to him again and Tom Manning never sent them a bill for his services. She later found out why.

She had arranged a meeting for them with Special Agent Paul Cox and Barry the following day. At the appointed time, Barry, with a driver, showed up looking very sick. He said Paul Cox couldn't make it. He took the floor and told her attorneys if there was anything he could do to help Shirley, anything at all, the FBI or anyone else that he would be there for her. They stared at him and listened in awe. When he finished, he kissed her on the check and left. When he walked out of the room, both of them, at the same time, said, "Wow". They felt as if they had just been in a movie and Al Pacino just walked out the door. Barry was indeed very sick and she was indeed very worried about him, whoever he was. One thing she was sure of was his loyalty.

Bruce and Jackie followed up their trip with a letter to the Congressman which said, "We met with Shirley in Wilmington last week to review the status of her case and her extensive research regarding potential contracting irregularities at the RTC. We also met with a law enforcement official who has been assisting her on various matters." Nobody knew whether Barry was law enforcement or not. He seemed to have a lot of connections.

They continued, "We have some definite ideas regarding where your office might start in evaluating the track record of the RTC in its liquidation of the Great Atlantic Savings Bank in Dare County. Billions of tax dollars were at risk in this and other thrift failures around the nation. As the ten year anniversary of FIRREA draws near in 1999, it is increasingly appropriate to look back and examine how the RTC discharged its stewardship of the S&L bailout. There are many signs that the agency fell woefully short in earning the "trust" in RTC. Shirley and we as her counsel are free to discuss the Great Atlantic matters with you without risk of violating the seal governing her pending qui tam litigation."

They continued, "We have taken the liberty of enclosing a newspaper article about our professional backgrounds and the work of our law firm. We are proud to have an ethics based practice with an emphasis on representing whistleblowers. As you will read, we are unusual in being attorney whistleblowers ourselves. We sacrificed our careers in government in conjunction with out campaign to expose rampant mismanagement at the RTC between 1992 and 1995. Those efforts included extensive work with both Senate and House committees with oversight jurisdiction over the RTC. We remain committed to the goal of promoting integrity and honesty in our federal government."

Bruce suggested to Shirley that they drop the case and go for the big picture meaning the exposure of the FDIC. He hesitated to ask this of her so used an analogy of the Battle of Gettysburg when the army was surrounded on all sides. He was suggesting that they needed to regroup if they were going to win the war. Bruce was a serious student of the Civil War. He likened her to General Robert E. Lee and himself to Stonewall Jackson. She shocked him when she said, "I think that's a great idea Stonewall. Let's do it!"

Chapter Twenty One

The Year 1998

February of 1998. Shirley was being sandbagged from all sides of the FDIC. Her requested information was being fouled up: addresses missing, names missing, and other types of mistakes. She wrote a formal letter to the FDIC complaining. The complaint was taken to the oversight manager for that particular database. The oversight manager confirmed the missing information and "reprogrammed" it. The FDIC "graciously" replaced thousands and thousands of pages of public information for which she had been charged.

She let the Congressman know that she was very mad at whoever in the FDIC was tampering with the software.

She wrote him a letter saying, "Again I report to you, I can expose the systemic fraud in the RTC contracting process as it relates to the RTC Asset Managers, their subcontractors and the servicing of the many assets. But I will not pick and choose. The exposure has to be complete."

She made a trip to St. Pete to see Dr. Morgenroth and told him of her dilemma with getting public records from the FDIC. They decided to ask for the entire databases. Surely they, whoever they were, wouldn't sabotage the entire databases. They wouldn't dare, would they? It was public information. Dr. Morgenroth wrote a letter dated February 18, 1998 to the Congressman, introducing himself and asking his help in obtaining the following two databases:

CARS	Contracting Activity Reporting System
REOMS	Real Estate Owned Management System

Most of her discovery came from these two databases and she wanted the official databases in order to backup her research center.

Dr. Morgenroth told the Congressman, "To introduce myself, I've been an advisor to Ms. Mays for her research – a friend for a dozen years. My background includes: Holder of Chair for the C&S Bank (a forerunner of NationsBank) and teaching business courses at the University of South Carolina, Ohio State and other schools for over 30 years. During World War II, I worked in the Middle East and Southeast Asia in Foreign Intelligence for our Navy."

Dr. Morgenroth didn't have to worry about credentials. He had more credentials than most entire business departments.

On March 10, Shirley wrote her attorneys, "It is clear and evident to me that extreme financial damages were incurred by the taxpayers and will be ongoing for many years but unfortunately, the FDIC and Congress created the problems and some individuals in the FDIC and other government agencies are now involved in the cover-up. Therefore I agree that qui tam is not the way for us to go. I'm glad you and Jackie put on your Stonewall hats and changed our strategy. This war will not be won in a courtroom. As far as I'm concerned it's a matter for Congress and it is definitely a matter of national security."

Pederson and Taylor filed a Notice of Relator's **Intent** to Dismiss The Complaint Without Prejudice' on March 11, 1998.

The players in the Department of Justice, who were deeply involved with the cover-up of this case, went crazy because their whole purpose was to get Shirley Mays into federal court where they could deal with her in a judicial manner to which they were accustomed. They had already proven themselves to be keystone cops but they were about to outsmart themselves after receiving this notice of *intent* to dismiss. She considered herself in good hands when Dr. Morgenroth planned a trip to Denver to meet with her attorneys. She knew that better strategists had never been born so she was just waiting for the results of this important meeting being held on her behalf. Her team was fearless and so was she. Their goal was to totally disarm the enemy and at this time, the enemy happened to be the people assigned to her qui tam action and the FDIC.

Her attorneys were having a hard time finding out who replaced Justin Castillo as the trial attorney for her case. There was a strong indication that no one wanted the job. After much effort Bruce finally got a new name from the DOJ in DC but when he wrote the newly assigned attorney on May 4, he never received a response. It had been almost two months since her attorneys had proposed a dismissal and no word from the Department of Justice.

While Dr. Morgenroth was in Denver planning a course of action with her attorneys she was in Wilmington fighting demons. The IRS had zeroed in on her with a charge that she had not paid some Dare County taxes from long ago involving the sale of her Sand Piper Quay condo. They sent the notice to an address in Charlotte where she had not lived for several years. Instead of developing stress over nothing she engaged an attorney friend to answer them and then she wrote a blistering letter to the IRS about harassment. She was well aware that the Dare County boys were very restless. Shots were coming from everywhere! Sometimes it was difficult to identify the origination point. In this case, she found that the local IRS office in Dare County was next door to one of the players so this must have been a coffee break decision to harass her.

She was disappointed that the Congressman had not been able to help them get the databases that Dr. Morgenroth had requested way back on February 18. She wrote to inform him of her concerns. Immediately after her letter, Dr. Morgenroth received a little sticky note from the Congressman's Chief of Staff, Glenn Downs, saying, "Mr. Morgenroth, per your request to Congressman Jones."

Glenn Downs, the Chief of Staff or someone in the Congressman's office had neglected for over two months to send Dr. Morgenroth the answer to his request. The Congressman had responded immediately to Dr. Morgenroth's request and the Director in the Office of Legislative Affairs had responded immediately in a letter dated March 31. Dr. Morgenroth received this very important information from the Congressman Chief of Staff on June 6. Who had been holding this vital information for over two months? Shirley thought she knew the answer but it presented a problem for her.

When she next talked to her FDIC contact, she was informed that strange things were happening in the FDIC. He said that over 300 software people came in at one time and the operating system was changed. They had been there a couple of months transferring data. No one understood why it was being changed. Shirley was beginning to wonder just how valuable her discovery really was and how high up the fraud went. It was a real coincidence that Dr. Morgenroth's request for the databases and the need for 300 people to change the operating system occurred at exactly the same time.

Dr. Morgenroth contacted Shirley with the concern that he just received a letter from the Criminal Division of the U. S. Department of Justice. He asked, "Did we write them?" She said, "No. Someone in the Congressman's office must have forwarded them a copy of your database request." He conveyed a little of the substance of the letter to her which stated, "Thank you for your letter to the Attorney General. She has asked me to respond to you on her behalf regarding the Department of Justice's investigation of possible violations of campaign finance law in the last election cycle."

The plot thickened at that moment.

"Good grief. I've always wondered how many of these RTC assets might have ended up in the hands of people who got them for almost nothing because someone owed them a big favor." She told Dr. Morgenroth, "I can actually prove the wrongdoings with the assets that were involved with Whitewater and the Buddhist Temple in California.

Many assets worth millions of dollars were given away for $1.00 or zero dollars. Many of the giveaways were falsely labeled environmentally impaired or affordable housing."

Dr. Morgenroth and Shirley were then beginning to wonder just how very high up her discovery was being sent. After all, Frank Hunger, the Assistant Attorney General who was the #2 man in the Department of Justice, directly under Attorney General Janet Reno, headed her case and he was Al Gore's brother in law. Vice President Al Gore did have a problem with donations from the Buddhist Temple. He also was known as Mr. Environmental and she had the biggest environmental scandal ever uncovered in the country. She was just having trouble getting it exposed.

Gary Shipman had evidently not forgotten about her. He was upset and concocted a bill for over $7000 and turned it over to a collection agency. She received a call from them trying to collect. She firmly informed them, "If you have a contract from me proving that I owe that amount you had better present it. If not, your next call will be considered harassment." She never heard from the collection agency again.

At the time she released Gary Shipman she was given all of the paperwork, including his private notes. She discovered that Gary had contacted the Banking Committee general counsel without her knowledge. He made notes during the phone call. It appeared from his notes that he suggested to someone, "Join the lawsuit with her. A few million would stop her." "No, she wants indictments." "Be sure claim covers us. Her research is over." Then his infamous note said, "Next case, conspiracy and obstruction of justice case – outlives the statute." Gary Shipman recognized a class action case when he saw it. He tried to persuade her to file a class action case in the beginning but she insisted on filing a False Claim Act on behalf of the taxpayers of America.

She also learned that other attorneys in the state referred to Gary as "Deep Throat" because he was known to work behind their backs and the backs of their clients with the FBI and the DOJ. He admitted to her in a letter that he had developed a good relationship with the DOJ in DC but she was also aware of the damages behind the scene which included his contacts with Rudy Renfer.

She felt sure that a lot of her problems were still coming from Gary and Rudy. They had much to lose if she won.

On August 11, 1998, she wrote her Denver attorneys, "Today, it has been five months since you filed the Motion with Intent to Dismiss with the federal court. I believe it would be proper and appropriate if you would ask the Congressman to make a congressional inquiry as to why and how the DOJ can respond in this manner concerning my very serious "In Camera and Under Seal" qui tam case which is causing so much personal turmoil for me. We need to know the legal interpretation of what they are doing. Let Congress decide. They voted to support this statute when it was amended in 1986."

She then wrote her Congressman. "In April of 1996, before I filed, you told me that I wouldn't have anyone standing beside me while I was struggling but many would be there when I succeeded. You also said you believed me and would be with me until I got to where I needed to go. I have the team. I just need to get to that "right" place. If it isn't the DOJ, would it be the Oversight Committee for Banking? It's not that I don't like your Chief of Staff. He just made a mistake in the beginning, when, after a very short time in the meeting with me, he said it was probably the 699th RTC complaint and he wanted me to get to my bottom line. It wasn't that simple then and it certainly isn't simple now. This is not just RTC fraud. It is ongoing fraud in the FDIC that is being covered up at the highest levels of government."

On August 19, the headlines of the Wilmington Morning Star's local/state section said, "Judge W. Earl Britt decides he's not the retiring type after all. Two weeks after announcing his intent to retire on Jan. 2, U.S. District Court Judge W. Earl Britt has changed his mind."

Shirley is trying to dismiss her case but the DOJ won't respond and the judge assigned to her case announces his retirement and abruptly changes his decision.

The article further states, "Earlier this year, Judge Britt ruled against the Morning Star and one of its reporters for reporting on a $36 million settlement between Conoco Oil Company and a community north of Wilmington. The case is on appeal to the 4th Circuit Court of Appeals."

Her gut told her that this judge has abused his judicial position for so long that his tail is now in a sling. He had covered for a big oil spill by putting the decision "In Camera and Under Seal." He sued the New York Times and teed them off. If he would go to that extreme for the oil companies, he would certainly stick his neck way out for the big banks right in his own backyard of Charlotte, North Carolina. The article further quoted the judge by saying, "he changed his mind after a lot of soul searching." "What is up with this powerful federal judge?" Her bottom line was that she was still stuck with him.

In September, she wrote her Denver attorneys, "I promise both of you this is my last whistleblowing case. I hate swimming in new discovery of fraud everyday of my life that appears to be going nowhere. Please just help me get this exposed and I will spend the rest of my life praying for you and your other cases."

She then flew to Idaho for an extended visit with her younger daughter and her wonderful grandsons. The biggest pleasures she had in life were visiting her daughters and her grandchildren. Her two granddaughters lived in Florida. They were growing up so fast and she had such little time with them. It made her wonder what her life was all about.

Bruce drafted a letter for the Congressman who immediately sent it under his letterhead to Attorney General Janet Reno, dated September 17, 1998 which ended by saying, "It appears that six months without a written response from the U. S. Department of Justice is excessive in litigation of this nature. The delay also stands to tax the patience of the Court. If a response has been filed with the Court, then I submit that, in all fairness, a copy should be sent to Ms. Mays and her counsel."

The Congressman's office followed up with a call to the DOJ and was told they could expect a response in four weeks from September 23rd when the letter was received in the *Civil Rights Section*. That would have been the proper division to receive it because Shirley was a minority certified government contractor; she was definitely experiencing discrimination. The DOJ followed up with a letter stating that nothing about this case ever went to the Civil Rights Section or the Criminal Division. As a matter of fact, it went to both. They had given the Congressman a file number.

The US Attorney's office finally responded to the *Intent to Dismiss* by filing a Government's Notice That It Does Not Object To Dismissal Of Relator's Complaint Without Prejudice on October 19.

At the same time, she asked the Congressman's office to check with the DOJ to see if Attorney General Janet Reno had answered his letter. They were told that a decision had not been made in that case. The Congressional Liaison Office reported to the Congressman that they had no response yet from the Civil Rights Division where it was sent but the DOJ thought the Civil Rights Division intended to ask for an extension.

It was blatantly obvious that once again Main Justice didn't know what the left hand in Raleigh was doing.

Shirley called her attorneys immediately and said, "Do not, whatever you do, submit a formal dismissal in this case. Let them hang themselves legally. With this group, it shouldn't take long." She knew she was holding an ace because Rudy Renfer made the motion not to join her case after he had been taken off of it. The #6 paragraph in the order from the judge, which backed him up read, "Should the relator or the defendant propose that this action be dismissed, settled, or otherwise discontinued, ***the Court will solicit the written consent of the United States before ruling or granting its approval.***"

She interpreted that to state that this powerful Senior U. S. District Judge, who had just sued the New York Times $600,000 for printing the truth, announced his retirement, then changed his mind was now taking the lead in her bank fraud case and saying in a formal order, filed in the records, that he would have the final word by soliciting the written consent of the United States before ruling or granting its approval.

Guess what? That had not been done so the case was hanging in space like a grenade with the pin pulled. She was told, as late as 2005 by the federal Clerk of Court in Wilmington that her case had never been archived and sent to Atlanta. Until the case is formally closed by the judge and brought out of seal, she is not allowed to view the materials that were too sensitive for her, the relator, to see.

"Secrecy, when imposed by a federal judge, is powerful and damaging." No one understands that more than Shirley Mays.

At the same time, in the summer of 1998, The White House was involved in a Filegate scandal involving the FBI, the one where information from many personal FBI files were downloaded into the White House computer database. Shirley read an article about the White House counsel secretary, Betsy Pond, who had downloaded the FBI info into the White House database for White House attorney William Kennedy who was presently in prison. That secretary's name was the same one from the criminal division of the Department of Justice who had just written the letter to Dr. Morgenroth answering a letter that he never sent her. She had to wonder if Betsy Pond and the FBI were still working together improperly using personal files of private citizens. Betsy Pond was now at the Criminal Division of the DOJ. Who gave Dr. Morgenroth's letter to her? How did she obtain it? She was now doing dirty work for someone at the Department of Justice Criminal Division just like she did at the White House and somehow Shirley's whistleblowing case had become a big issue.

She questioned the actions of the Congressman's Chief of Staff and the actions of the FBI special agent she was working with and she had to wonder, "Is Paul Cox working directly with the Chief of Staff without the Congressman's knowledge? How did Betsy Pond, secretary at the Criminal Division of the DOJ get the letter that was addressed to the Congressman? Shirley wrote the Congressman asking him that very same question. Dr. Morgenroth was very concerned because it was his personal letter to the Congressman that was in question.

Shirley Mays was after a bunch of government lawyers and a bunch of government lawyers were after her. It was becoming very difficult to distinguish the good from the bad.

In November of 1998, she wrote a letter to the Chief of the FDIC Reading Room. She wanted to be sure her letters of complaint were being sent to the FDIC Inspector General. Cyber-fraud is bad but cyber terrorism is worse and she had reason to believe the government should be concerned about their software contractors. They should definitely be concerned about the people in charge of the two databases that Dr. Morgenroth had requested on her behalf. She knew the names and addresses of the contractors and would be glad to share them. Dr.Morgenroth agreed and suggested she directly alert the FDIC Inspector General

Her public information problems really heated up after that letter. There was no more doubt in her mind. Someone who had close access to those two databases knew everything she was ordering and was trying desperately to sabotage the information before it was sent to her. Who were they and why would they risk tampering with public records?

Chapter Twenty Two

The Year 1999

Shirley again wrote her loyal Congressman. It was February 29, 1999. She said, "Dear Walter, there are some FDIC oversight and internal control people who should be under house arrest for what they are doing to our nation. They are in key positions to help expose the domestic cyber terrorism that is taking place within our banking agencies and institutions. I am talking about white-collar corporate crime involving environmental and affordable housing rules. These are very big issues. As I told you in the beginning of my case, what is happening to our country in the banking world is just a continuation of the BCCI scandal. The DOJ has really fouled up my federal <u>qui</u> <u>tam</u> case. They are in a terribly bind as to what to do about me. Once again, I want to remind you of my concern for my personal safety."

That same day, she read a disturbing article in the press. The Wilmington Morning Star headline read, "Jury decides clown's threats were no joke. A prominent Wilmington lawyer Gary Shipman said this week that a man posing as the famous clown Ronald McDonald targeted him with threatening messages and made him fear for his life." It appears that Ronald McDonald actually was an ex-deputy in the Sheriff's department in the county next to Wilmington. The night the first message was left, a picture of him as Ronald McDonald was taped to the front of Shipman's office door with a note which said, "Hey Kids. Beware. This attorney is a snake, a liar and a thief." Gary Shipman had represented him and his mother, ten years earlier, in a contract dispute. "Ronald" accused Gary Shipman of improprieties, which the lawyer denied.

After Gary swore out a warrant for the note and several phone calls, "Ronald" was arrested during a routine traffic stop. The officer testified that he found a double-barreled shotgun in the car. "Ronald" contended he used the weapon to kill snakes, an assertion the police officer found odd because it was loaded with slugs rather than the traditional varmint-hunting buckshot. It appeared that Gary Shipman, a Wilmington civil attorney, the one who was involved in several high-profile lawsuits, including a class-action stucco lawsuit, litigation opposing Wilmington's annexation plans and a dispute over beach-access right on the Outer Banks was also the one that she had earlier released.

Can you believe Shirley Mays' luck in the judicial world?

- *Her local Wilmington attorney is being threatened by "Ronald McDonald" for being a snake, a liar and a thief.*
- *The judge who is assigned to her whistleblowing case in federal court, has not only gone against the advice of Janet Reno, the Attorney General of the United States but has sued the New York Times $600,000 for printing public information exposing Conoco, one of the biggest oil companies in the world for an oil spill right in Wilmington.*
- *The Chief of the Civil Division with the US Attorneys office in Raleigh, working closely with her defendants in the FDIC, made the motion not to join her case AFTER he was removed from her case.*
- *Main Justice said her case had been sent to their Criminal Division and then they denied it.*
- *Main Justice said her case was sent to the Civil Rights Division and then denied it.*

There was no doubt in her mind that our judicial system was broken and it looked broken beyond repair.

She again wrote her Congressman on March 29, 1999,

"Dear Walter, the twenty S&L Nature Conservancy scandals that I have involve the Outer Banks, Austin, Texas, and the State of Florida. Sam Gwynne, the National Editor of Time Magazine who was an international banker, along with Jonathan Beatty, an investigative journalist with Time broke the BCCI story. BCCI was known as the Outlaw Bank. Gwynne lives in Austin, Texas at this time. I spoke with him last week just to plant my seeds. He vacationed last summer with his family at the beach near Wilmington. He visited the Cotton Exchange and is familiar with the location of my office. If anyone in the United States would understand and appreciate my discovery, it would be the two of them. The BCCI scandal involved three administrations, Carter, Reagan and Bush. The S&L scandals involve all three of those administration plus Clinton. The BCCI scandal was covered up at the highest levels of the White House, DOJ, NSC, FBI, CIA and others. It was all about Iran Contra and the CIA. My story is going to be very hard for anyone to believe but I'm sure you are aware that I have it well documented and in a safe place."

On April 1, 1999, she received a letter back from the FDIC Reading Room Chief which said, "The Acting Chief, Operations Unit, Systems Support Section of FDIC's Acquisition and Corporate Services Branch, after analysis and system testing, informed me that there was a program bug. I was subsequently notified on March 24, 1999 that the bug was fixed. In response to your request letter, I will forward copies of your correspondence referenced in this letter, as well as a copy of my response letter, to the Office of Inspector General."

Shirley had worked within the system for a long time, even though she was positive the system didn't work. She was now trying to get her discovery to the FDIC Inspector General.

On April 6, 1999, she documented a letter, by Certified Mail, to the FDIC Inspector General.

S.L.M. & ASSOCIATES

Shirley L. Mays, Real Estate Broker / License No. 96641

(910) 815-0037 – 321 N. Front St., Suite 113 – Wilmington, NC 28401

April 6, 1999   **Certified Mail**

Office of Inspector General
550 17th Street, NW
Washington, DC 20429

Dear Sir:

Reference is made to a letter that I received from Ms. R. Teresa Neville, Chief, FDIC Public Information Center dated April 1, 1999, copy enclosed. She has handled my past complaints with the CARS database and sent a copy of them to you at my request. She suggested, in her April 1 letter, for the sake of expediency, that I deal directly with you.

Her April 1 response included an explanation from Ms. Nancy Matzke, the Acting Chief, Operations Unit, Systems Support Section of FDIC's Acquisition and Corporate Services Branch. *Ms. Matzke is responsible for the CARS database.* I am not satisfied with Ms. Matzke's answer. I do not think it addresses my question or the problem. Ms. Matzke said that she was unaware of this "bug" until I brought the data discrepancy to her attention. She said "after analysis and system testing, there was a program bug that failed to reset the counters to zero for closed contracts/task orders or terminated contracts/task orders when running a report with multiple firms".

This was in response to my question as to why the task order information is disappearing from many contracts – active and closed – in the CARS database. As you are aware, in the beginning of RTC, there were only

12 service listings. This increased to 36 and on October 7, 1994, a 37th service listing was added to the public information database, which was Purchase Orders –PO. Within these 37 service listings, there are 2,168 zero (0) contracts, which involve 14,752 task orders. The total amount of these 14,752 task orders is $1,818,517,150 according to the statistical data listed in the public records at the end of each of the service listings.

On April 1, 1999, The Washington Times reported that the General Accounting Office, (GAO), Congress' investigative arm and the government's official auditor reported that $3,400,000,000,000 of taxpayers' money is missing. The U. S. government can't balance its books and can't properly explain how it spent a grand total of $3,400,000,000,000. The upshot is that "once again, billions of taxpayer dollars were lost to waste, fraud, and mismanagement" says Rep. Steve Horn, chairman of the House government reform and oversight subcommittee on government management, information and technology. Article enclosed.

On July 24, 1996, I filed a Whistleblowing Case against many SAMDAS and the unnecessary and unauthorized subcontracts issued by them which would involve waste, fraud and mismanagement. I am a minority contractor and certified to do work in the areas of selling and consulting in real estate and environmental matters with FDIC/RTC. Several of your OIG Semi-Annual reports to Congress *confirm* the unnecessary and unauthorized contracts that were issued by RTC Asset Managers (SAMDAS).

Oversight and Internal Controls *should be aware* of these problems since they have been reported to Congress several times. According to the OIG reports that I have, there have been Hotline Calls and Congressional inquiries about some of these same concerns. I have discovery of many contracts that are listed under UNKNOWN, in the names of Nancy Matzke and Rick Miller. Mr. Miller, I believe, is listed in both the NY and DC offices of FDIC. These people need to be aware that their names are being used in public information associated with "unknown" contracts in most of the 37 categories of service listings. I am enclosing a listing of the examples in the service listing of SE –

Securities. I also have documentation on the other 36 service listings. They need to be aware that data is presently "disappearing" from some of these contracts.

On January 11, 1996, after RTC sunset, a report concerning internal controls was presented to Congress with a cover letter to Honorable Robert E. Rubin, Chairman of the Thrift Depositor Protection Oversight Board from John E. Ryan, Deputy and Acting Chief Executive Officer which *"continued" to identify six high risk areas:* contracting systems and contracting systems oversight; accounting, financial management and reporting; asset management and disposition; information systems management; legal services; and transition management. These were the same areas identified in previous internal control reports to Congress and Mr. Rubin.

One new material weakness was identified for 1995 in that report to Congress and Cover Letter to Secretary Rubin. It was and I quote "general controls over some of the Corporation's computerized information systems did not provide adequate assurance that data files and computer programs were adequately protected from unauthorized access and modification."

I am concerned about the unauthorized access and modification of the CARS database. I have experienced problems since January of 1998 concerning deletion, modification and disappearance of data. I have kept my government sources informed at all times of these problems. They are well documented.

Following the Qui Tam Statutes, I first took my discovery to government sources before filing my case. I have continued to keep them informed for the past three years. If you wish to discuss any of these matters, you should contact one of those parties:

Congressman Spencer Bachus, Chairman
General Oversight and Investigations
212 O'Neill House Office Building
Washington, DC 20515-6056

Congressman Walter B. Jones
422 Cannon House Office Building
Washington, DC 20515-3303

Mr. Bruce Pederson
Pederson & Taylor, LLC
143 Union Blvd, #900
Lakewood, Colorado 80228-1829
Phone: (303) 980-9091
Fax: (303) 980-8991

Sincerely

Shirley L. Mays
SLM & ASSOCIATES

CC: Congressman Spencer Bachus
Congressman Walter B. Jones, Jr.
Bruce Pederson, Pederson & Taylor, LLC

On May 4, 1999, Shirley wrote the Congressman to tell him the silence coming from everyone was deafening. She ended her letter by saying, "We have a war going on in the United States, which involves the control of our government. It involves our national security. I hope God finds some leaders in Congress real soon because some of his Christian soldiers out in the field are getting weary."

Breaking News! May 12, l999, Treasury Secretary Robert Rubin to Resign.

On May 22, 1999, Shirley wrote Bruce Pederson, her Denver attorney, "I am very disappointed in the FBI's participation or lack of participation in my case. I told the Congressman in June of 1996, before I filed, that I didn't trust the FBI. I trust them even less now. Frank Ruerkheimer, a former US Attorney, who is now a professor at the University of Wisconsin Law School says, "A big part of the F.B.I.'s power is passive. They usually don't fight you, they just wait you out. They know you will be gone in a few years, but they will not." The Director of the FBI, in his testimony before the House Judiciary Subcommittee on Crime on June 5, 1997 summed up why rigorous oversight is so important for them. "We are potentially the most dangerous agency in the country."

The Director of the FBI said that, not Shirley Mays.

By June 9, 1999 the Congressman and her attorney, Bruce Pederson got a letter ready for Frank Hunger who was the #2 man in the Department of Justice. It stated, "The purpose of this letter is to ask for an explanation as to how the U. S. Department of Justice (DOJ) went about performing its review of the allegations contained in the subject lawsuit for purposes of deciding whether to intervene in this matter. As you know, relators who file such actions often place themselves at great financial, emotional, and sometimes, physical risk. Ms. Mays is no exception. With that concern in mind, and the historic track record that such cases have recovered billions of dollars for American taxpayers over the years, I would like to be satisfied that the DOJ has thoroughly investigated the alleged false claims contained in the qui tam complaint filed by Ms. Mays."

The Congressman then listed 11 dynamite questions. The 11th one being, "Are you aware of three letters, that Ms. Mays sent in connection with this case wherein she expressed concerns for her physical safety? These letters were sent to: AUSA Fenita Morris in Raleigh (1-17-97); Judge W. Earl Britt in Raleigh (4 -21-97; and Attorney General Janet Reno (8-18-97). Did DOJ take any actions regarding these concerns? If yes, what were the actions?"

Frank Hunger left the government before answering the Congressman.

On August 10, 1999, David Ogden, the acting Assistant Attorney General who was handling the big tobacco cases attempted to answer the 11 questions that were asked of Mr. Hunger on June 9. He was relying on someone who had not given him accurate information.

On September 23, 1999, The Congressman wrote Mr. Ogden back saying "Your last correspondence failed to address the majority of questions contained in my letter of June 9, 1999. I am at a loss to understand why you, or your staff, would not simply answer each of the eleven questions that were set forth in my inquiry. Even a generous reading of your letter reveals that the following items have yet to be answered. Finally, your response to Question No. 11 is incomplete. Who is the staff attorney referenced in your letter? When did he speak with Ms. Mays about her safety concerns? Is he still employed by the Department? If not, how was his conversation with Ms. Mays memorialized? I would like my questions answered as soon as possible. I was disappointed to receive so little information from you after waiting over 60 days for your last letter. If you believe that a briefing in my office would expedite this process, please let me know. Thank you for your assistance in fully resolving this inquiry. Given an historic intervention rate of approximately 20%, it is critical that taxpayer confidence in the Department of Justice's stewardship of the False Claims Act remains intact."

Shirley was very confident that her Denver attorneys and the Congressman were on her side. She just wondered how long they would have to deal with these incompetent attorneys in the DOJ.

She wrote John Edwards, her United States Senator at this crucial time, who later ran for Vice President. "I am a whistleblower. I have a False Claims Act in Federal Court at the present time. I am writing you not as a lawyer but as my Senator. I am trying very hard, working within the system, to expose the environmental and corporate fraud ongoing within the FDIC. It is of interest to me that you serve on the Banking, Housing and Urban Affairs, Governmental Affairs, Small Business and the Year 2000 Technology Problem Committee. The government person I took my findings to before I filed my case is a close and personal family friend. My present attorneys are from Denver, Colorado. They were FDIC/RTC employees. One of them headed the Public Integrity Office for the RTC in Denver. His office was responsible for closing the institutions west of Denver. He and his partner have testified before the Congress four times, twice in person and twice in interrogatories, trying to expose the wrongdoing in the FDIC. They finally left the government and decided to concentrate on representing whistleblowers like me. Susan Schmidt of The Washington Post gave me their names. The below figures represent four contracts handled by Financial Conservators, RTC Asset Managers. An asset you purchased was handled by the first one listed. Someone changed the date, the 4th and 5th figures so the asset wouldn't be picked up by the auditors. I filed my case on behalf of the American people. I do not want it to become a partisan issue. If you would be interested in having more information, please feel free to contact me."

Shirley gave John Edwards, US Senator from North Carolina, her name, business address and phone number. She never received a response. That didn't look good for the Senator, especially with him owning that RTC property, and not even being concerned that his closing information was falsified in the official corporately owned FDIC database which was used for reports to Congress. Definitely not with him being on a Banking Committee.

So many people in Congress were compromised with good deals that no one wants this damaging discovery to reach the public. Many, many good books have been written by top investigative journalists about this biggest financial scandal in the history of this country and one of them is the Mafia, The CIA and George Bush by Pete Brewton. In his book he states, "Another reason journalists are still unable to follow the money is that some of the crucial documents that would allow them to do so are not public. Federal and state Freedom of Information acts and open records laws exempt the relevant financial documents from disclosure. In our case the necessary records are the loan documents, particularly the Title company disbursement sheets. (Title companies collect the loan money from the S&Ls and then cut checks to all the parties getting money.) These documents, along with the federal and state examination reports, which are also not available to the public, are the "Rosetta Stones" of the savings and loan debacle. Any journalist, federal agent or *self-styled expert* who claims to know what happened to the money without actually having studied the title company disbursement documents and examination reports is shooting in the dark.

Without even knowing it, Shirley was acquiring the "Rosetta Stones" of the S&L debacle. She considers herself a self-styled expert who definitely has NOT been shooting in the dark. REOMS, the FDIC official real estate database has closing information.

The Washington Times headlines on October 4, 1999 read, "House Committee probes document destruction". It stated, "This investigation started out as simply an inquiry into how fish and wildlife conservation funds were being spent. It now appears that the situation at the Fish and Wildlife Service and Department of Interior is rotten to the core", quoted the House Resources Committee Chairman. One of the auditor's from the General Accounting Office was quoted as saying, "the Administration of the conservation program funds in question is "one of the worst managed programs we have ever encountered."

Another headline on October 4 from the CBS news, "U. S. Vulnerable to Cyberterror" It read, "There is a growing risk of a terrorist nation doing real damage to U. S. infrastructure through a computer hack attach and the federal government is not doing enough about the threat, according to a report by congressional investigators to be released Monday." "At the federal level," the report says, "these risks are not being adequately addressed."

On October 6, 1999, she again wrote the Congressman,

"My case will expose the fraudulent use of the environmental buzz words listed below by the FDIC and RTC Asset Managers. The assets were listed in the official database with false contract numbers. It has to be the biggest environmental real estate scandal this country will ever experience. It is systemic. Many of the asset managers are holding companies for the big banks. They don't have to find a place to launder their money because they own the laundromats. Dare County's Great Atlantic Savings Bank and the other eight S&Ls in North Carolina are no exception. They were definitely in the loop of collusion and commingling. I now have almost twenty years experience in what I am trying to expose. And don't forget I work with one of the best geologist in the country. Thank God he is honest like us. I feel sure the Senator from Utah, who just wrote the GAO report saying "Our nation's computer based critical infrastructures are at increasing risk of severe disruption" would be interested in my discovery." She closed by saying, "The big problem is that our government agencies have no oversight and no internal controls that can be trusted. The problem is definitely a matter of national security."

By the end of 1999, Shirley, Bruce and the Congressman had managed to start getting the attention of the DOJ regarding her case that she filed it in July 1996.

Chapter Twenty Three

The Year 2000

By January of 2000, the correspondence became heavy between the Congressman, the DOJ in DC and the FDIC IG. The Congressman was very dedicated in his efforts to get Shirley's discovery properly recognized.

She was very concerned about obtaining the "written investigative report" involving her that was mentioned in a letter from FDIC IG Gaston Gianni to the Congressman. In January the Congressman wrote the DOJ and requested the written investigative report. Maybe she could figure out their strategy if she could get that report. She especially wanted Exhibit 1 which the DOJ declined to send. They refused to send their internal memoranda, "in view of the need to protect the confidentiality of their internal deliberations." They were claiming executive privilege.

In July, the Congressman wrote FDIC IG Gaston Gianni and questioned him about the April 6, 1999 letter Shirley had sent to his office. She had addressed a lot of serious issues that needed to be answered.

In less than a month, which is very fast for the government, Shirley got a response to Congressman Jones' letter from the Office of the FDIC Inspector General. The letter was from Rex Simmons, Assistant Inspector General for Management and Resources. He acknowledged that her letter was never received by the Office of the Inspector General and suggested she address further issues with the Chief of Operations Systems Branch.

Unfortunately, that was someone she was complaining about.

The Congressman got a letter from the OIG on the same day as Shirley which acknowledging that the OIG never received her April 6, 1999 letter. They then said "Accordingly, we are releasing Exhibit 1 to you without redactions."

BINGO!

Exhibit 1 was a letter dated September 4, 1996. It was four years old. It was marked *Privileged and Confidential*. It was from Michael F. Hertz, Director, Commercial Litigation Branch, Civil Division, U. S. Department of Justice, Washington, DC and it was hand carried by messenger to Mr. Thomas A. Schultz, Assistant General Counsel of the FDIC.

In that September 4, 1996 privileged and confidential letter, Mr. Hertz, head of the Civil Division, had informed Mr. Schultz, Assistant General Counsel of the FDIC that "a copy of the complaint and other materials are enclosed. Please note that named defendants include several employees of the RTC as well as Mr. William C. Thomas, former director of the RTC."

That clearly meant that the Department of Justice had not only informed the FDIC that her qui tam case involved them but sent them the entire case and supporting evidence. She had sued a dozen FDIC employees including William C. Thomas, RTC Director from Atlanta who had personally signed the quitclaim deed for the Nags Head Woods.

She now realized why she had been harassed by so many. The defendants were in charge of her harassment and fully aware of her "In Camera and Under Seal" accusations. The DOJ put her in that position. Their hand carried letter had shown copies to Laurence A.

Froehlich, Counsel to the IG and Honorable Janice McKenzie Cole, the US Attorney in North Carolina. Shirley knew the US Attorney and had thought since the filing of her case that it would become political. Janice Cole was appointed by President Clinton and Shirley was working closely with a Republican Governor. That alone made her an enemy in Northeastern North Carolina where a diehard one party Democrat system has reigned forever. Her Whistleblowing case had become political. She had little doubt.

One thing was very clear to her in August of 2000 after receiving that privileged and confidential internal memo from the DOJ dated September 4, 1996. "If you blow the whistle, the DOJ will destroy you."

Shirley Mays became very mad at the DOJ and our "judicial system." She was determined to make a difference.

The North Carolina Real Estate Commission was teaching a course about SCAMS and FRAUDS all over the State. The Great Atlantic Savings Bank, FSB in Manteo was their role model.

She was more motivated than ever to get her discovery exposed. Out of the blue, Special Agent Paul Cox called and casually asked for a meeting. It appeared to her that she was being babysat by the FBI so she called her attorney in Denver and asked him to fly in and attend the meeting. The FBI had a reputation for shelving information. In April, the FBI Director took an early retirement. She was now aware that the DOJ and the CIA had accounts in many of these defunct S&Ls and the S&Ls did a lot of money laundering especially in the case of Iran/Contra where the CIA was so involved. It was a very good chance that nobody wanted these skeletons to surface.

The FBI meeting was arranged and confirmed for June 6, 2000. She spent a lot of time and a lot of money in preparation for that meeting. *It was a bust.* Special Agent Cox had other obligations and didn't arrive until late afternoon. Agent Cox had managed to avoid the first meeting with her attorneys back in 1998 and it appeared he was trying to avoid them again. She and Bruce waited all day for him. She was thoroughly disgusted when he finally arrived in late afternoon. Not much was accomplished at that meeting.

She requested another meeting with Special Agent Paul Cox on September 1. She fully intended to kiss the FBI goodbye and she wanted to do it formally. The meeting had hardly started when Paul Cox got a phone call and said he had to go to school and get his daughter. She was sick. Another FBI meeting down the drain. They rescheduled it for September 13 at which time she presented him with a thank you letter for all of the past meetings and a letter to be given to Rudy Renfer to inform him that she now has substantial and credible evidence that she wished to present to him. Paul Cox said he didn't know Renfer, the Civil Chief of the NCUSAO. She insisted that he take the letter anyway. Shirley didn't care how Renfer got it – just that he did.

While letters were going back and forth from the Congressman to the DOJ and the FDIC OIG office, Dr. Morgenroth called her and said he had found the name of that nice chap who had befriended him during his two week trip to Norway. "Who was it?" He said, "Rudy Renfer."

It appeared to her that Rudy Renfer had gone out of his way to befriend her senior advisor *before* they boarded the vessel for a two week trip to Norway and even told him, "If you ever need me, feel free to call." What a coincidence! Shirley figured it was time to feel free to call that nice chap. She headed to St. Pete to see Dr. Morgenroth.

While in St. Pete, she called Paul Cox to see if he had given the letter to Rudy Renfer. He said he had put a coversheet on it and sent it to his supervisor. She figured that supervisor might just be the one who had drafted all those brilliant letters for the Congressman to send the FDIC. The FBI drafted letters were on the verge of exposing the FDIC when Paul Cox wrote that personal memo to the Congressman telling them that the FDIC must be right. It appeared that somebody very influential put the skids on the FBI just in time.

Dr. Morgenroth said to Shirley when she arrived in St. Pete, "Call Rudy Renfer now and arrange a meeting." "Will you go with me?" "Absolutely." She called the NC US Attorney's office. Rudy Renfer answered the phone and seemed shocked that it was her. She immediately asked, "Did you get my letter?" Without having time to think, he said yes. She asked for a meeting and he started giving excuses about having to go out of town, etc. "I can come anytime at your convenience. Dr. William Morgenroth, my senior advisor will be coming with me. I believe you know him."

Rudy Renfer acted as if he had no idea who she was talking about. Unfortunately for him she was using Dr. Morgenroth's phone. Dr. Morgenroth looked very disturbed and said to her, "Ask him if he remembers having lunch last week with my twin brother Bobby in Chapel Hill?" Rudy Renfer said, "Oh, that Bill."

Rudy was trapped and he knew it. The meeting was arranged for October 2 at 11:00 a.m in Raleigh, North Carolina. He asked Shirley to do a critique. She planned to do one based on the Report of Investigation that the Congressman has received from the FDIC IG showing why they decided not to intervene in the subject False Claims Act lawsuit. The information in the ROI had been falsified and she could prove it.

Dr. Morgenroth advised Shirley that they needed to specify charges that she could show:

- Defrauding the U. S. Government through record falsification whose purposes are to block trails of values

- Or Defrauding the U. S. Government by creating false trails to hide fraudulent transactions, etc.

Three days later, after arriving back in Wilmington, she received a *personal* letter from Gaston Gianni, Jr, FDIC IG apologizing for her lost April 6, 1999 letter. He wanted to thank her for her continued concerns about the efficiency and effectiveness of FDIC operations.

The IG personally acknowledged the loss of her April 6, 1999 letter now that he had now received a copy of the certified mail receipt from the Congressman. The proper groundwork had been laid for her upcoming meeting with Rudy Renfer, AUSA.

She and Dr. Morgenroth arrived at the Federal Building in Raleigh, checked in, got badges and headed for the US Attorney's office. Dr. Morgenroth had a strange feeling before they went into the building that they were being watched by a group of three men who appeared to be following them. Rudy Renfer acknowledged Dr. Morgenroth and was trying to make up for the embarrassing phone call when he denied knowing him.

You just don't forget meeting the Professor. He is a very imposing figure. Besides Rudy Renfer had spent two full weeks with him on the cruise after he befriended him. It just didn't add up.

Needless to say, it was a very awkward meeting. Renfer insisted, right off the bat, that her *qui tam* case was closed. Shirley insisted that it wasn't. Renfer excused himself. He went to the Clerk's office and returned without saying a word. Evidently he found out the case wasn't closed. She knew that it wasn't closed because paragraph #6 had not been exercised by the Court. Her top concern that day was being sure Rudy Renfer knew that she was concerned about the two official databases, CARS and REOMS being falsified. Rudy Renfer escorted Shirley and Dr. Morgenroth into their meeting room and at the same time, the three men they saw outside the building were escorted into an adjoining room. The meeting lasted about an hour with nothing being resolved. The last thing Renfer said was, "This case is closed and I speak for the US Attorney's office and the FDIC." She said emphatically, "This case is not closed."

She had a strong feeling that the three men overlapping their meeting that day were bankers.

She wrote Mr. Gianni, told him about her meeting with Rudy Renfer and sent him a copy of the critique. She wanted to be sure all of the players knew what game was being played. She was concerned about the CARS and REOMS databases and wanted everyone to be aware of their deficiencies.

She had definitely gotten the attention of the FDIC IG. The Congressman wrote Mr. Gianni and asked him to arrange a meeting in Wilmington with Shirley Mays. The IG assigned one of his senior auditors to call her. The auditor's name was Marshall Gentry. He had someone else on the phone listening to their two hour conversation. She later found out that it was Stephen Beard, who had responsibility for oversight for the $7.2 billion dollar pool that her case was built on. It appeared that Marshall Gentry worked for him. Evidently, besides having the personal attention of the IG, she had locked in on the attention of several of his senior auditors.

Maybe those senior auditors knew something about her lost April 6, 1999 letter. She intended to talk to them, as soon a meeting was arranged, about the man she had sued, William C. Thomas, the Director of the RTC in Atlanta, and his involvement in the legislation that gave non profits first choice of all of the assets in all of the defunct S&Ls all over the country.

Shirley wrote a letter to Congressman Jones on March 5, after getting back from meetings in St. Petersburg with Dr. Morgenroth, thanking him for requesting an FDIC meeting. In it she said, "We are very pleased with your letter to Mr. Gianni asking for a meeting in Wilmington. I asked Bruce to compose letters to the IG and the DOJ without any wiggle room. If the IG doesn't respond favorable to the Wilmington trip then I will very shortly move in a different direction. The organized crime evidence I have affects both the FDIC and Wall Street. Fortunately, the SEC has admitted to the presence of Organized Crime on Wall Street and appears to be trying to expose it. As I understand it they can pursue the auditors like Coopers and Lybrand under Rule 102(e)P which is an administrative proceeding where the judge is a SEC employee."

Shirley continued saying to the Congressman, "My goal is the same as it was when I first came to see you in Greenville in April of 1996, retribution for the taxpayers. I have spent a great deal of time and money in addition to my damages trying to achieve that goal."

Not the End of the Story

The Year 2009

POLITICAL CORRUPTION

The Congressman, Bruce Pederson and Shirley Mays continue to this day trying to expose the FDIC, the agency responsible for the giveaway of the last bailout. The FDIC IG sent two people to Wilmington on May 22, 2001. Marshall Gentry was a senior auditor from DC and Edward Slagle was a criminal investigator from Atlanta. Both of them had worked for William C. Thomas, Director of the RTC in Atlanta, Georgia who signed the quitclaim deed for the Nags Head Woods. Throughout the important meeting in her conference room they kept referring to him as "Billy." "Billy" had been involved in the mishandling of many assets from the Great Atlantic Savings Bank, FSB which was on the Outer Banks of North Carolina in the Congressman's district. He was Shirley Mays' most important defendant.

Against great odds, she has managed to acquire the two official FDIC databases. One is the real estate database (REOMS) which also includes loans. The other is the contracting database (CARS). Both of these official corporately owned FDIC databases have been falsified, with intent, to block the trail of value of over 400,000 assets. Both of these databases, with intent, have falsified federal ID numbers, to block the trail of the IRS.

Shirley Mays can prove, with official FDIC documents, the who, where, what, when and why of each of these assets and the names of the private contractors and the oversight people who were responsible for them. She can give you their federal ID numbers. She can show, with official FDIC documentation, the systemic environmental and affordable housing violations. She can show, with their own databases, the violation of the National Housing Act by the RTC and the FDIC.

Shirley Mays believes that she has the Rosetta Stones of the S&L bailout.

It is of great concern to her as a taxpayer that the FDIC at this present time is promoting a "bad bank" for the toxic assets from all of the banks that they would control. The American taxpayers should not inherit those problems. The banks created the junk or "toxic" loans and they should have to deal with them.

The FDIC is claiming that the RTC was a success while Shirley can prove it was the biggest real estate scam in the history of this country. The FDIC should not be in charge of anything before their RTC software fraud is exposed.

Shirley was told by Mark A. Brenneman, the Deputy Director of the FDIC Division of IT that the RTC software was designed exclusively for them. She was told that in a meeting on July 16, 2008 in the Rayburn Building. The meeting was arranged by Deborah Silberman, Senior Counsel for Barney Frank, Chairman of the Financial Services Committee for the House of Representatives.

MEETING: July 16, 2008
2:00 P.M.

PLACE: Rayburn House Office Building
Room 2222

PRESENT: House Financial Services Cmte, Deborah Silberman, Senior Counsel
House Financial Services Cmte, Michael Beresik, Senior Policy Dir.
FDIC IG, Fred W. Gibson, General Counsel
FDIC IG, Leslee A. Bollea, Congressional Relations Specialist
FDIC Office of Legislative Affairs, Eric J. Spitler, Director
FDIC Division of IT, Mark A. Brenneman, Dep. Director
Bruce J. Pederson, Counsel to Relator, Denver, Colorado
Shirley L. Mays, Relator, Wilmington, NC

SUBJECT: Falsification of Public Records – FDIC
Qui Tam Case
Civil Action No. 7:96-CV-117-BR(2)
United States of America ex rel
Shirley L. Mays
Graimark Realty Advisors, et al

After leaving the meeting that day, Bruce Pederson, her whistleblowing attorney from Denver who had been with the FDIC and the RTC and was instrumental in closing the S&Ls west of Denver, said to her, "You should consider Room 2222 in the Rayburn Building your sacred ground where you were allowed to speak the truth on behalf of the American public for over two hours with no interruptions."

Ben Bernanke, Federal Reserve Chairman had met with Chairman Barney Frank and the Financial Services Committee from 1:00 to 2:00 p.m. in an open hearing. She met with Chairman Frank's top staff and the FDIC on the same day in the same building from 2:00 to 4:00 p.m. in closed session.

Why would the Department of Justice, on behalf of the taxpayers of America, not be interested in Shirley Mays' discovery of FDIC falsified databases?

DRUGS

And why would the United States Coast Guard not be interested in investigating Edgar Styron, Jr. who deliberately attempted to deceive them into believing that the boys were at sea in trouble when in fact he knew it was a lie? It was a huge search and cost the taxpayers a lot of money. Jock MacKenzie told Shirley Mays when meeting with her and Dick Ruffino of Missing Persons that Edgar told him, *during the search*, that the boys were OK. That is powerful evidence coming from the last person to see them offshore on November 13, 1980.

Jock changed his story after Shirley Mays wrote her first book, "Outer Banks Piracy, Where is My Son Jeffrey?" First he had told Bob Eck, his ex-brother in law that he knew nothing. After the book he told Bob that maybe he did see Edgar bring some raingear aboard that day and put something under it. Jock divorced, moved to Florida, lives on a little island off the coast of Fort Myers, grew a beard, lives at the end of a dead end road in a single wide trailer and doesn't leave there even to visit his family. Coast Guard investigators should question that behavior.

Edgar was a drug dealer at the time working directly under Harry Williams who was also a drug dealer and whose brother was the local District Attorney. Edgar was piloting a boat named The Easy Ryder owned by Jock MacKenzie. Harry Williams personally told Shirley Mays in 2004 that the boys were at Edgar's place in Avon, North Carolina earlier that fatal morning of November 13, 1980. He also told her that Edgar was "under" him. That is exactly what kicked her into her first book.

How much more does the Coast Guard need to know in order to do an investigation on what happened to the boys offshore that fatal day of November 13, 1980 at 1:30 p.m?

They have the best rescue people in the world. Drug dealers should not be allowed to lead them astray.

Why would the United States Coast Guard, on behalf of the taxpayers of America, not be interested in this information?

Where The Rubber Meets The Road

There is not a dime's worth of difference in all of the above issues   All of the above issues are about drugs, law enforcement corruption, political corruption, money laundering, etc. etc. and how they commingle, intermingle and destroy American families all over the country.

All of the issues in this story have one thing in common, the power of money. The bad guys in the world would be crippled terribly without the accessibility of the banks and the ability to use banks to launder their illegally obtained money to destroy us.

It is the responsibility of the Obama Administration and this Congress to make sure the banks don't destroy our country.

And it is the responsibility of the American people to **Stand Up and Be Counted** and make sure President Obama and Congress do not shirk that responsibility.

Epilogue

Shirley Mays is a mother who has spent the last 29 years of her life looking for her missing son Jeffrey who went fishing one day and didn't return. His disappearance created one of the largest United States Coast Guard searches ever on the East Coast. There was international drug dealing that fateful day off the Coast of Cape Hatteras. Jeffrey was in his boat with another young man, Ted Wall, also 21, who owed some money to Edgar Styron, Jr. a local drug dealer. The boys were reported to have been at Edgar's house earlier that morning. Because Ted owed Edgar money; she feels they may have been used as a decoy for a big drug deal going down 16 miles offshore in international waters. Edgar was the last person reported to have seen them at sea. She thinks he was part of the deal going down that day and when the boys went against his orders, he told them to get the hell out of the area and don't come back.

Her journey has taken her deep into the world of drug dealing and political corruption. She has been given information by many people, some reliable, some not. She knows many of the locals involved and is convinced they have been untouchable because of their relationship with local law and powerful politicians. One of the powerful politicians at the time was the District Attorney H. P. Williams, whose brother Harry was caught drug dealing while driving the DA's car. Edgar Styron, Jr. worked "under" Harry. Most of the locals involved were related and had relatives at the top of the search.

To her knowledge there was never an investigation by the Coast Guard or local, state or federal law enforcement although all of them were aware of the major drug dealing going on off the Coast of Cape Hatteras during that time. She has tried for years to get someone to look at her discovery as to what transpired that day. The moment anyone shows interest, steel doors come crashing down.

It's a total mystery to her as to why the United States Coast Guard would not be interested in questioning Edgar Styron, Jr., who was responsible for lying to them about the location of the boys. Edgar gave them a location that he knew the boys had left and he knew they were OK. She has dedicated her life to fighting the environment that surrounded her son on November 13, 1980.

She is a real estate broker and ironically her fight against political corruption lead her to being a whistleblower who filed a <u>qui</u> <u>tam</u> case on behalf of the taxpayers of America. Her case involved the S&L Banks where a great deal of illegal drug dealing took place.

She has been trying to blow the whistle on the FDIC for over twelve years. Her efforts and those of her Congressman and attorney have never stopped. She is in possession of the official FDIC databases for contracting and asset management for 747 institutions. She can prove that the information has been falsified; with intent, to block the trail of value. She can give you the falsified contract numbers of the private asset managers and/or the government personnel who handled these assets and their falsified federal ID numbers. The falsification of the FDIC databases is systemic. Those databases were used to compile report to Congress. She has been stopped at the highest level of government.

Her discovery reveals how drug dealing and political corruption run hand in hand and together created one of the biggest nightmares this country has ever seen, the failing of our financial system.

Why is Congress not interested in all of this? Just how high does this drug dealing and political corruption go and when is it going to come to *Full Circle*?

Acknowledgments

I want to once again thank God for my sanity and my health.

I want to thank the United States Coast Guard for *THE SEARCH*.

I want to thank my family and friends for the comfort they have given me.

I want to thank two of my dearest friends for editing this book.

I want to thank all the many people who have sincerely tried to help my whistleblowing team get the FDIC falsified information to the American public.

Most of all, I want to thank my team:

Congressman Walter B. Jones, (R-3rd District), North Carolina
Millie Lilley, Director, Greenville, NC Office for Congressman Jones
Bruce J. Pederson, Esquire, Denver, Colorado
Dr. William Morgenroth, Senior Advisor, St. Petersburg, Florida
Robb Porter, Geologist, Heaven

Printed in the United States
146478LV00004B/1/P